ABOUT THE AUTHOR

Michael Dane was a professional investigator for over twenty-five years.

His Frank McBride stories are entirely fictional but inspired by his own experience as an officer in H.M. Customs & Excise's National Investigation Service.

Michael re-trained as a lawyer and joined the private sector where he investigated cases of fraud, corruption, smuggling, money laundering and breaches of international sanctions on five continents.

He now writes full time and lives in England's Vale of Belvoir.

Learn more about Michael at

https://www.michaeldaneauthor.com/

ALSO BY MICHAEL DANE

The Frank McBride novels
The Rutland Connection
The Rutland Identity
Coming Soon
The Rutland Legacy
The Rutland Assassin
Prequel Novella
McBride Undercover

THE RUTLAND VOLUNTEER

BOOK THREE IN THE FRANK MCBRIDE SERIES

MICHAEL DANE

DEER ISLAND BOOKS

Copyright © 2024 Michael Dane

The right of Michael Dane to be identified as the author of this

work has been asserted by them in accordance with the

Copyright, Design and Patents Act 1988.

All rights reserved. No part of this publication may be

reproduced, transmitted, or stored in a retrieval system, in any form or by any means,

without permission in writing from the publisher, nor be otherwise circulated in

any form of binding or cover other than that in which it is published and without

a similar condition being imposed on the subsequent purchaser.

This work is entirely fictitious and bears no resemblance to any persons living or dead.

For my parents.

Foreword

You have to remember. It was all a long time ago now. It was back when Customs and Excise investigators were respected, feared even. Of course, a lot of things have changed. What was cutting edge technology then are quaint antiques now. Cars ran on four star. Mobile telephones were exotic. Society had different attitudes, different tolerances.

Some things haven't changed though. People are the same, the good, the bad, the ninety-nine percent of us that are somewhere in between. Complicated, contradictory each with their own set of values, their personal code. Each with their own motivations, fear, greed, love, hate. That hasn't changed.

Criminal masterminds, infallible sleuths, all the nonsense served up as drama or entertainment. They weren't true then. They aren't now. Reality is more complex, more imperfect. Always was.

Sherlock Holmes is a fiction. Moriarty too. But people are real.

Prologue

Seville 1999

Bryan took a sip from his *café con leche* and looked up. Even at a quarter to eight, the sun was already high and streaming through the window. The grime cast shadows on the wall behind him and the smears on the table reflected a greasy kaleidoscope of colours. He could see the Irishman walking towards him across the yard.

There were half a dozen other drivers, all Spanish, sitting at the handful of tables outside the café, but Bryan had been ordered to remain indoors. It was cooler and, in any case, he was less likely to attract attention to himself or to become drawn into any conversation that might cause somebody to remember him. In light of his limited Spanish, such an eventuality was unlikely, but Bryan had been told to be cautious.

The Irishman had reached the door now. He pushed it open and walked in. He didn't march or stride. He didn't saunter or wander. He just walked, but somehow, he managed to convey a chilling menace with this simple act of perambulation. Bryan couldn't have told you

'It's Tony.'

'It's Bryan.'

'Where are you?'

'Leicester.'

Tony gave him the address of the meeting place – Customs would have called it 'The Slaughter' – and instructions on how to find it. He made Bryan repeat the instructions back to him.

'See you in an hour.'

'Just over,' said Bryan, thinking of his sandwich.

*

It was one of those farmyards that aren't farmyards anymore. This one had probably been a haulier's nest. Now it didn't even seem to be that. Bryan was a little later than he'd said. He preferred for them to be waiting for him, not the other way around. He was pleased to see there were already four vans and a forklift truck there when he arrived. He'd barely applied the brakes when the forklift was at the back doors, and barely out of the cab when he heard those doors open. The whole unloading operation took less than fifteen minutes.

Steve thought he was intimidating. He actually put quite a lot of effort into it. Not just the clothes and the hair and the car. Or even the tattoos. He practised. He practised his stare, his growl, even his walk. And to some extent his hard work paid off. A lot of people were intimidated by Steve. He was a hard man, a bit of a legend on the terraces, or more realistically, in the car parks a few miles from the terraces. He appeared to be a genuinely frightening character. Unless you had met the Irishman.

Bryan leant against the side of his cab, chewing a piece of nicotine gum, and watched Steve walk across to the ageing and slightly rusty Jaguar that he doubtless thought contributed to his image. He was why he was frightened, but it wasn't an irrational fear. The small, softly spoken Irishman was utterly terrifying. Perhaps it was something about the eyes. Nobody forgot those eyes.

The Irishman sat down. He pulled a thick envelope from his back pocket and put it on the table. 'Five thousand.'

Bryan looked at the envelope. He briefly, very, very, briefly, considered opening it, and counting the contents. Then he remembered the eyes. Instead, he picked it up, and put it into the holdall on the chair beside him. Bryan didn't know very much about the man opposite him, but he knew it wouldn't be wise to insult him.

'You remember the code?'

Bryan nodded. 'One is six, two is seven, three is eight...'

The Irishman passed him a scrap of paper. 'Call when you get to Leicester.'

Bryan folded the paper and put it in the breast pocket of his shirt. He dropped a handful of pesetas onto the table. He glanced at the Irishman. He'd never quite mastered the currency. The Irishman nodded. Bryan rose, picked up the holdall, and headed for the door. Behind him he heard the Irishman speaking to the café proprietor in rapid, and apparently fluent, Spanish.

*

It was a little after noon when Bryan's rig pulled into Leicester Forest East motorway services two days later. He climbed down from the cab and walked stiffly to the building. He visited the toilets and then purchased a takeaway coffee and a sandwich. The prices were shocking.

He fished the piece of paper from his breast pocket, slightly crumpled, very sweaty, and approached the small bank of public telephones. He squinted at the piece of paper where he'd written the decoded numbers in pencil under the original message and dialled.

using his 'gangster' walk, but it was wasted on Bryan. He'd seen the real thing.

He returned with an envelope and handed it to Bryan. 'Five grand.'

This time, Bryan counted it.

CHAPTER 1

Nottingham 1999

It had taken Andi Woodhead a long time to rise to the rank of Senior Investigation Officer and it hadn't been easy. Pursuing a career firstly whilst also an international footballer and later a mother. The twins were now six. But she had made it. And now this.

She was forty, would be forty-one by the time the 'late blessing' arrived. Was she willing to do it all again? The sleepless nights? The nappies. The chaos? The exhaustion?

Damn right she was.

*

The speculation began almost immediately. An investigation team needed a leader, a Senior Investigation Officer. Nottingham A would need a temporary SIO. Would it be an outsider? Would somebody be temporarily promoted? If so, who? The discussions lasted several months, and each day Andi's changing profile brought the necessity for a decision closer.

The senior members of the team mentally calculated their own chances and the prospects of each of their likely rivals. Every one of them arrived at the same conclusion. Others had powerful cases but, in reality, only one candidate possessed all the qualities required for the role. The new SIO would surely be them. They were all wrong. Instead, it was going to be somebody who hadn't expected it at all.

*

Joe Lake normally preferred to avoid the branch headquarters in Birmingham. He didn't have anything particular against the city or the members of the six investigation teams based there (Nottingham had only two teams). He just generally preferred to stay away from management and office politics. Today, he could avoid neither. Andi hadn't actually told him why they were on their way to see Alan Hawkins, the Assistant Chief Investigation Officer and Andi's boss, but having eliminated every other possibility Joe was left with only one. And he didn't like it at all.

He didn't want to be made a temporary SIO. He wasn't sure he could do it. He was pretty confident most of his colleagues didn't think he could do it. Even if they did, he was sure they thought somebody else could do it better. And worst of all, after six months of trying to manage a team full of jealous and resentful former teammates whose ranks he would eventually have to re-join. He spent most of the journey trying to think of convincing excuses for turning the role down.

Lake had only been in Hawkins' office once before. It had been a tip, with every available surface covered in paperwork, or pieces of equipment, or what in any other circumstances could only be described as litter. This time, it was worse. The piles of paper were even taller. It looked like somebody had tried to recreate Manhattan using management memos and copies of the *Angling Times*.

What made it worse was that Hawkins had obviously been tidying up because opposite his desk were two chairs which had been cleared of the detritus everywhere else. Hawkins nodded to the chairs and pulled a cigarette from behind his ear. Then he remembered the purpose of the meeting and returned it.

He began by congratulating Andi, but swiftly switched to a series of anecdotes about his own grandchildren. It was quite sweet, actually. He appeared to be utterly devoted to them. There was a fifteen-minute highlight reel of adorable things they'd said and early evidence of what fine people they would become and successes they would achieve. It was a side of Hawkins Lake had never seen before. He risked a sideways glance at Andi and saw that she was experiencing it for the first time, too.

Lake felt his attention starting to drift, his mind turning to pressing questions: how did Hawkins find anything in this office? Did he know that he'd done the buttons of his shirt up in the wrong order? Did he care? How long could it realistically be before he retired? He tried to re-focus while Hawkins interrupted a story about his granddaughter shouting out random answers at *University Challenge* to have a coughing fit that suggested that he probably didn't need to worry about retirement. When it finished, he reached again for the cigarette behind his ear before remembering. Finally, he came down to business. He did so suddenly, and Lake wasn't really ready for it when it came.

'Joe, I want you to take over as SIO while Andi is away. Be about six months?'

This last line was delivered to Andi who gave a sort of affirmative shrug.

Lake waited for an explanation, some sort of outline of Hawkins' reasoning. It didn't come. And Hawkins hadn't framed it as a suggestion or request. He hadn't solicited Lake's opinion or sought his agreement. This was going to make it more difficult.

'Err...some people might be surprised that you've asked me...'

He didn't even get to finish his sentence, which was just as well, because he hadn't fully decided where it was going to go.

'I don't care. It's my decision and I've made it. You're temped up for the duration. Andi can show you the ropes. I'm sure you'll be fine. Now, there is a second reason I've asked you here.'

And that was it. The chance to object, to refuse, to somehow wriggle out of it was gone. The conversation had moved on.

*

Lake dropped Andi off at her home. He probably should have gone straight to his own and told Bella about his temporary promotion. But she wouldn't understand. She would have thought it was good news, grounds for celebration, or something. So instead, he veered off to the south-east, through villages and market towns, and finally down winding country lanes and across the border into England's smallest county.

Rutland is the sort of place you see in jigsaw puzzles with Morris Minors, smiling policemen, and schoolboys in blazers and caps looking in toy shop windows. In some places, there were more thatched roofs than tiled. One of those places was Leighton Parva, a tiny village of cottages made of honey-coloured stones, verdant cricket pitches, hanging baskets, and The Old Volunteer.

The lounge bar of The Old Volunteer looked like a thousand other country pubs. There were prints on the wall depicting bucolic scenes and old sepia photographs, a man standing beside a plough-horse, a cricket team from nearly a hundred years earlier. There was even a hunting horn over the bar. There were horse brasses too. One of them depicted Yuri Gagarin, a private joke between Lake, the politics graduate, and the landlord, a lifelong communist.

Lake headed instead for the public bar Just crossing the county boundary into Rutland felt like travelling half a century back in time. Walking into the public bar of The Old Volunteer was like the other half. The floor was plain stone flags. The furniture simple wooden benches and stools. There was a dog bowl and a dartboard in the corner and behind the bar was Frank McBride, polishing a glass.

He must have been very tempted to say something like, 'Oh, Mr Lake, I've been expecting you.' But instead, he just pulled him a pint. He paused for a moment, and then helped himself to a bottle of tonic water, slimline tonic water, from the shelf. He rang in the sales on a till that looked like it had been salvaged from the *Titanic* and picked up a small glass. No ice. McBride put both drinks on the table. He sat on the bench and took his pipe and tobacco from his pocket.

Lake nodded at the slimline tonic.

'I'm a publican now. A publican who drinks doesn't last long.'

McBride started to fill his pipe. The same slow methodical procedure Lake had seen a hundred times before, or a thousand.

'I believe you've given up. Very sensible. I'm too old to be sensible.'

'You look well. I like what you've done to the place. It's very…' Lake didn't really know how to put it into words.

Phosphorous scraped against sandpaper. Frank extinguished the match with a swift flick of the wrist and put it in the ashtray on the table between them. He drew upon his pipe to get it started. Staccato bursts of smoke drifted upwards until they were replaced by gentle clouds. Lake took a sip of his pint.

'If you're expecting an apology, you won't get one. Yes, I had a word with Alan. He asked me what I thought, and I told him. Now, you were wise to try to get things straight in your mind before you see the team. Whether you were wise to seek my counsel, well, time will tell.'

Frank spoke for fifteen minutes. He shared his experiences, and some of them were not good at all. His career had been less of a steady ascent, more of a game of snakes and ladders. Nobody had been promoted, demoted, temporarily and substantively more than Frank McBride. Even almost two years after his retirement, he was a legend in customs investigation.

Lake never really understood why McBride had taken him under his wing, or made him his personal project, depending on your point of view. It was even less clear why he was still doing it. Lake resisted the urge to take notes.

'And now I have to get on. It's the quiz tonight and we usually get a good crowd.'

'It's doing well, is it? The pub?'

'Very well. People seem to like the fact that it's—'

'Traditional?'

'A bloody time capsule. Someone asked me last week if we had a shove ha'penny board.'

Lake laughed. 'Have you?'

'Have now.'

Lake finished his pint. 'We've got a target job. Cigarette smuggling.'

'I know.'

'Of course you do.'

*

Frank hadn't been making excuses. The weekly quiz was a big event at The Old Volunteer. There had been one for years. The previous landlord seemed to enjoy organising and hosting it, but Frank was too busy pulling pints to act as quizmaster. He'd delegated that task to The Old Volunteer's actual owner, Bernard Taylor. Bernard had bought the place a year earlier to prevent it from becoming yet another local facility converted into a private residence. Leighton Parva already had an Old Forge, an Old Post Office, and the Old Reading Rooms. Bernard himself lived in The Old Vicarage.

Brigadier Sir Bernard Taylor KBE MC had spent a lifetime in the pursuit of what he called skulduggery and mischief. For over thirty years, he'd been an officer in Military Intelligence stationed in West Berlin. For ten years after that, he'd performed a similar role in a less official capacity. When the wall came down, he and his German wife, Karin, had retired to the village where Bernard had been born and that he'd left at the age of three. Karin loved the gentle quiet of the English countryside. Bernard had been bored. When Karin had died two years ago, it got worse.

And that was how the knight of the realm who'd spent a lifetime trying to thwart the Stasi and the KGB, had become friends with Frank McBride, the Glaswegian Marxist. Bernard had seized upon an opportunity presented by some less than accomplished drugs smugglers to coach his grandson Michael in the ways of covert operations.

The gang had been being targeted by McBride in his last operation prior to retirement. Frank knew what Bernard had done, and Bernard knew he knew. But the gang was now in prison and Michael was now an officer in the Intelligence Service, MI6, and everyone involved seemed content to let things lie.

*

Bernard was nearly eighty now, but his appetite for manipulation and deceit was undiminished. He could no longer play the great game, but he enjoyed playing smaller games of his own devising and of whose existence he alone knew. One of these games was the weekly pub quiz.

Bernard didn't merely rig the outcome, he orchestrated it. He would determine not just who won but in which place every team would finish.

Although nobody participating knew, it was actually the reason why the quiz was so popular. Everybody won from time to time. Everybody had an occasional exasperating second place. Teams would fall steadily in the rankings each week before pulling off a startling victory. It was all choreographed like professional wrestling except nobody knew or even suspected. Except Frank. Well, of course Frank knew. He was almost as devious as Bernard.

Actually, that's not quite true. Not every team won. Simon Roberts' team never won. It used to. Before Bernard had become the quizmaster Colonel Roberts, as he insisted upon being known, regularly won – except on the occasions when Bernard decided that he and Karin would beat him. Karin loathed Roberts so Bernard would beat him as a special treat for her.

Bernard tortured Roberts because he simply didn't like him. He was a bumptious, opinionated old bigot who disliked and mistrusted Karin. And so, Bernard teased him with a succession of second places, followed by humiliating oblivion.

But one day Bernard learnt of something that Roberts had once said about Karin. And he decided to destroy him. Roberts liked to think of himself as the foremost and most senior member of the village. His entirely misplaced sense of superiority was in part due to his chairmanship of the parish council.

Bernard was a mischievous old man, and because he thought it was amusing, he decided that Roberts should be defeated by Frank McBride. The idea of Leighton Parva's foremost citizen being a Clydeside communist tickled him.

In truth, Roberts wasn't that popular and could hardly point to a record of stellar achievement at the parish council. Defeating him ought not to have been particularly difficult simply by employing traditional means. Frank McBride, by contrast, was very popular in the village. To the surprise of many, including perhaps himself, he'd been an innovative and enterprising pub landlord.

Frank had opened the pub for coffee mornings, allowed the Women's Institute and other local groups to use the function room free of charge and started selling newspapers, bread, milk, tea, and coffee. Bernard had even managed to persuade him to sponsor the village cricket team.

Only Bernard knew of his dedication to Leninist dialectic and the fact Frank's father had died fighting against Franco. To most of the villagers, he was an amiable retired civil servant who had swiftly put himself at the heart of village life. But winning fair and square would have been unsatisfying to Bernard. If victory didn't involve a bit of skulduggery and mischief it simply wasn't worth having.

Roberts came eighth, and last, in the election to appoint the seven members of Leighton Parva Parish Council.

Bernard laughed so hard he cried. And Simon Roberts put his house, Windmill Cottage, up for sale the next day. It was purchased surprisingly quickly by a company registered in the Isle of Man.

CHAPTER 2

His birth certificate read James Christopher McKenna, but he hadn't used that name in years. He'd used dozens of others, some for months, some just for a few days for a specific mission. But the one that had stuck was a childhood nickname. 'The Scholar'. That was the name on the front of his file.

He'd been born on the Creggan estate in Londonderry. He would have called it Derry – and so would you if you knew what was good for you – in 1960. One of six children. He had two older brothers, Kieran and John, two older sisters Una and Niamh, and a younger brother, Joseph, the baby of the family.

His father, Eugene, was a mild-mannered man who worked as a carpet fitter. He did his best to ignore politics, and for a while that had been possible. He was sympathetic to the civil rights movement in the 1960s, but not an active participant. He wasn't active in most senses. A lifetime spent on his knees had taken its toll. If you'd pressed him, really pressed him, he might have conceded that his preference was for a united Ireland. But he was no rebel. He was just an ordinary man trying to live an ordinary life and raise an ordinary family.

Eugene hadn't really approved of Kieran and John and Una attending the civil rights march through Derry on 30th of January 1972. But he hadn't objected. He wished he had. Wished it for the rest of his life. He did prohibit James from attending, though. He was just eleven and although the march was intended to be peaceful, well, you couldn't be entirely sure.

The reports said that he had been a normal, happy little boy. A little quieter than most, a little more studious, and a lot brighter. He'd been in the bedroom he shared with his brothers, reading the *Blue Peter Annual* he'd got for Christmas, when he heard the scream. He'd never heard his father scream, never heard any man scream. He didn't know men could, did.

They didn't want him to see. His mother, covered in blood. John's blood. They told them to stay in the room, but he saw through the bannisters. Later, he would say that he saw his brother die, witnessed his last breath. He didn't know if that was true. Literally true. But it was true figuratively. True in essence. True enough for the purposes of grief and anger and republican folklore.

James McKenna, the Scholar, saw his brother bleed to death in the front hall on Bloody Sunday. That's what everyone said. So, it was true. What it did to him wasn't immediately apparent.

The McKennas were peaceful people. The rebels were all on his mother's side. The Cartys.

The Cartys claimed a heritage of resistance dating back to 1798. They'd fought with the United Irishmen, fought with the Fenians, fought in the Tan War and the Civil War, and now they were going to fight in this war.

The day after John's funeral, Kieran, the eldest, joined the IRA. His father was so consumed with grief he pretended he didn't know. His mother didn't tell him about the balaclava she found under his pillow in the room he shared with James and Joseph. History does not record what Saoirse McKenna née Carty thought about Kieran. But it was clear she thought one dead son and one volunteer in the family were enough.

James was a bright boy, and he was at an impressionable age. An uncle, a priest, had a few connections. James was sent away to a boarding school over the border in Donegal, away from trouble, away from the Troubles. Even when Kieran was interned in 1974, James showed no sign of following in his footsteps. He continued to do well at school, very well. Young James had a gift for languages. He was fluent in Irish, Spanish, and French. He'd been offered a place at University College Dublin, in European modern languages. His route out of danger was established. His parents' prayers would be answered. He could leave Derry behind.

And then Kieran died.

*

His name would appear on the roll of IRA war dead, Volunteer Kieran McKenna, killed in action. But he wasn't. Not really. Kieran and another volunteer had been assembling a car bomb. Kieran had done this a few times before. The other volunteer had not. Somebody made a mistake.

The day after Kieran's funeral, the Scholar joined the IRA. He was welcomed. He had the pedigree. One brother a martyred volunteer, a second a victim of Bloody Sunday. And then there was his mother's brother, Uncle Paschal, although now he had to call him Commandant. Perhaps he'd been intending to join, anyway. Perhaps Kieran's death, or the combination of Kieran and John's deaths, had caused something to snap. The psychiatrists would continue to debate this.

The Scholar was considered too valuable to be a mere gunman. He swiftly became Paschal's aide-de-camp. Then he was sent abroad, first to Boston, Chicago, and then New York to raise funds. Later to Libya to spend them. He was sent to liaise with ETA, the Basque separatists, with representatives of other like-minded national liberation movements.

The earliest reference to the Scholar in Military Intelligence's files was in 1979. He'd been named by an informant, a tout in the vernacular of the republican community, as one of those who administered punishment beatings. By 1985, there was a whole dossier, filled with rumours and reports from informants, from interrogated prisoners, from telephone intercepts, and a hundred other sources of intelligence. Rumours of republican courts martial, of kidnappings, and executions. But nobody knew his name.

While the Scholar had been travelling the world in the cause of Irish freedom, the Derry Brigade of the IRA had undergone a lot of changes. Of the handful of people who had known his real name, some were in prison, some were dead, some had simply drifted away, and some had just disappeared. The disappearances became fewer after Paschal Carty had gone to prison in 1992 (possession of explosives, weapons, narcotics, and conspiracy to rob a wages van just outside Strabane). But they didn't stop entirely.

In the mid-nineties, the rumours began. Rumours of negotiation, or disarming, putting weapons beyond reach, whatever that meant. Rumours of peace. The psychiatrists discussed this too. What was the effect of this on a man who had been a warrior since his teens?

Mammy had died in 1983 and Daddy just two weeks later. More trauma. Una had married a man from Letterkenny and they lived in

Dublin now. Niamh had gone to university in England and wasn't expected to return. That left James, now a lieutenant, and Joe, the baby of the family.

On the positive side, Joe wasn't in the IRA. On the negative side, it was because they wouldn't have him. And he'd tried the Irish National Liberation Army too, but they'd heard what he was like.

Daddy had tried to get him an apprenticeship as a carpet fitter, but he hadn't lasted long. Various aunts and uncles had pulled various strings, but Joseph never took advantage of the opportunities that had come his way. He drank. And he drifted. And he drank.

The Scholar pretended he didn't know. But he knew. He just didn't know everything.

He was on the road a lot, out of the country. He saw Joseph less and less frequently. By the time he had no choice but to confront reality, it was too late. The clues had been there for a while, but you don't want to believe that about your little brother, do you? Your last brother.

It was probably a dirty needle that gave him the virus. It didn't matter. It was the second needle, or the thousand, and second needle, that killed him. Not an overdose. The doctors were very clear. He was poisoned. Poisoned by the brick dust, or the strychnine, or the scouring powder. One of the lethal cocktail of diluting agents. The IRA was supposed to be preventing this. All those warning visits, the threats, implicit and explicit. All those kneecaps shattered. And Joseph was dead. Thank God Mammy and Daddy didn't live to see it.

The Scholar made inquiries, very, very discreet inquiries. He spoke to the junkies, the street level pushers. He even asked questions of the nuns at the at the drop-in centre. He sifted through what he heard, what he learnt. It all pointed to the same answer. There was one last piece of the jigsaw. And that would require a special trip. But in his heart, he knew.

Actually, if there was a single event that flipped a switch in his brain, this was probably it.

The ceasefire. Nineteen ninety-seven. Nineteen ninety-eight. The Belfast Agreement. But everyone called it the Good Friday Agreement. The referendum. Peace for those who wanted it. Freedom for the prisoners, including Paschal.

*

Brendan Behan used to say that the first item on the agenda for any IRA meeting was 'The Split'. In 1998, it was every agenda item. Gerry Adams and Martin McGuinness, the republican movement's leaders had delivered...what had they delivered? Peace? Betrayal? Opportunity? Paschal decided that it was betrayal. At least, that was what he said, but he was thinking 'opportunity'. Paschal knew a thing or two about capitalising on opportunities.

Most republicans accepted that the Good Friday Agreement signalled the end of the armed struggle. But some didn't. A few formed what they called the Real IRA, others Continuity IRA. Paschal formed the Irish Republican Volunteers. It was, at least, a more accurate name. Can an army really have fewer members than a football team?

Where Paschal went, the Scholar followed. He became Deputy Commander of the IRV. They could field a football team if they wanted to. Provided they didn't need too many substitutes.

Where the IRV was concerned, the first agenda item was the oath. And the second was honouring its dead. James didn't know what to think when he learnt Kieran had been retroactively recruited and was considered a martyr of the IRV, or the Volunteers as they (Paschal) like to style themselves.

The third item on the agenda was fund raising. This was the Scholar's department, but Paschal had some ideas. The fourth item was 'the split' or, more accurately, what the attitude of the IRV was to be towards the other dissident republican groups. This final agenda item was discussed at a subcommittee level. That is to say by Paschal and the Scholar alone.

'Listen, Jimmy, I want the Volunteers to be the only representative of physical force republicanism in Ireland. We cannot fight a war without funds, and we cannot gather sufficient funds if we're fishing in the same pools as the other groups. So, we need to do two things. We need a source of revenue, and we need to eliminate the opposition.'

The Scholar said nothing. Was his uncle seriously suggesting that they go to war with the other factions?

'The source of revenue we have discussed. The elimination of the opposition is more delicate. The path to national self-determination is always a winding one. Sometimes it can look a bit like a crooked one.'

The Scholar said nothing, but he said it slightly louder.

'I want the Brits to do it for us.'

The Scholar was determined not to react, to betray his reaction, but he wasn't prepared for this, and his face gave him away.

'I know. I know. It's a dirty business. And I hate talking to them. But I can't. They know me. I've been inside. And, in their eyes, at least, I'm a fanatic. They just wouldn't buy it. it's gonna to have to be you.'

'You want me to turn tout?'

Paschal thought for a moment. He had a little speech prepared about how this was for a noble cause, about the greater good, the destiny of the Irish people...but somehow it didn't seem appropriate. He realised he wasn't looking into the face of the little boy he'd dandled on his knee, or even the young man who'd volunteered to avenge his brothers' deaths. And Paschal knew he wasn't clever enough to persuade the Scholar much less to bamboozle him. He opted instead for a much shorter speech.

'Yes. That's exactly what I want you to do.'

The Scholar said nothing. His empty, dead eyes gazing ahead as if at some distant object. After a minute or two, he said, 'Okay.'

And Paschal shivered.

*

British Military Intelligence knew, or at least anticipated, that there would be elements of the IRA who wouldn't accept the Good Friday Agreement, but they didn't know who or where. For Paschal, it was easy.

For the last year of his imprisonment, republican prisoners had discussed little else, and he had at least half a dozen contacts among the dissident groups. Very carefully, he set about contacting them. He learnt their organisations' names, their locations, and their strengths. It took months, but gradually he learnt of their objectives, their command structures, and their plans for gathering finance.

After a while, discussion tended to centre upon plans for cooperation or even a merger, but considering the personalities involved, their philosophies and political ambitions, everybody really understood that a merger was unlikely. They were allies of convenience. Temporary allies.

Meanwhile, James set about the task of gathering the necessary funds to begin operations. He had a little seed capital, but he needed to secure a rapid and substantial return on that investment. James began to leverage his contacts and connections. He started in a small way, but in a few months, word had got around that the Irishman with those eyes was a reliable partner.

By re-investing profits, he'd begun to build up an operation that would eventually make the IRV a well-funded and financially secure organisation. On New Year's Day in 1999, he bought the factory.

Within a month, he had the machinery and equipment. Phase one was complete.

*

You've probably never asked yourself how you'd go about making contact with the British Security Service and explaining to them that you were in a unique position to provide them with operational and tactical level intelligence about a number of active terrorist organisations. Neither had Paschal. And neither had the Scholar.

It's a tricky question, even if your motivation isn't rooted in the fact, you're a leading member of a rival terrorist organisation that's funding itself through a large-scale international criminal operation. The Scholar needed to give the matter a great deal of thought. And so, he did what he always did when he needed to think things through carefully. He picked up a rod and a few of his favourite flies and headed for Lough Anure.

After two days, he had a plan that he was sure would work. In fact, it contained a flaw. No, not a flaw, an error. Instead of approaching the Security Service, MI5, he approached the Intelligence Service, MI6. An easy mistake to make.

Chapter 3

Monday morning, Michael Butcher walked the short distance from Vauxhall station to the slightly absurd concrete wedding cake that housed the Secret Intelligence Service. He didn't look for a tail, or double back, or dart into a shop doorway. He wasn't that type of spy. He didn't have a compass hidden in the sole of his shoe or a revolver strapped beneath his left armpit. His work was of a less glamorous variety. He'd been at MI6 for almost two years and spent most of that time at his desk. He expected today to be just like any other. But when he reached his desk, there was a note.

It was short. An independent observer might have described it as peremptory, but anybody who knew its author would have called it ominous. Phillipa Templeton wasn't Michael's boss. She wasn't even his boss's boss. Michael hadn't seen her more than once or twice since she'd recruited him. She occupied an office that was literally and figuratively far above Michael's. A summons from Phillipa Templeton required an immediate response. Michael glanced ruefully at the coffee machine as he walked to the lifts.

You know those glamorous but severe powerful women that you see in spy films? Self-assured and no nonsense and ever so slightly terrifying. That was Phillipa, and the fact that she was the sister of Michael's best friend, Giles, somehow made it worse. He knocked at her door and took a deep breath.

Phillipa had a file open on her desk. She closed it and put it in a drawer as Michael entered. She took a much slimmer file from a different drawer and nodded towards an empty chair. It was one of a pair and on the second was seated a young man of about Michael's age.

It was hard to be sure since he was sitting, but he appeared to be about eleven feet tall. He sat upright, and with his heels together directly in front of him. The whole sight gave the impression of a locust sitting to attention.

Phillipa scanned the file's contents. Her eyes darted to and fro with an alarming purpose. Michael stole the opportunity to take a sideways glance at his companion. He looked like he might be a minor member of the royal family, or possibly one of those experts you see on BBC 2 talking enthusiastically about Dresden porcelain or the abdication crisis or the protocol for some obscure state occasion.

Phillipa looked up. 'Do you know Richard?'

Michael indicated that he didn't and Phillipa appeared displeased, bordering on exasperated. 'You'll be working together.'

Michael turned and gave Richard the sort of half nod that people do on these occasions.

'Ireland,' Phillipa said. 'Specifically, dissident Irish republican organisations.'

'Those I know.'

'I should hope so.'

Even when you told Phillipa something positive, she managed to express dissatisfaction and disapproval. It was extraordinary that this woman was related to Giles. Giles was the most affable, modest, and generous person Michael knew. His sister was like a character Roald Dahl would have rejected as too lacking in humanity or empathy.

'We have an informant—'

'A covert human intelligence source,' Richard said in what he thought was a helpful manner. Phillipa shot him a glance that would have rendered most people dumb until Christmas and would have carried those with less robust constitutions off all together.

'I want the pair of you to babysit him. Debrief him. Empty him of any and all information. Don't worry about how useful you think it might be, or how truthful. We have analysts for that. You know the drill. Establish a relationship, gain his confidence, win his trust, and then wring every last drop out of him. Talk to Margaret about a safe house. Try to find somewhere where he might be able to do a little fly-fishing nearby. And under no circumstances trust him an inch. All clear? Any questions, talk to Margaret.'

Phillipa picked up the file. Richard bent forward to take it from her, but she gave it to Michael. 'Calls himself Diarmuid Geraghty. That's not his real name. Right, off you go.'

Michael took the file and rose. Richard sort of unfolded himself like a loft ladder in reverse, nearer eleven foot six, thought Michael.

*

Margaret was Phillipa Templeton's assistant. Nobody knew exactly how long Margaret had been at Six, since the Boer War at least, though. She'd previously been the assistant to four different heads of the service. The fact she was working for Phillipa now didn't represent a demotion, but rather a strong indication that Phillipa, despite being only in her thirties, was the heir presumptive.

That, at least, was the working theory of some of those who concerned themselves with that sort of thing. Every office has such people, self-appointed professors of office politics, who spent far too much time hypothesising, speculating, and hunting for little clues, indications, or hints. Sometimes they're called Kremlinologists, but not in the Secret Intelligence Service. Where that term was applied literally.

Sir William Potts must surely retire soon. He'd been chief since the mid-eighties. He'd steered the service through some extraordinary times, the fall of the wall, the rise of Islamic terrorism, and the end of conflict in Ireland. He was tired. And he was frequently ill. The office wits hypothesised that he'd had so many internal organs replaced it was doubtful he was still one hundred per cent British and probably ought to have his security vetting renewed. But he hung on for now. He made fewer and fewer public appearances, and each time he was seen, he looked visibly older, visibly sicker.

Those in the know, or at least those who claimed to be, speculated that he was waiting for a successor to emerge. Others said that he'd already made his choice, and he was waiting for his protégée to rack up a little more experience and a few more achievements. Those who subscribed to this theory thought Phillipa Templeton would be the next chief. Others thought that a more conservative and less radical candidate would get the nod. What Margaret thought, nobody knew.

Quite a lot of people in MI6, people who would travel alone and unarmed into some of the world's most dangerous regions, were frightened of Margaret. The rest were utterly terrified. But not Michael.

Margaret must have been past mandatory retirement age. Perhaps nobody had the courage to tell her. There was a rumour that even Phillipa Templeton was slightly wary of her. She came from that school of English spinsters who usually ended up as headmistresses of girls' boarding schools, or particularly exacting judges at Crufts.

For reasons he'd yet to learn, Margaret had a soft spot for him. He didn't really understand why, but he suspected it had something to do with his grandfather. Bernard Taylor had never been in MI6. At least not officially. He'd retired from the army as head of Military Intelligence in West Berlin in about 1980 and then there were about ten years unaccounted for. Michael had once heard Margaret sigh under her breath. 'So like him. So very like him...when he was young.'

Anyway, whatever the reason, Michael enjoyed a special licence where Margaret was concerned, so he wasn't the least bit nervous when he went to see her. Richard wasn't nervous either, partly because he was so new he didn't know Margaret's reputation, but mostly because nervousness had been bred out of his family sometime around the restoration of Charles II.

Margaret gave Michael a beaming smile. Then she saw Richard.

'You're a Perceval.'

'Why yes, how awfully clever of you—'

He was cut short by a loud and disapproving sniff.

'Diarmuid Geraghty, doesn't matter. It's not his real name of course. He's in a hotel at the moment. You don't need to know where. Still with the reception team.'

'The reception team?'

'Oh dear, definitely a Perceval. Yes, dear, a reception team. You don't need to worry about that either. I assume you've both read the file.'

Michael nodded.

Richard said, 'Yes, and I have a few questions—'

'Well, since your job is to interrogate the wretched man, I should fucking hope you do.'

Thereafter, Margaret completely refused to acknowledge Richard's presence. She spoke exclusively to Michael concerning various logistical considerations; recording equipment, security, arrangements for providing reports and updates, and all the other rather boring details that are part of debriefing an informer/defector/turncoat in a safe house. Finally, the subject turned to the house itself.

'I think I may have found a perfect spot,' said Margaret. Was there a little smile?

'It's one of our new ones, actually. Recently acquired. Rural, but not suspiciously so, not too far from London and it's even got fishing nearby. I think it will suit you very well.' Perhaps it was a smirk, not a smile. She handed Michael a set of keys. The address of the safe house was written on a small parcel label. Windmill Cottage, Leighton Parva.

*

Windmill Cottage was far too modest a name for the place. The Scholar hadn't had a chance fully to explore it. It hadn't explicitly been forbidden. He just didn't sense that it would be appropriate. But from what he'd seen, and from what he'd been able to deduce, it had at least six bedrooms. His own had a nice en suite bathroom. There were several rooms downstairs, all decorated in the style that you see in magazines called *Stylish Chintz Life* or *Aspirational Snob*. There was even a grandfather clock in the hall. The Scholar had seen Little Chris winding it.

Little Chris was one of his three...what were they? Chaperones? Guards? Hosts? Little Chris was about six foot three and built like a rugby player, the sort who gave other rugby players nightmares. But it wasn't one of those ironic nicknames, like calling a bald man curly. Little Chris was Little Chris because Big Chris was simply enormous. An absolute giant of a man, he had to duck going through every door and turn sideways through quite a lot of them. Tony fitted in somewhere in between. They each looked like they were special forces troops as indeed they had been. They clearly loathed the Scholar. That didn't matter. He loathed them, too.

But they weren't important. An interview team would be arriving from London shortly. That was when the real challenge would begin. In the meantime, he waited. Sitting in a wing-backed armchair in what the previous residents would probably have called the drawing room, sipping a cup of tea. Black, lemon, no sugar. While he was waiting, and chiefly to amuse himself, he speculated as to where the hidden cameras and microphones were.

There was a camera in the speaker of the television set. There usually was, but you could actually see this one when the direct sunlight shone through the window. And if you knew what you were looking for, of course. Microphones? Well, there was likely to be more than one. One would be in the table lamp. Another in the television, although James couldn't see it, so possibly not. One in the light fitting in the ceiling. Might be a camera there too, although he couldn't see it. None of it really mattered. He wasn't going to be caught in an unguarded remark.

The real business would take place next door in the interview room. James had seen that. It wasn't an interview room like you see in police dramas on television. It wasn't a stark room with a heavy table surrounded by tubular steel and plastic chairs bolted to the floor. This was entirely different. It was like a cross between a recording studio – the walls had a special acoustic cladding – and the sort of setting for a late-night panel discussion television show. Not one of the ones with politicians insulting each other. More of a BBC 2 show featuring four old academics discussing the latest novel by a barely functioning alcoholic or an interpretation of Bizet's *Carmen* entirely in rhyming slang.

There were four comfortable armchairs, not like the ones in the drawing room, modern, in primary colours. And there was a sort of coffee table in the middle with microphones pointing at each chair. Nothing remotely covert about any of it. There was even a switch next to the light that said, 'Recording' and a little red light to let you know it was on. This was where the real fun would take place.

*

Michael picked up Richard the following morning from his home in Fulham, a rather grand block of what estate agents call mansion flats.

Richard tossed a leather holdall onto the back seat and hopped into the front. Ten minutes later, as they passed Hyde Park Corner and headed up Park Lane, Richard began to study the road atlas.

'You won't need that. I've been before.'

'Margaret said it was a new safe house.'

'Not the safe house, Leighton Parva. My grandfather lives there.'

Michael had been brooding on this overnight. Leighton Parva was a tiny place. Ninety-nine dwellings, he had counted them once. The idea that MI6's latest covert premises should, by chance alone, be in his grandfather's village, defied the laws of probability. More importantly, it defied the reality of everything Michael knew about the old man. He wasn't even sure that his grandfather wasn't still on the payroll of some government agency or other. He rather hoped he was, because he had first-hand experience of what the old man got up to when he had time on his hands.

The file on Diarmuid Geraghty had been very thin. He claimed to have been a member of the IRA for twenty years and wished to provide information on various dissident republican groups. He hadn't said why. He'd undergone a preliminary round of questioning in London and the results were in the file.

Whoever he was, he wasn't Diarmuid Geraghty. There was no such person. He almost certainly had spent some time in the IRA, or at least been very close to it. He knew people. He knew procedures. He hadn't fallen into any of the traps set for him. He appeared to be the real thing.

There was only one area of concern, not his name, that was to be expected, and in any case, there were people working on that. They would know who he really was by the weekend. No, the issue was that he refused to disclose his motivation for becoming an informant. That needed to be cleared up.

*

It took two and a half hours to reach Leighton Parva. They drove past The Old Volunteer and The Old Vicarage. There was no sign of the net curtains twitching, but Michael hadn't expected them to. His grandfather probably had a periscope sticking up through his chimney or a CCTV link to a camera disguised as a bird table in the front garden. He wouldn't have been totally shocked if he'd found his grandfather sitting in the safe house sipping tea and discussing improvised explosive devices with an Irish terrorist.

Windmill Cottage was the last house in the village on the Oakham Road. You could even make a case that it wasn't in Leighton Parva proper at all. It was at least two hundred yards from the nearest building and its entrance drive was about two feet inside the sign welcoming careful drivers.

Michael swung in through the open five-bar gate and his car, the government's car actually, made a pleasing crunch on the gravel. The gate swung shut behind him, controlled by some unseen hand. The drive curved behind the house, and Michael followed it to a parking area in front of a triple garage. There was a Land Rover Discovery and a powerful BMW parked there already. Standing at the open back door was Little Chris, looking like Tarzan in a polo shirt.

*

The Scholar looked, at first glance, fairly unremarkable. He was a little below average height, or so it seemed. It's hard to judge a man's height when he's sitting in an armchair and harder still when your entire sense of perspective and scale has been thrown out by the presence of Chris, Tony, and Chris.

He was about forty, maybe a year or two younger. Grey curly hair, clean shaven, and wearing a T-shirt bearing the logo of a company that made fishing reels and, finally, jeans, not expensive ones. But the thing Michael noticed was the shoes: expensive Italian loafers. He was a sort of sartorial contradiction. He was drinking from a fine china cup. Michael could see the slice of lemon floating on the top.

'Hello. I'm Michael. This is Richard.'

The Scholar looked up.

'We'll have a much longer chat later, but if you like, you can start by telling us your real name.'

Michael had been thinking for the whole journey about how he would handle his first interaction. Nothing aggressive or hostile. Businesslike. He needed to ensure that Geraghty, or whoever he was, didn't think Michael was a gullible fool.

The Scholar took a sip from his tea and looked up. It was like looking at a portrait painted by somebody who wasn't very good at eyes. 'For now, you can call me Mr Geraghty. Perhaps later I shall permit you to call me Diarmuid.'

Michael had lost round one. And Richard appeared to have enjoyed that.

Chapter 4

Lake had decided to start as he meant to go on, and that meant being the first person in the office each morning, and, if necessary, the last to leave. The small petty part of him considered that this would be revenge on his wife Bella who hadn't understood why Lake was so unhappy about being promoted.

'Temporarily promoted,' he said with a heavy emphasis on the first word.

But she'd given him a rather harsh lecture, touching upon themes such as matrimonial and parental responsibility, the suggestion that he couldn't spend the next thirty years crouching on the back of observation vans and sitting in parked cars eating food from petrol stations. Then she moved on to some character observations and forecasts. Phrases such as 'self-indulgent man-child' and 'playing cops and robbers' kept cropping up. She suggested that he get over himself, pull himself together, and start showing a little self-belief. Finally, she suggested that if he wouldn't take any notice of her, he should go and see Frank McBride.

Lake didn't say anything in response. Didn't have time, really. His face must have given him away.

'You've already been to see him, haven't you? You've been down to that bloody Edwardian museum of brown ale and spittoons in Rutland, haven't you?'

She would have said more, but their daughter, Caroline, toddled in carrying her story book. Lake seized upon the opportunity to escape and swept her up in his arms and headed for the stairs. Hopefully, by the time the *Little Red Tractor* had rescued the farmer from whatever minor catastrophe had occurred in chapter five, Bella would have calmed down.

So, he would be first in, last out. And if Bella said anything, he would throw her own words back in her face. Except he wouldn't. Partly because he wasn't that brave, partly because he loved her too much and partly, and this was the really annoying part, he knew she was right. Again.

'I saw Monster and Amy on Saturday.'

'Hmm, hmm?' Lake had realised he'd put Caroline's nappy on back to front and he was inwardly debating whether it could be adjusted or whether he would have to remove it and start again.

'Yes, in Mothercare, looking at car seats.'

'Hmm, hmm?' It was no good. He would have to start again.

'Infant car seats.'

'Really?'

'Yes, and later on I saw them looking in a jeweller's window in Wheelergate.'

'That's interesting. What did they say?'

'Oh, I didn't speak to them.'

Lake had finally fixed the nappy. 'Hang on, Mothercare is in that retail park. That's at least a mile from the city centre.'

'Hmm.' Bella was affecting vagueness now.

'You saw them in two different locations and spoke to them on neither occasion, don't tell me—'

'Well, you know, I saw them in Mothercare, and I just sort of thought, and so when they left, I just sort of…I thought it would be easy, but following people without being spotted is really hard, actually.'

'Yes, I know. I do it for a living, remember?'

'But not so much now that you're management.'

'Temporary. Temporary management. Bella, I know that you think I ought to be chief, but the reality is I am just a humble customs officer.'

Bella decided to say nothing.

*

He was usually among the first to reach the office anyway, but there were always two or three people there before him and he wasn't exactly sure when they arrived. He was pretty confident that it wouldn't be before seven fifteen.

The Customs and Excise, National Investigation Service, Branch Eleven, Nottingham Sub Office wasn't an impressive building. But it was discreet. Lake parked behind the building, two large Victorian semi-detached villas knocked through into one slightly higgledy-piggledy set of offices, let himself in, and was pleased to see that he needed to disarm the alarm. He was first in. He headed first for the break room where he filled a kettle and hunted for his mug. He dawdled as long as he could, but he couldn't put it off forever. He eventually turned the key in the door of his office, took a deep breath, and walked in, almost tripping over the litter bin.

On his desk was a single envelope, addressed to 'Joe'. He recognised Andi's handwriting. It contained a single piece of paper bearing the words, 'Good Luck' and the spare key to his office.

Lake had hoped it would be a couple of months before Andi went on maternity leave. It would give everyone time to get used to the fact he was the temporary SIO. It would also give him a bit more time to decide how he was going to handle it. Frank McBride's advice had been well meant and sincere. And the approach that he'd suggested would probably work well...if you were Frank McBride.

Joe Lake was no Frank McBride. He had a fraction of the experience for a start, but that was less important than the fact he simply didn't have anything like his...what would you call it? Presence? Well, yes, but not exactly. Charisma? No, not unless you had a pretty unusual definition of that quality. Frank McBride was Frank McBride, and Lake wasn't confident that he could even carry off a cheap imitation. He sat at his desk with Andi's note in his hands and that was when he understood the real meaning of Frank's advice.

Andi was organised. And professional. She had a plan. She was going to gradually delegate her responsibilities and workload to Lake. She'd persuaded Alan Hawkins that there should be an overlap of at least a month when she and Lake would be joint SIOs. She'd even made plans for a second desk to be moved into her office. It was a little cramped, but that didn't matter.

Andi was also, in strictly medical terms, a geriatric mother. The doctor must have known how she was going to react to this characterisation. Presumably, most mothers reacted in a similar way. Anyway, he pushed ahead, and went on to explain that this was quite common in geriatric mothers. He clearly had some sort of death wish, or perhaps there is a quota after which you get given some sort of medal for bravery. He managed to get away with it though because his next sentence completely knocked Andi off kilter. She would need to cease work immediately. She managed to negotiate a couple of further days, but the message was clear. Her maternity leave would start at the end of that week. Joe Lake was in charge.

Lake was in London when Andi had received her news. He was attending a meeting with the officers from 'The Other Office' who would be handling the intelligence end of the operation. Customs officers always called it the Other Office. People weren't supposed to know who they were or what they did. Mostly they didn't. Lake was given as much information as was known and told that he would start to receive intelligence next week. He was told to choose a case officer and an operation name.

Lake had already chosen both. He just hadn't told anyone. The case officer was to be Chris Bolton, known to one and all as 'Monster' because of his size and his appetite. It was a nickname that fitted him less well than in the past because, after having spent his twenties on the rugby pitch or in the bar, Monster had found love and a ready-made family. He was living with Amy and her two daughters. He'd even started eating vegetables, not just the gherkins on cheeseburgers. He was studying law in his spare time. Lake knew that Monster was planning to leave the world of investigation, get a sensible nine to five. And, courtesy of Bella, he knew his plans for the immediate future, too.

Monster was usually among the earlier arrivals. He'd found the note left on his desk and Lake could hear him in the break room. Lake had never known anyone who could make so much noise just putting a spoon of instant coffee in a mug. There were crashes and curses, muttered profanities, and at one point it sounded like he'd drop kicked the bin across the room. Eventually, he put his head in at the open door. Lake nodded towards the chair behind the second desk. As Monster squeezed into place, Lake shut the door.

'Do I call you Guv or something now?'

'I wish you wouldn't.'

'Why are there two desks still in here? Can't swing a cat.'

'That one's yours. We've got a target job. You're the case officer.'

Monster beamed, then he seemed to think of what Amy might say. The beam faded, but then regained its earlier luminescence. After all, it was probably his last job. Why not go out in style?

'Is this Andi's decision, or yours?'

'The queen asked for you personally. It was you or one of the corgis.'

'What can I say? That girl's been spoilt and now nothing but the best will satisfy her. What's the job?'

'Cigarettes.'

Monster's face fell. 'Fags? Fags? We're supposed to be a drugs team. Why are we targeting some chancer who's smuggling a few ciggies?'

Lake took a sip of coffee. He'd had all this set out in his head last night. He'd anticipated that some might think the investigation of cigarette smuggling less worthy, less glamorous, less sexy than drugs smuggling. But he was sure he could change that. Well, almost sure.

'The Other Office thinks that there is a target on the continent – not sure who, or where at this stage – who is coordinating the entire operation. They estimate he's moving five or six loads a month. Lorry freight, Channel ports. We don't know the vehicles, the drivers, or the ports of entry. You can get ten million fags on a lorry. Bit less if they're concealed, obviously. That's the thick end of a million quid in duty and VAT per load. Packet of fags is what? Three fifty? These are probably being flogged at two quid a pack. So maybe a million quid per lorry, most of it profit.

'Now, no one is going to sell millions of fags off the back of the lorry, or even out of a single corner shop, are they? So, there's some sort of warehouse, or something. We do have a couple of targets who we think are heading the distribution network here. We're talking serious money, and that's why it's a target job.

'So that's the job. It's yours if you want it. But if you'd rather investigate some loser with a hundred grams of coke up his arse, that's up to you.'

Lake reached for his mug, that was the longest speech he'd given for a while. Monster picked up his mug and put it down again.

'What's the operation name? And when do we start?'

'Operation Bridegroom. And we start now.'

'Bridegroom?'

'Bridegroom. And congratulations, by the way.'

Lake enjoyed Monster's reaction enormously. Perhaps this was how Frank McBride felt all the time? If so, Lake rather liked it. McBride wouldn't have smirked, though.

*

While elsewhere in the office, the rest of the team indulged themselves in gossip and speculation, Lake and Monster wrestled with the planning for the operation. By twelve thirty, all they had to show for their efforts was a bin full of crumpled paper and a powerful desire for a pint.

It was quiet in the Limelight, the bar to Nottingham's Playhouse Theatre that served as the team's local, even for a Monday. The two men found a quiet corner and attempted to summarise the fruits of their morning's deliberations.

'It's just really hard.'

'We don't know enough. We don't know where the stuff is coming in, or what happens to it next. Will we get enough notice to be at the port when it arrives? Will we be able to follow it wherever it goes without being spotted? And what are we going to do if the lorry parks up in some lonely spot and a dozen big blokes turn up in Transit vans? That'll be a punch-up for certain and we won't necessarily win. Even if we do, where are we going to put a dozen prisoners at short notice? And if we charge them all, we'll be tied up for months preparing for an enormous court case and all we'll have to show for it is some pretty weak evidence against a bunch of low-level chancers and wide boys.'

Lake nodded. 'Let's not worry about stuff we couldn't or shouldn't do. Let's focus on what we do know and what we can learn.'

'Which brings us back to these two targets the Other Office knows about. Eamonn Walsh and Tony Castle.'

'So, we focus on them to begin with. Maybe one of them will lead us to a warehouse or something.'

'Okay, get Nick to prepare files on them both. Full background checks, we'll start the mobile surveillance next week.'

*

Eamonn Thomas Walsh was born in Leicester and had lived his whole life less than a mile from the Leicester Royal Infirmary in the network of narrow streets between the hospital and Leicester City FC's ground at Filbert Street. Despite this, he was considered one of the leading characters in Leicester's small Irish community, due in no small part to his proprietorship, in recent years, of The Walnut Tree.

Frank McBride had put quite a lot of thought and effort into returning The Old Volunteer to its appearance in about 1914. It would have taken Eamonn Walsh a lot less effort because a lot less had changed in his establishment. The Walnut Tree wasn't the sort of pub that appears in Sunday colour supplements, as The Old Volunteer had. It didn't even appear in good beer guides. If The Walnut Tree was on a list of establishments, it was convincing evidence the list was comprehensive and complete.

The clientele of The Walnut Tree, while not especially well-heeled, were loyal, or, if not actually loyal, very reliable. They expected little from their local except drinkable beer at a reasonable price. This Walsh was able to supply, and he would have survived, if not exactly prospered, if this had been his only source of income. But it wasn't.

The Walnut Tree had a large function room that served as a venue for birthday parties, anniversaries, wakes, weddings, and the numerous other family occasions that the Irish diaspora simply cannot acknowledge without a licensed bar. Walsh also owned a mobile bar that could be set-up in church halls, at Irish dancing competitions, and at barbecues. He also rented out fruit machines, pool tables, dart boards, and cigarette machines.

And he sold and distributed approximately half a million smuggled cigarettes every week.

*

On 30th May, 1979, Nottingham Forest had astonished just about everybody with the exception of Brian Clough, by becoming the champions of Europe. A year later, they did it again. In the nearly twenty years since, the number of people who claimed to be either at Munich's Olympic Stadium in '79, or Madrid's Bernabeu in '80, had grown far beyond the capacity of either venue. But, so far as is known, only one person has claimed to have been present in both cities but spent the duration of both games in a police cell. That person was Anthony Mark Castle.

Of course, he was a much younger man then. He now considered himself a businessman, a trader in various goods. Electrical household appliances mostly, compact and portable, the kind that can be passed through a window. Oh, and a few car radios. Not much in the way of accompanying paperwork as a rule, but very affordable. Oh, and cigarettes, also very affordable and if the printing on the packs was a little blurred or if Marlboro was spelled with two Ls, or two Rs, or both, never mind that, two quid a pack, bud.

Chapter 5

Nine thirty on Wednesday morning, the sun was shining at an angle through the French windows. In an hour or two, Michael calculated, it would begin to shine into the face of Diarmuid Geraghty. At that point, Michael would courteously close the blinds, but probably not the curtains. This wasn't the sort of interrogation where a light is shone in the suspect's eyes.

The atmosphere in the interview room was more like the studio of a chat show where young celebrities would be invited to gush their much-rehearsed routine about how astonished and how lucky they were to be starring in the latest Hollywood blockbuster. Or some much-loved national treasure who had done something similar thirty years ago would have an opportunity to let slip some faux-indiscreet anecdotes about dear, dear Johnny Wayne, or that rascal Peter Sellers before moving on to the serious business of hustling their autobiography filled, it would be intimated, with similar stories from a life spent attending glamorous parties or waking up in gutters with people who were now showbiz royalty.

It wasn't just the surroundings, although perhaps subconsciously they played a part, but Michael had decided that this interrogation was going to be conducted the way Michael Parkinson would do it.

Michael had a plan. He would interview Geraghty the way people make polite conversation with strangers at parties. The emphasis would be allowing him to talk, for as long as he wanted, on just about any subject, nudging him back to the interesting stuff ever so rarely, ever so gently. That part ought to be easy. People like talking about themselves.

He would not set traps. He would not try to catch him out. He would just let him talk, and later, who knew how much later, he would very gently press him for details. Details that could be referenced, cross-checked, verified...or disproven. There was no time pressure, no ticking bomb somewhere, no deadline. It was all going to be very Michael Parkinson. All he needed was a small orchestra to play Geraghty's theme tune as he skipped down a curving staircase beaming at the audience.

Richard had a plan, too. But he was keeping it to himself.

And the Scholar had a plan.

The Scholar had been considering his plan for weeks. At first, he'd thought the task difficult, maybe even impossible. He didn't know how the interrogation would take place. Perhaps it would be in a damp basement with a hundred watt right in his face. Some musclebound ex-para shouting at him from a range of six inches, a hood over his head, white noise at a million decibels. Or perhaps it would be conducted on a chesterfield sofa in a country house library where he would be interviewed by a man in a smoking jacket with a cigarette holder. You never could tell with these Brits.

He didn't know exactly what they would want to know. Just as at a dinner party, it's a mistake to think that what you think is significant or fascinating is what somebody wants to hear. He didn't know what the questions would be or how they would be asked. It was like trying to play poker without knowing what was in your own hand, either.

But none of that mattered. The best poker players didn't need cards. They weren't even playing cards. They were playing their opponents. The Scholar would play his opponents.

*

Michael had laid out a pot of tea on the table, and a cafetiere of coffee. There were mugs, not cups and saucers, and a plate of biscuits. But when the Scholar entered, he was already holding a demi-tasse in a matching black saucer. He placed it on the table in front of the single empty seat. He raised his eyebrows, nodded ever so slightly towards the seat, and said, 'May I?'

'Please,' replied Michael, and he rose from his own seat and crossed the room to press the *record* button beside the light switch. A little red light lit up. It signified nothing at all. The recording controls were operated by Little Chris next door and the room had been 'live' for ten minutes.

'Case number ninety-nine slash one four oh four,' Michael began. 'Wednesday 8th April 1999' – he glanced at his watch – 'Nine thirty-one.'

He sat down and drew the cafetiere towards him. 'I'm Michael. This is Richard. May I call you Diarmuid?'

Diarmuid leant back in his chair and took a sip of his espresso. 'Of course.'

Inside both men's heads was the sound of the bell signalling round one. Richard's private contest had actually already begun.

*

They broke for lunch at one. Beans on toast. Whatever branch of the military Tony had been in, it wasn't the Catering Corps.

It was agreed that they'd reconvene at two thirty. The Scholar retired to his room, Richard paced to and fro in the garden talking on his mobile phone. Michael decided to stroll into the village and see if his grandfather was at home. It took less than five minutes to walk into the village proper, past the war memorial, and the entrance to the cricket club to where The Old Vicarage stood, diagonally opposite The Old Volunteer. There was something different about the pub. It took Michael a few seconds to work out what it was. The sign had changed. Some things had to change in Leighton Parva occasionally.

Michael walked down the gravel drive, and through the little gate that led to the kitchen door. The gate now bore a tasteful little brass oval, 'Beware of the Dog'. He paused and looked in at the window. His grandfather had his back to him. He was fiddling with a teapot. For a moment, Michael considered the possibility that the old man had known he would be coming but that was impossible. He hadn't decided himself until a few moments ago. Then he saw him add a second scoop of tea to the pot. His grandfather still made tea in a pot and still made it with loose leaves rather than teabags. But a second scoop? He was expecting someone. He knocked and opened the door in one movement.

'Hello, Mikey.'

The old goat had done it again. He hadn't changed. He turned to face his grandson. Still the same retired military officer. The silver hair perhaps a little thinner. The gap between the collar of his check shirt and his neck perhaps a little wider, the knot of the tie perhaps a millimetre lower. But the same man. And The Old Vicarage, or at least its kitchen, had changed little too, with one exception. In the corner was a dog bed, empty.

'Of course,' said his grandfather, 'you haven't met Brunhilde.' He hadn't lost his gift for telepathy, either. He opened the door that led to the hall, pursing his lips in preparation for a whistle, but it wasn't necessary. Brunhilde came bounding in, mouth wide open, long pink tongue at four o'clock. Her four paws were struggling to gain purchase on the tiled floor, and she looked like a speed skater who'd forgotten how to slow down. Eventually, she came to a halt at Michael's feet in a sitting position.

'She's a Weimaraner. Twelve months old. Some of my friends thought I needed some company since my grandchildren visit me so seldom.'

'Well, I'm here now.' Michael nodded at the teapot. He couldn't help himself. 'Were you expecting me?'

'Good Lord, no. How could I? No, my friend Ron will be here in a moment. We were going to give Brunhilde a training session.'

As if on cue, the back door opened and in walked a man who must have been Ron. If his grandfather was the retired Rutland colonel archetype (actually, he'd been a brigadier) then Ron was the salt of the earth countryman. He didn't actually tug his forelock as he crossed the threshold, but he looked like the sort of man who might.

Michael didn't know many countryman types. His social acquaintances were mostly people who couldn't tell a mangelwurzel from a mango and certainly couldn't identify a Massey Ferguson model by sound alone, and yet there was something about Ron that seemed familiar to him.

Ron was clearly familiar to Brunhilde too. She immediately rushed and sat to attention, if that's what gundogs do, beside him. Ron patted and fussed the dog with what seemed genuine affection.

'Time for a cup of tea before we go, Ron? This is my grandson, Mikey. Michael, I should say. He's up from London for a few days, staying locally.'

Michael shot a glance at his grandfather, but it was no good looking for any embarrassment or sheepishness on his face. The old schemer was completely without shame.

Ron nodded at Michael and sat down at the kitchen table. He gave his head another movement, even smaller than the first, and Brunhilde trotted over to the bed and lay down.

Michael's grandfather brought him up to date with developments in Leighton Parva in the two years since he'd spent a summer in the village. The cricket club had started a second team and there was an open coaching session for children on Friday evenings. Leighton Hall, the stately pile on the outskirts of the village, had been bought by a company that specialised in corporate training. The Old Volunteer had a new proprietor (Bernard didn't mention that it was him) and a new manager.

'Is there still a quiz?' Michael knew that the quiz at The Old Volunteer had been a highlight of his grandfather's week.

'Well, yes, but a slight change. I'm the quiz master now. It's tomorrow evening, actually. You might want to pop down. It's quite well attended.'

Michael said that he would try. He finished his tea and, sensing that Ron and Brunhilde in particular wanted to get on with their programme for the afternoon, he rose to leave, promising he'd return soon.

*

The Scholar was ready at two thirty. Ready to be Diarmuid Geraghty. He sat in the same chair, folded his hands in his lap and with his expression, his eyes, in fact his whole body, he seemed to say, 'How may I help you?'

They'd spent the morning discussing how he'd come to be involved in the republican movement. He'd talked about life in Derry in the sixties, about the discrimination, the gerrymandering, the disparity in employment and education opportunities. All standard stuff. If Sinn Fein had made party political broadcasts, these were the type of messages they would have contained.

He was able to tell the story fluently. He'd recited some version of these stories many times in Boston, Chicago, and New York, a little difference in emphasis according to his audience. Sometimes he emphasised the famine of the eighteen forties that had driven so many of his audience's forefathers to America in the first place. Sometimes he emphasised the monarchy and referenced regiments with some of the odder names. Some Americans had only the shakiest understanding of the role of the crown in the British constitution and they would often get perversely agitated by references to The Black Watch and The Duke of Cornwall's Light Infantry.

Now he was consciously dialling back the fluency. The character that he was creating for himself wasn't supposed to be a slick operator. He'd decided that he was a disillusioned republican, driven into the movement by circumstance and now appalled by the cynicism of the movement's leaders: those who now wished to be regarded as politicians or statesmen, those who wished to continue the cycle of violence and mayhem and those who merely wanted to enrich themselves, turning their companies of soldiers into criminal gangs. He was, in turn, frustrated, tearful, bitter, sorrowful, but mostly just disorientated and confused.

He knew that if he provided too much information too freely that it, and he, would be treated with suspicion. So, occasionally he would lapse into a sulky silence or claim that he didn't want to say any more. Sometimes he would insist that he still hated the Brits or tell a long story of some terrible injustice that had been done, not to him, but to the cousin of a friend of his, sometimes to a friend of a cousin. Some of these stories were true, some were common urban myths that most people knew to be, at the very least, grossly exaggerated. One or two he just invented.

He was starting to enjoy himself, weaving his imagined persona into a real character live and in person. Now and then, he had to check himself. He couldn't afford to get carried away.

The two men opposite him seemed to be drinking it all in. The tall one occasionally made a note or two. The other one, the one he thought was probably the senior of the two, wrote nothing. But he was the one who asked the questions, did the coaxing, made the correct reassuring noises at the right moments. They were buying it.

They were buying it all, both of them. He could tell. He could tell from the body language. Sometimes the tall one would underline things in his notebook. The Scholar couldn't see it. But you call tell if someone is underlining something, can't you? You can tell. They were lapping it up, and he hadn't told them a damn thing. They probably hadn't realised that yet. But this evening, they would go over what'd been said, and they would realise. And then in the morning they would be back again, trying to pin him down, trying to get something specific. And they would believe anything he told them.

*

The grandfather clock in the hall struck five. Michael stretched and glanced across at Richard. He gave a slight shrug.

'Well, Diarmuid, I think we've made a good start. But I don't want to tire you out, so let's call it a day. I believe dinner's at six and afterwards the evening is yours.'

Diarmuid nodded and rose. He turned and headed for the door. 'Shall I?' he asked indicating the switch with the little red light.

'Please,' said Michael.

Diarmuid flicked the switch. The light went off. He opened the door. Michael could see Big Chris winding up the grandfather clock. Diarmuid headed for the stairs. Michael waited a moment and then went and closed the door.

'What do you think?'

'Espresso.'

'Yes, I thought so too. And the almond biscotti.'

'All the rage on the Bogside, almond biscotti. I wonder who he really is.'

'His prints will be on that mug.'

'I'll give it to Big Chris. Have him run the checks.'

'And his eyes?'

'If the eyes are the windows of the soul...I think his have been boarded up.'

Chapter 6

Andy Bishop had moved to Spain in 1988. He hadn't needed to, but he didn't know that at the time. All he knew was that Terry had told him that the police were looking for him. He didn't even say why. It could have been several things. Some of them petty. Some of them, well, not exactly trivial. So, he had fled.

The fact is, he'd panicked. He'd believed Terry and so he just took off. Maybe it had been true. Maybe it hadn't. But he'd since heard that Terry had been exposed as a police informant and he'd had to leave Leicester in a hurry, too. Bishop wasn't expecting him to show up in Murcia, but it was possible. After all, he had. He wasn't exactly sure what he would do if he saw Terry in the Bow Bells Bar in Cartagena. Ignore him, probably. Or hurt him.

By the time he learnt all this, it was almost two years later, and by then, he'd met Selena and he had to stay. No. He'd *wanted* to stay. They had married. Then Jose came along, they always called him Pepe. A year later Carla had been born. He had a family. He had a life. He was happy.

Selena's family welcomed him into the fold, but very much on their terms. Their acceptance and approval were very much dependent upon his behaving in exactly the way they thought a model son-in-law should. And that was just the start of it. Selena seemed to have about a thousand cousins, and he had to meet and impress every one of them. On the plus side, he found that his Spanish quickly improved; it had to.

But it wasn't just the approval process. The family seemed to think they had the right to exercise total control over his life. His attempts to find an apartment were constantly thwarted. Landlords would mysteriously find objections or rents would double. In the end, he'd bowed to the inevitable and moved into his parents-in-law's house.

Uncle Pedro had found him a job. After a few years, that became too stifling and so he found another, driving for a local firm. It didn't pay all that well and then...then an *opportunity* had presented itself.

It was nearly eight o'clock when his rig rolled off the ferry from Le Havre. He had managed a hurried breakfast. He would eat again when he reached Leicester. He crawled through the port in first gear. Passport control was a formality, Customs likewise. He tuned his radio to the BBC and caught the end of the news as he joined the M275. Behind him, unseen, the surveillance team took up their positions for the long drive north.

*

Fifty miles to the west, and an hour later, Bryan Sharpe drove his lorry through similar controls at the smaller and quieter port of Newhaven. There was no surveillance team to meet or follow him. There was bad traffic on the M25. He didn't make it to the Midlands until late afternoon.

Tony Castle was impatient and angry, but Bryan wasn't in the mood for that.

'If you've got a problem, take it up with the Irishman.'

From the look on Castle's face, it was obvious he'd met him. It was obvious he'd looked into those eyes. And it was obvious he wouldn't be directing any complaints or grumbles, even the slightest hint of dissatisfaction, in that direction.

Unloading was swift and efficient. Castle was good. A different rendezvous point every time. All the customers present and ready. The wagon was empty in a little over thirty minutes and everyone was away and clear. Bryan and Castle waited fifteen minutes until Castle had received the all-clear from each of the customers. Then Bryan turned around the empty rig, empty apart from two pallets of well-travelled oranges, and left, leaving Castle sitting in his Jag counting his money.

*

Every time Bishop came to Leicester it felt a little less like home. He never sought out any of his old friends or frequented his old haunts. He just dropped his load, turned around, and headed home. Home was in Spain, now. But he'd felt a little sad when he learnt that Leicester City would soon be leaving its ground at Filbert Street. He'd spent many happy hours in the old double decker stand behind the goal. Of course, he'd spent many more frustrated, bitter, and unhappy hours. But that wasn't the point. The point was that Filbert Street was a monument to his connection with the city of his birth and it was one more connection that was going to be taken away.

He could see the stadium now, on his left. The double decker stand had now gone. He passed The Walnut Tree and turned right, and then right again, each street narrower than the previous, each turn sharper. He pulled up outside some blue gates, left the engine running, and reached for his mobile phone and sent a one-word text message. While he waited for a response, he pulled a packet of Camels from his breast pocket and lit one.

He'd never got on with Spanish cigarettes, Ducados and Fortuna, filthy things. But he got used to Camels. And Camels were cool. Humphrey Bogart had smoked Camels. Of course, they'd killed him, but that wasn't the point. Bogey was cool, ergo Camels were cool, ergo Andy Bishop was cool.

He'd only been there a minute or two, barely time to smoke half his fag, when he heard the creaking, groaning, protesting sound of the blue gates opening. Eamonn Walsh half raised a hand in greeting and swung the two wooden gates, painted in Leicester City blue, but peeling in places, open. Bishop wound down his window.

'Eamonn.'

'Andy.'

He tossed the cigarette out of the window and turned the keys in the ignition.

For most drivers reversing from a narrow street through narrow gates and into a tiny yard would have been a tricky manoeuvre, but Bishop had been steering an articulated lorry through the narrow streets of south-east Spain for almost ten years. For him it was no problem. He reversed up to the doors of a building that looked like it had been assembled from the spare parts of condemned Scout huts and held together with snot. He hopped down from the cab and shook Walsh's hand. Then, together, they shut the gates.

Forty-five minutes passed while the surveillance team sat around waiting, listening to a commentary on events taking place behind the blue gates.

Monster had seen and heard enough. He reached for the transmit button.

'*All mobiles, from commander. Stand down. Stand down. Rendezvous back at the office. Debrief there.*'

*

The team was tired. Most of them hadn't reached Portsmouth until late the previous evening and they'd all been up at six. Kevin Cleary who had ridden the motorcycle for nearly two hundred miles was especially weary.

The story of the journey from Portsmouth to Leicester hadn't taken very long to tell. What had happened behind the blue gates was the important part. Nick Harper had somehow got himself to the top floor of a block of flats that overlooked the yard.

'He backed it up to a sort of shed or warehouse. The other man. He had a forklift. He took off two pallets and put them to one side.'

'What were they?'

'Couldn't tell for sure. Onions, if I had to guess.'

'Okay.'

'Then he unloaded sixteen pallets into the shed. Shrink-wrapped in blue stuff. Couldn't see what they were. Then they put the onions, or whatever, back, and closed the doors.'

'Shed or lorry?'

'Both.'

'Then the man went inside, came back a couple of minutes later with a bag and gave it to the driver. Bag contained cash.'

'Are you guessing again?'

'No, I saw it. He counted it, well looked at it. Definitely cash. Then he left.'

'And the lorry was empty?'

'Apart from the onions, yes.'

Monster looked at his watch, then he looked at Lake. Lake shook his head. Monster raised an eyebrow.

'Right!' said Lake. 'Get the radio batteries on charge, fill the cars with fuel, make sure your notebooks are complete.' He glanced at his watch. 'See you in the pub at six.'

*

Monster and Lake withdrew to the office they shared. It had been designed for single occupancy and only represented about eighty per cent of the space that two people needed. Or seventy per cent if one of them was Monster.

'I've got my sums right, haven't I? Sixteen pallets. Eight million fags?'

'Yep.'

'How many fags does, say, a corner shop sell in a month?'

'I don't know, not eight million, though.'

'So, there're multiple customers?'

'Presumably. We should know soon. Walsh will presumably tell them he has stock in and they'll start to arrive. We'll have to get a camera installed. Get the number plates of the customers when they arrive, trace them, and have the local excise office raid the shops.'

'Supposing he delivers?'

'Then we'll need a new plan. For now, let's get a camera stuck outside his yard. We can probably hide one of the new tiny ones in that lamppost. We've probably got a few days.'

'They could be collecting now. He might have moved it all by tomorrow.'

'He might. We just have to do the best we can as quickly as we can. But if he has to split it up into packages for his customers. That will take a day or two.'

Lake was far less confident than he sounded. But, in fact, he was right. It *was* two days before the first customers started to show up at Eamonn Walsh's yard. By then the camera was in place. In the next few days, a dozen different vans visited the yard.

*

In earlier days Lake would have spent the whole evening in the pub. But not anymore. Not because he was the SIO, if anything that would have made it more likely. But now he was a husband and father and since he'd spent the previous night at an unremarkable hotel on the outskirts of Portsmouth, he wanted to go home. Bella had just started back at work. Caroline had just started at nursery, and he didn't just feel that he *ought* to go home. He *wanted* to.

Even at half-past six, Nottingham traffic could be very frustrating. Lake crawled the mile and a half to Trent Bridge and it wasn't until he was past Radcliffe and into the Vale of Belvoir that he was able to pick up speed. Sometimes he deliberately diverted through villages like Granby or Redmile so that he could enjoy the bucolic scenery. He found it restful, even if it added a few minutes to his journey. But not that evening. He was tired, and he wanted to be home.

As he crossed the threshold, he heard the sounds of splashing and gleeful screaming from upstairs. Caroline was having her bath. At least he hoped that was what it was. Somebody had bought Caroline a plastic Noah's ark for her first birthday. It was her favourite and Bella had been teaching her the names of the animals. Lake could hear her as he climbed the stairs.

'Rarf! Rarf!'

'It's Jee Rarf, darling.'

But Caroline had moved on. 'Zebba! Zebba!'

Bella was kneeling beside the bath. She'd heard Lake enter the room behind her and turned now and looked up at him. She looked exhausted. 'Oh good. You're home. How was it?'

'Fine. It went fine.' That was enough about his job. 'How was school?'

'Oh fine, I mean I want to murder the lower sixth, but otherwise fine. I'll go and see to dinner.'

Lake felt guilty that Bella, after a day's work, and a couple of hours of entertaining Caroline should now be cooking, but they both knew that if they wanted something edible that didn't come from the chip shop, that was how it had to be. She climbed to her feet – she looked so weary – and headed downstairs.

'Zebba, Zebba!'

'That's right. It's a zebra. Now, what's this one?'

'Lion!' Caroline was pointing at the floor where about a third of Noah's menagerie had been cast. 'Lion!' She pointed to the bin. And that's when Lake saw it.

*

It took Lake almost half an hour to dry Caroline and get her ready for bed. Then he read her a story, one about something called a Gruffalo. Then he read it again, then *Little Red Riding Hood* and finally his own notebook recording the events of that day's surveillance.

Bella had cooked spaghetti bolognaise and was apologising. Spaghetti bolognese would have represented the most ambitious dish that Lake would have attempted, and even that would have resulted in a mediocre heap of vaguely edible slush and a mountain of washing up that you normally only see on television commercials or student houses.

'How did Caroline get on at nursery?'

'Oh, okay, I think. There were no complaints, anyway. She seemed to like the building blocks. When I dropped her off, she toddled away without so much as a backward glance. She seems to have made friends with a boy named Luke. She seems very happy.'

'And you? Are you missing her?'

'A little, but I'm so busy at work I hardly have time to think about her.'

Well, that was a lie, but Lake let it go. He was just preparing the ground, building up to the main topic.

'Luke's a nice name.'

'Yeah, I suppose so.'

'But you can't really have a child called Luke Lake.'

Bella looked at him.

'And, of course, it might be another girl.'

Bella looked again. 'How...?'

'I am an investigator.'

A tiny point scored and probably a temporary one. Before long, Bella would remember that she'd left the test in the bathroom bin.

Chapter 7

'Shall I?' The Scholar's hand hovered over the switch that purportedly operated the recording devices.

'Please,' said Michael while pouring himself a coffee.

The Scholar flicked the switch and as he did so, he became Diarmuid Geraghty again. The little red light came on. He placed his demitasse and saucer on the coffee table and settled into his chair, or at least the chair he'd been assigned to the day before. He was expecting that today's questioning would pick up where they'd finished yesterday. If he'd wanted to, he could have fended off questioning like that for weeks. But that wasn't why he was there.

Go slowly at first, by all means. Win their confidence, that was essential. But sooner or later he had to provide this pair with the information that he wanted fed into the security services, or at least, the apparatus of the British state.

He thought he had the measure of the two men. Very relaxed, very unhurried, but sharp. They were letting him talk because they wanted to see if he'd just arrived with a pre-scripted message (which he had).

They wanted to test whether he was using them (which he was). And they wanted to give him the opportunity to expose himself (and that he was not going to do).

The second day started with a slight change of pace. The two men were each sitting in the chair that the other had occupied the day before. Surely, surely, they weren't going to try good cop, bad cop, were they? That would just be insulting. But apparently not. It was just a slight change of tone.

'So, Diarmuid, if you were me, which dissident republicans would worry you most?'

*

Heather Hobday had overreacted. She knew that she'd overreacted. All her friends had told her for a start...more than once, usually. Sometimes they told her in earnest head-to-head conversations, sometimes quite late in the evening in the pub, and once as part of a badly orchestrated and most unwelcome 'intervention'. This was all unnecessary. She knew she was overreacting. She wanted to overreact. She wanted to overreact spectacularly, run away to sea, or join the French Foreign Legion. Except that she'd once been seasick on the Isle of Wight ferry and she wasn't even sure that the *Legion Etrangere* accepted women. And even if it did, she was pretty certain that the haircut wouldn't have suited her.

But she had to overreact. The sheer scale of the betrayal demanded it. Anything less would have been to accept the pain, the horror, the humiliation. And she couldn't do that. She just couldn't.

She'd been so happy. To be young, to be in London, and to be in love was to experience the nearest thing to heaven on earth. She enjoyed her job, teaching in an inner-city primary school. She enjoyed the chaotic lifestyle that came with sharing a house with Louise and Lucy, her university friends.

And she had had Julian. And everything was going to be just perfect. He hadn't actually said so. They hadn't been shopping for rings or saving Saturdays in the summer exactly. But it was understood. At least Heather had thought it was understood. They'd paused hand in hand and looked in estate agents' windows. They'd joked about baby names. He even called her parents 'the in-laws'. And that's what had made the betrayal so awful and that was why she had to overreact. Well, that, and her grandmother dying.

She'd been a sweet old lady. Twinset, pearls, beaming smile, and just a hint of mischief behind the eyes. She knitted and made jam and attended the Women's Institute. She hid shortbread in a vase on the mantlepiece, who knows from whom because she'd lived alone since Heather's grandfather had died twenty years before. She'd always welcomed Heather on visits to see her in the country as a little girl, gave her sweets and, scandalously, allowed her a sip of her sherry. Heather had hated the taste, but the thrill of the illicit made her desire it, anyway.

As she'd grown older, Nana had done her best to keep up her role as a bad influence. She'd given Heather an ivory cigarette holder on her sixteenth birthday.

'Don't let your father see it. It was a present from an admirer, before your grandfather. A pilot he was. Very dashing.'

And there would be increasingly risqué stories of Nana's time in the WAAF. Racing through Lincolnshire lanes in a sports car. Canoodling – Nana always called it canoodling – in air-raid shelters, standing at the end of the runway as the Lancasters dragged themselves into the air and turned east towards danger and terror. Nights in the officers' mess, high jinks, the raucous laughter of young men who partied like there was no tomorrow, because for some, there wasn't. The way she told it, Nana had dated half of Bomber Command. She would wink and giggle and break off stories with, 'And that's all I'm going to say about that.'

But as the level in the sherry decanter lowered (of course it was in a decanter) the mood would become more sombre and the emphasis of the stories would change to boys that she'd known who didn't come back. She became maudlin and young Heather found it, if not exactly frightening, certainly disconcerting.

Then she'd change gear again and talk about the grandfather Heather couldn't remember.

'Harold wasn't like the others. They were all so dashing, so devil-may-care. He wasn't like that at all. He was very sober, very reliable, always reliable. The others thought he was boring. But he made it through. He always came home. Even that one time. Always came home.'

And she'd disappear to the kitchen, dabbing her eyes with a handkerchief and return with a leather casket, and it would have to be opened. Heather would be shown the black-and-white photographs of the handsome young man in uniform, the Navigator's brevet, and the medals, the newspaper clippings, frail as ancient gossamer, faded to a jaundice yellow. And the handkerchief would be in near constant use.

Nana would have understood about Julian. She would probably have gone down to London and set about him with her walking stick. Would have served him right. But Nana was gone and the leather casket belonged to Heather now. Everything did, including Primrose Cottage, Leighton Parva, Rutland.

*

It had all happened so fast. It had to really, before the anger and the hurt had worn off. She saw the advertisement in the *Times Educational Supplement*, applied without thinking. And now here she was, no longer a young metropolitan surrounded by like-minded friends. She was a resident of a tiny village in the county that time forgot. And it wasn't just her surroundings. Everything had changed. She was a senior teacher now, a sort of deputy head, at a primary school in Oakham. Nothing like London. There, a quarter of the children arrived unable to speak English. Here, three-quarters of them arrived in Range Rovers.

And the staff was different too. They were all very nice, very, very nice, but there wasn't one of them under the age of fifty. Perhaps that was why there'd been so many questions about her willingness to supervise games. The rest of the staff looked like a brisk walk across the car park might be their last. They all seemed to be clad exclusively in tweed. One or two of them might even have been made of tweed. They were like slightly younger versions of Nana.

She wasn't regretting her dramatic gesture. Well, not yet. And there were definitely upsides. She owned her own house. She didn't know anybody else her age who could say that. And she'd been able to buy a little car. But where could she go in it? And who would she see? Her friends had all promised to come and see her, to spend weekends in the country. But she knew that the novelty and the appeal of Rutland would quickly wear off. Jasper's in Oakham could hardly compete with the Ministry of Sound. Perhaps, after all, she was regretting it.

But for now, she was determined to enjoy herself. She would spend a year in the country. Buy some green wellies, attend a point to point, find out what a 'point to point' was, something to do with horses perhaps, or was that a gymkhana? Perhaps she could get a cat, or a dog. Perhaps she could buy a loving, loyal dog. A dog who would adore her unconditionally, a dog that would always be pleased to see her, a faithful friend who would never hurt her, never betray her, never sleep with her best friend.

Of course, the idea of a dog was absurd, utterly impractical. But she couldn't quite let it go. The idea had been put there by the three old men she'd met on the hills behind Leighton Parva. She'd decided she needed a brisk walk to think things through and she'd met them somewhere near the beacon.

Actually, she'd met the dogs first, a pair of them. One was a spaniel of some sort. Heather knew little about dogs. The other was possibly some sort of gun dog too, but it was of a variety that she'd never seen before, grey as a ghost with amber eyes. They'd come scampering up the hill towards her, playing a game of their own invention, running alongside each other, occasionally colliding, rolling over, and wrestling. When they saw her, they galloped forward, mouths open, one tongue pointing to four o'clock, the other to eight. They each gave one friendly, or at least it seemed to be friendly, bark and then turned and raced off back in the direction they'd come.

A moment or two later, the three old men had breasted the brow of the hill. The dogs circled them three times and then tore back to Heather and circled her twice. They'd been very friendly, the men and the dogs, too. She'd fondled their ears and asked them searching questions like, 'Who's a good boy?' and 'Do you want a belly rub?'.

The spaniel was called Rocky and the grey dog, a Weimaraner it transpired, was called Brunhilde. They ran and played and…frolicked, there was no other word for it, they frolicked. The men looked on fondly and introduced themselves.

One of them asked her if she was, or could see herself becoming, an enthusiast for crown green bowls. At least that's what she thought he said. His accent was pretty thick.

Another, the Scotsman with the beard and the pipe, introduced himself as the landlord of the village pub. Heather had seen it, of course, but it didn't really look like her kind of place. But then, if she was honest with herself, Leighton Parva wasn't really her type of place.

The third man, the oldest of the three, seemed to sense this. He suggested that she might like to pop in on Thursday evening. That would be the quiz night, and half the village would be there. He hinted, ever so subtly, that if she were to make a personal appearance, it might quell some of the speculation that was already starting to occupy some of the more inquisitive locals. Heather gave a promise to look in if she had time. She was polite that way.

*

Less than a mile away the Scholar was starting to enjoy being Diarmuid Geraghty. Until now, it had been rather too easy. And the Scholar enjoyed a challenge. He hadn't been expecting the change of gear in his interrogation. Despite the *Antiques Roadshow* surroundings, the unfailing politeness of his inquisitors, this was an interrogation. And he had to admit that the two men opposite him were actually rather good.

Good!

A grand master deserves a worthy opponent. He was pleased that the difficulty level had been turned up a notch or two.

He spoke at length about the republican movement. From time to time, he would remind Michael and Richard of the importance of context and use this as a justification for going off on lengthy, and often irrelevant, tangents. He knew everything he said would be checked and verified, so he made sure he included plenty of accurate details. And a few less accurate ones. And one or two that were just plain incorrect.

He knew that he'd fallen into the lap of the intelligence services, and he needed to be sure that he didn't appear to be 'too good to be true'. Things and people who were too good to be true weren't true. That is what the expression meant, although the world seemed to be full of people who didn't fully understand this.

So, he told them stories about the IRA in Derry, in Fermanagh, in Belfast, and in Armagh. He told them about the protection rackets, a few verifiable facts there. He told them about the armed robberies, and named names, men who'd been caught, or were on the run, or who'd retired.

He told them about local councillors and 'community leaders' and the positions they'd held and the actions in which they'd participated. He told them about the time he'd met Martin McGuinness. He told them about the time he'd met Gerry Adams. He told them lots of things that the general public didn't know. And he made a few errors, just little ones.

Michael and Richard just sat and nodded. Very occasionally they would ask a question. They affected polite interest, but he could almost hear the cogs whirring and the gears grinding behind their impassive faces. By lunchtime, he still hadn't answered the question they'd posed at one minute past nine.

When they resumed at two thirty, Michael had done exactly what the Scholar had expected. He returned to the issue of the current threat. And the Scholar did the opposite of answer the question. He told them who wasn't a current threat and why.

He told them all about Declan Higgins. Higgins was notionally a farmer. He had about forty-five acres between Cullyhanna and Castleblayney. Crucially, forty of those acres were in Northern Ireland, but five were in the republic. Higgins' unique circumstances had made him a crucial member of the Armagh IRA.

Guns, ammunition, and explosives had crossed the border for years simply by moving from one field to another. The European Union's Common Agricultural policy had provided him with a useful additional income as cattle, both genuine and fictitious, had passed from one country to another.

He had a sideline removing the dye from rebated diesel, and there wasn't a petrol station within ten miles that sold diesel at the full price.

Most recently of all, according to the Scholar, Higgins had got into cigarette smuggling. He was making so much money that he had neither the time nor the inclination to continue the armed struggle.

And because he was the South Armagh Brigade's quarter master his retirement from terrorism had effectively rendered the brigade ineffective as a force, even if there were some among them that might be opposed to the Good Friday Agreement and the peace process in general.

'They do say he's making a million a month.'

*

They broke at five. Tony had been promising, or perhaps it was threatening, to attempt chilli con carne for dinner.

Richard screwed his eyes up and pinched the bridge of his nose. 'What do you think?' he asked wearily.

'He's playing us along. Telling us only what he wants to tell us. Ninety-nine per cent of what we've heard today is useless.'

'So why is he here?'

'I don't know.'

'The prints have come back from the lab. No trace. Maybe if we knew who this guy is, we could knock him off balance, regain the upper hand somehow.'

'We've never had the upper hand.'

Michael rose and stood by the French doors, looking out over the back garden. There was a small bird, a finch of some kind, or a tit, perched on the bird table. He turned back to the room.

'Okay, how about this? I get him out of this place for a couple of hours. You turn his room upside down looking for some clue that might identify him.'

'All that's been done.'

'Do it again. I'll get him out of here, change the environment. Perhaps he'll let his guard down. And I'll subject him to a different type of questioning.'

'What do you mean?'

'Diarmuid and I are going to a pub quiz.'

Chapter 8

Heather had only been to a pub quiz once, and she'd hated it. And that had been in the company of her friends. She certainly wasn't going to The Old Volunteer on a midweek evening on her own. She hadn't even been in the pub. It was very much not her sort of place. She'd glanced through the window once and there had been horse brasses. Horse brasses!

But on the other hand. What else was there to do? And the three old men had been so kind and nice and welcoming. Would it be rude not to go? It might be a little bit. And she was sure to meet them again. And could she, in all conscience, fondle Rocky's ears if she hadn't been to the pub quiz?

That was an absurd reasoning. Rocky wouldn't know or care and the old men must understand that a quiz night in a village pub was hardly her scene. Except, perhaps it was. She had after all bought a pair of green wellies. She'd been quite shocked at the price. And she had a waxed jacket. What was happening to her? She was a few short steps from a headscarf and jam-making.

She stood in front of the full-length mirror on the back of the wardrobe door. A million years ago, or was it two months, she'd spend hours deciding what to wear on a night out. It hardly mattered now, did it? She wasn't going to meet the love of her life at The Old Volunteer, was she? And anyway, all men were bastards, and she didn't need any of them.

But perhaps she could shock the locals. She held up a sequined top that would have been quite daring in the West End on a Saturday night. She giggled to herself. Perhaps she'd give a couple of village gossips a heart attack. She had a mini kilt somewhere. That ought to do it. Better not, on the whole. What about a Nirvana T-shirt? Or one of Nana's dresses? There were still a couple of those in the house. She could go as a Rutland spinster in a fancy dress. No. That would be taking it too far. Or she could just go as she was. Jeans, her second-best pair, and a nice top. Now, make-up? Yes? No? Perhaps just a little.

There was an easel outside the pub announcing that the quiz began at eight. She'd seen it earlier. She planned to arrive a little early and if it was as awful as she expected she could make a hasty exit. So better go now. A dab of perfume behind each ear. Why had she done that? Habit, she supposed. Silly, really. Not as silly as the scarlet ankle boots, obviously. But she put those on too.

*

Michael had expected that he would have to cajole Geraghty into going to the quiz, but he'd been surprisingly acquiescent, which should have sounded alarm bells, but Michael had had a long hard day, too.

They walked the short distance into the village. The sun was starting to set and its reflection of the honey stone of the buildings made a pleasing ochre colour. Michael sometimes wondered what love of queen and country really meant. He certainly wasn't an intelligence officer because he was motivated by patriotism in the way his grandfather was or the way it had inspired the men whose names now existed only on the village's war memorial. He wondered if some notion of patriotism lay behind the actions of Diarmuid Geraghty, or whoever he was.

At twenty to eight, the place was surprisingly full. Michael had been to pub quizzes at The Old Volunteer before, but they hadn't been as well attended as this. As he approached the bar, he was intercepted by his grandfather. The old man glanced at the Scholar.

'Ah! Hello. Here for the quiz? Just the two of you? Would you mind if we buddied you up with another couple of lost souls? Make up a scratch team?'

Michael appreciated the tradecraft. An uninformed observer could have reached the conclusion that the two men were total strangers, or casual acquaintances, or close family. The phrasing, the tone, the vocabulary, everything lent itself to multiple interpretations. And he'd done it all naturally, with no notice at all. A lifetime in the pursuit of skulduggery and mischief, as his grandfather called it, never really left you. *I wonder if I'll be like that when I'm eighty?*

He indicated a table occupied by a man almost as old as his grandfather, Michael recognised him as Ron, the dog training countryman and a young woman of roughly his own age. Without being aware that he was doing so, Michael dropped his shoulder, blocking the Irishman's path, and sidestepped neatly so that he was in pole position to take the seat next to her.

'Oh hello, I'm Michael, this is my friend Diarmuid. Would you mind if we, if we...err?'

'Arr!' said Ron in what appeared to be an affirmative manner and without waiting for anything to throw him off course, he sat next to Heather.

'Michael.'

'Yes, I know, you said.'

Okay, so not the ideal start. But what Michael didn't appreciate was that the real source of Heather's coolness wasn't that she'd taken an instant dislike to him. It usually took women at least five minutes to do that. It was because she'd just decided that she could stand it no longer. She'd been there five minutes and was ready to flee. Michael had closed off her avenue of escape.

Diarmuid took the seat beside the old man.

'Diarmuid.'

'Ron.'

'Heather.'

'Michael.' Oh God, what a klutz! This was why he was single. Fortune had contrived to place him in proximity to an attractive young woman, and she was attractive, and he'd advertised himself as a prize ass in the first thirty seconds by telling her his name three times.

In a desperate effort to regain ground already, and perhaps irrevocably, lost he offered to buy a round of drinks. Ron wanted a mild and bitter, at least he thought that was what he said. It's what he was getting, anyway. Diarmuid, after much deliberation, opted for a pint of lager and Heather...Heather fixed him with a hard stare and said,

'A pint of Rutland Best Bitter please.' And she delivered this request with the same blend of defiance and aggression that's usually associated with a boxer, defeated unjustly on points, demanding a re-match.

Michael was in love.

This had happened before. More than once, actually. And it tended to go one of two ways. Either he took his time and pursued a meticulously planned campaign, in which case he was sometimes successful. Or he allowed his heart to rule his head, went with the flow, was spontaneous, and allowed the girl to see the real him from the outset. Under the second scenario, he had a one hundred per cent record of abject failure.

But these circumstances were even less promising than usual, for a number of reasons. First, he was at work, even here in the lounge bar of The Old Volunteer he was working very hard. Second, Michael was fairly hopeless with women at the best of times, but when he was in love, he was absolutely awful. And finally, he was in love with a woman who he'd probably never see again and who clearly thought him an absolute arse, which so far this evening, he had to concede he had been.

The first task of any pub quiz team is to choose a name. For many participants, this was the most difficult question of the night. You want to be clever and witty, but not too witty. You don't want to look like you're trying too hard. Puns are almost mandatory, but for some reason that nobody knows certain puns are considered out of bounds.

Then there is the issue of vulgarity. A little sauciness might be tolerated, but outright profanity seldom is. And even that has to be calibrated according to circumstances. What might be rather tame by the standards of the Students' Union bar might be considered utterly obscene in a pub in rural Rutland.

And the whole thing is even more awkward if your team consists of people who don't know each other. And if one of them is an actual terrorist informant and one of them is an MI6 officer who can't decide if he's going to pretend not to know his own grandfather, and if one of them only seems to communicate via the sound 'arr' and a Rutland dialect unknown since the invention of the spinning jenny and if one of them has eyes of the brightest emerald and a way of brushing loose hairs behind her left ear, and a tiny, tiny dimple right on the point of her chin. Oh God!

Actually, it wasn't a problem at all. When they were given their answer sheet, the name of the team was already written on the top, 'Ron's Team'. So, that's all right then.

At eight o'clock, the quiz began. Bernard stood at the end of the bar, the questions in one hand, a microphone in the other. It might as well have been a baton. Bernard conducted the event as if he was conducting an orchestra. He pointed at the string section and the room filled with the sound of crying violins, or rather he announced the next round was on sport and brought the 'Don't ask Us' team a little higher up the rankings.

He was toying with the idea of creating a season long league next year. It would encourage teams to turn out every week to protect their position in the table. Bernard hadn't bought The Old Volunteer in order to make money, but it would be nice if it remained profitable.

*

The first round, popular culture, was an absolute disaster. If Ron hadn't known the answer to a question about *The Archers* (the definition of popular culture used in Rutland differs from some of those used elsewhere) they would have earned no points at all. As it was after one round, they were firmly in last place.

Things improved a little in round two, science and nature. Ron was pretty strong on flora and fauna, and Heather knew a lot about astronomy, geology, and the atomic weight of chlorine. Ron's Team rose to number eight in the rankings.

In round three, Michael began to make a contribution. He was good at sport, and he knew how his grandfather, the question master thought. Michael was able to spot the little traps he had set. At the end of the round, they were fourth. But so far, Diarmuid hadn't uttered a single word. He just sat there in a near catatonic state. He had barely touched his pint. The others had finished theirs, so Michael went to the bar again. He brought back four drinks, just the same.

Things changed in round four, art, and literature. Question one met with blank expressions from seventy-five per cent of Ron's Team and Michael was just about to enter a blind guess when Diarmuid spoke.

'Harriet Beecher Stowe.'

Heather looked at him. She'd almost forgotten he was there. '*Uncle Tom's Cabin* was written by Harriet Beecher Stowe. Put it down.'

Michael did as he was instructed.

'Eric Arthur Blair.'

Michael wrote it down.

'Arles.'

'Boston, everyone thinks he came from Virginia, but he was born in Boston.'

Michael wrote it down.

'Rembrandt van Rijn.'

Heather was starting to feel impressed. Michael was starting to feel jealous. He glanced up at Heather. She was looking at Geraghty. He was pleased to see that it wasn't in admiration or rapture. But he was puzzled by the expression on her face.

Geraghty was more puzzling still. His eyes had changed. Normally, they were sort of dark and empty. They looked like those of the victim of a soul-sucking alien in an episode of *Doctor Who*. But now they were different. Somehow, they were worse. And Michael wouldn't have believed that was possible.

Geraghty's eyes hadn't just altered slightly. They seemed to have taken on a new level of malevolence. He looked like a schoolboy who had just learnt to pull the legs off spiders.

'It was actually published in two parts: 1605 and 1615.'

'What should I write down?'

Diarmuid shrugged. 'Sixteen-O-Five, I suppose.'

The eyes had changed again.

*

Ron and Heather were dismayed when Diarmuid didn't know the answer to the next. But Michael did, and he was sure, so after waiting a decent interval after Diarmuid's shrug, he started writing.

'What are you putting?'

'Shall I compare thee to a summer's day? Thou art more lovely and more temperate.'

'You sure?'

'Very sure.'

He was blushing he knew he was. He couldn't help it.

'Well, write it down then!'

But she seemed to be a little warmer. Or was he imagining that?

'John Synge.'

Diarmuid again.

'Peter Breugel...the younger.'

Diarmuid.

'Mark Twain.'

Diarmuid. But Michael had known it too. And Heather.

Michael's grandfather read out the answers. Ten out of ten and Ron's Team was now tied for second. Diarmuid's fingers closed into a fist under the table. A tiny, tiny gesture of satisfaction and triumph, but Michael saw it. The Irishman drained his glass, which had been two-thirds full, and took a healthy draught of the next one. Michael noticed that too.

Round five was history. Everyone contributed. Nine out of ten, now tied for first place.

The final round was geography. Tricky. One or two guesses. Two questions were about Rutland. Ron saved them there.

There was time for another round of drinks before the final set of answers and the final rankings were read out. Diarmuid announced that it was his round and asked Ron where the gentlemen's toilets were. Ron indicated a door beside the bar and said something that might have been,

'Through there, second left.'

Diarmuid rose and Michael returned to the discussion he was having with Heather about the exact whereabouts of Burkina Faso. He let Diarmuid out of his sight and unsupervised. And at that point Diarmuid Geraghty became the Scholar again.

The Scholar went through the door indicated by Ron. It led to the public bar, which was smaller and more sparsely furnished. There were only a couple of customers playing darts in the far corner. The Scholar saw what he needed at the end of the bar. He fished a handful of change from his pocket and drew the pay phone across the bar towards him.

He dialled slowly and deliberately. He hadn't time for a misdial. When the phone was answered, he pushed a fifty pence piece into the slot. He spoke clearly but urgently for two minutes in Irish. The darts players ignored him. The barman, or probably the landlord judging by his age, entered the bar for a few seconds, but if he overheard anything at all, he wouldn't have understood. When he finished, he ordered the round of drinks and visited the gents while they were being prepared. He returned to the table bearing a tray just as the final standings were being announced.

'And we have a tie for first place, on forty-seven points. It's Shake Rutland Roll and Ron's Team.'

Diarmuid placed the tray on the table and resumed his seat.

'Now, you all know the form here. There shall be one tie-breaker question. And it's this...'

The question master paused for dramatic effect. *You old ham!* thought his grandson.

'Who was the author of *Madame Bovary*, first published in Paris in 1856?'

Michael glanced over at the group of elderly men and women known collectively as Shake Rutland Roll. He was rewarded with five blank faces. Ron and Heather's faces were blank too, but Diarmuid's wasn't. He was wearing an expression of smug satisfaction. It wasn't appealing.

'Pass the paper to the Scholar,' he said extending a hand. Michael passed it across. Diarmuid drew it to himself and wrote two words. He spun the paper round so the others could see and raised his eyebrows, but nobody had anything to offer. Either Diarmuid's confidence was well founded, or it wasn't. Michael couldn't decide which outcome he preferred. Diarmuid folded the paper and handed it to the quizmaster.

'Geoffrey? Any answer from your team?'

'Sorry, Bernard. We haven't got a clue.'

'Guess?'

'Marcel Proust?'

'Sorry, no.'

Michael's grandfather unfolded the paper. 'We have a winner, Ron's Team who correctly identified the author of *Madame Bovary* as Gustave Flaubert. Well done everybody.'

Diarmuid beamed in triumph, and Ron clapped him on the back. Geraghty's, or was it the Scholar's, hand clenched in a fist again, but this time Michael didn't observe it. Michael wouldn't have observed it if he'd grown horns and a tail and burst into flames because in the excitement...well...

*

Diarmuid and Michael returned to Windmill Cottage. Diarmuid went straight to bed, but Michael had a little conference with Richard in the garden.

'Anything in the room?'

'Nothing. Not. A. Thing. Clean as a whistle. How about you? Learn anything?'

'Not much. He has a competitive streak, tries to hide it, but it's there. He knows a surprising amount about art and literature. Bit of a scholar. Actually...'

'What?'

'It's probably nothing, but let's check it, just in case...'

*

Heather was furious with herself. Absolutely furious.

Not just because she'd somehow allowed herself to take the silly quiz seriously. Or because she'd enjoyed herself. But most of all, above everything else, in spite of herself, her instinct, her reason and all common sense at the moment of triumph, and how absurd to think of it even in those terms, at that moment of triumph she'd kissed Michael.

Not a proper kiss, not a snog, nothing like that. But she'd kissed him and the thing that made her angriest of all was...she didn't regret it.

Chapter 9

The interview or interrogation, perhaps it was a battle of wits, whatever it was resumed on Friday morning. Michael decided to start the session by treating Richard to his and the Scholar's account of the pub quiz the previous evening. He thought perhaps it might somehow plant the idea in the Irishman's head that they were all on the same side. He needn't have bothered. The Scholar had already decided that today was the day Diarmuid Geraghty was going to provide the Brits with some genuine intelligence. But he was going to make them work for it.

The first hour, after they'd re-lived their quiz triumph, was largely covering topics they'd discussed the day before. The Scholar waited until an opportunity presented itself and then resumed his bitter denunciation of those who had used their position in the republican movement to line their own pockets.

This had to be handled carefully, no matter how much he wanted to tell them about Declan Higgins. He railed against what he called the profiteers and then drifted away on to the subject of those who treated being a volunteer as some sort of celebrity. Michael tried to steer him back to the profiteers.

'That's what I'm talking about. Men who've done very little. Men who've never shivered in a ditch as part of an ambush or smuggled a sniper's rifle through the Falls, strutting around like they were Che Guevara. And the diaspora! They just lap it up! These gobshites, propping up the bar at the Irish centre or in a pub telling tales from the front line and the English fools just can't get enough of it. And the next thing they know they're lining the pockets of men like Declan Higgins and thinking they're doing their bit for Irish freedom.'

'I don't follow.'

'So, what I mean is...take Declan Higgins. All he's done for twenty years is move a few things across the border. These days he's more or less a full-time smuggler. But that's a pretty competitive game in Ireland, so now he's just smuggling fags into England, and he's got this network of clowns buying and distributing his fags. They think he's a hero. They think they're helping. But all they're doing is making your man a millionaire. The size of that place he has in Spain. Two swimming pools. Two!'

'So, he's not active in the armed struggle at all?'

'Well. He contributes, financially, you know? Maybe kicks in hundred grand a month. But he's making ten times that himself.'

'He's funding a dissident republican group to the tune of a hundred thousand pounds a month?'

'Chicken feed. Chicken feed for him!'

'I think we'd like to hear about this in a little more detail.'

And so, the Scholar let them have it. Everything he knew about Declan Higgins's cigarette smuggling operation. The bits he didn't directly know he was able to fill in from his own experience. Higgins was making regular deliveries to St Anselm's Social Club in Exeter,

The Christy Ring, a pub in Sheffield, The Walnut Tree, a pub in Leicester, and a Celtic Supporters Club, somewhere in the north of England. He told them that the cigarettes were smuggled in lorries carrying goods from Murcia and that deliveries were made almost every week.

Michael nodded. Richard made notes. By the time the Scholar had finished, it was time for lunch.

*

Richard was in the garden of Windmill Cottage, smoking a cigarette and tapping the ash onto a bird table. He hadn't really understood why Michael had been so interested in the cigarette smuggling. It had been made clear to him in London that Michael was the lead interviewer and he should take instruction from him, but Richard was frustrated at the slow rate of progress so far. It was Friday afternoon and most of what they'd heard so far was a mixture of whining and second-rate republican polemic.

It was all pretty poor fare, and Richard would rather be planning his weekend's social activities in the fashionable parts of West London. He would like to have been urging Michael to pick up the pace. He had written off this weekend, but at the current rate of progress he'd still be stuck in this dead and alive hole next weekend. And he had serious plans.

He couldn't make his case because after a hurried sandwich, Michael had set off to see his grandfather, not that he'd told Richard where he was going. He was on his second intelligence mission of the day. He wanted to know more about Heather.

Bernard Taylor was in the kitchen, a reference book on British birds open on the kitchen table, when Michael knocked on the back door and entered.

'You're an ornithologist now?'

'Hello, Mikey. Good Lord, no. I wouldn't know a buzzard from a blue tit. It's for next week's quiz. Perhaps I shouldn't be telling you, giving you an unfair advantage. If you're coming next week, of course. Be a shame if you didn't, having enjoyed yourself so much last night.'

'Well, that's why I'm here, actually.'

'Her name's Heather. She's Millicent and Sid Hobday's granddaughter, lives at Primrose Cottage. Inherited the place a few months back. Moved up from London. I believe she's a teacher, possibly in Oakham. A primary school, I think. So, she won't be home now, but I have some notepaper somewhere, you know, if you were thinking of dropping her a little note, a billet doux.'

Michael was used to his grandfather. There was simply no point in expecting him to mind his own business or to refrain from the urge to move people about like they were on some sort of chessboard.

'You mean you don't know her blood group, shoe size, and date of birth yet?'

'I could probably have that information for you in a few days if it's really important. But surely, you'd rather discover these things yourself. I'll get you that notepaper, shall I?'

The old man rose, closed the book, and shuffled off towards his study. Brunhilde, in her basket, lifted her head and decided that she wasn't required to accompany him and lay back down again with a small sigh.

*

Michael had never spent more time on a shorter note. He was back on home territory now, weighing every word, calculating the impact of every phrase. What exactly was he trying to convey? Well, that he liked her, and would like to see her again. That he didn't want to wait until next week's pub quiz. That ought to be easy. Would she think it odd to return home and find a hand delivered note from a man who wasn't supposed to know her address?

In London, and Heather was from London, it would be odd, downright creepy actually, if not bordering on restraining order territory. But this was Rutland. If Heather had been here any time at all, she would know what Leighton Parva was like.

*

Primrose Cottage was halfway down Forge Lane between the Old Reading Rooms and Alma Villa. It wasn't a long journey, but it gave Michael time to second guess himself several times. Was he being bounced into premature action by his grandfather rather than thinking things through carefully? Perhaps he was. Or perhaps he needed to be jolted into action.

Michael walked up the very short path to the front door, took a deep breath, and pushed his note through the letter box. It wasn't easy. It was one of those wrought iron ones with a spring strong enough to bait a mantrap. He glanced at his watch. Time to hurry back for the afternoon's session.

*

Although he was a sworn enemy of the British state, the Scholar's knowledge of its various departments and functions was less than perfect. It was this gap in knowledge that led him accidentally to approach MI6 rather than MI5. Did MI6 liaise with customs? Was all the information that he was providing going to lead to Declan Higgins' arrest for smuggling? He just didn't know. In truth, Higgins wasn't really a threat to the British state. He was too old for sniping at military patrols, not that there were any anymore. And he could no more plant a bomb than he could build a flying saucer.

But that didn't matter. The British state's priorities were not the Scholar's priorities. Uncle Paschal wanted Declan Higgins taken off the board, and this was the only way of doing it. So, the Scholar was doing his best to steer the Brits that way.

He had to be careful, though. He didn't want to seem too keen. And he couldn't afford to provide too many details or to make it too easy for them. That would be suspicious. He had to put just enough pieces in front of them so that they, or customs, or whoever, could put them together, and take action.

What he didn't know, couldn't know, is whether the two men opposite him would pay any attention at all. He assumed that they were more concerned about the prospect of an Active Service Unit planting a bomb in a mainland shopping centre than a few smuggled fags.

Richard, the tall one, was starting to look bored. He'd stopped taking notes half an hour ago. Michael was still attentive but the Scholar, was running out of material.

'Is it Friday today?'

'It is.'

'So...so...will we be doing this again tomorrow? Over the weekend, I mean?'

Richard shifted fractionally. His body language switched from borderline asleep to vaguely interested.

'We might give it an hour or two in the morning. Why? Is there somewhere else you'd rather be? Or something you'd rather be doing?'

'We're near a big lake or something aren't we? A reservoir or something?'

'Rutland Water.'

'So, I'm assuming there might be a few fish in this water.'

Michael had no idea. He assumed Richard hadn't either, but he was wrong.

'Oh yes. Trout mostly, including quite a few nice ones. Predators too, if that's your thing.' It was obvious from Richard's tone that anglers who sought to catch pike and zander were a bit common.

'Oh, I wouldn't be interested in those lads at all. Now a few hours fly-fishing for trout, that would be something else entirely.'

'Well, I expect that we could probably organise something.' For the first time that day, Richard appeared genuinely engaged. Within a minute, they were talking animatedly about pink squirrels, black ghosts, and various nymphs and buzzers with increasingly preposterous names.

'Of course, it's likely to be a bit busy at the weekend, but if we crack on and get a bit more done, maybe we could take a look on Monday.'

Michael sat back and let the conversation flow. This was very good. Geraghty, was opening up. There had been flashes of it at the quiz, too. You just needed to hit a sweet spot. His competitiveness, or was it his desire to show off? Or his passion for fishing. They were starting to see the real man. A man that was educated, competitive and above all very focussed and sure of himself.

All of which meant that the rambling, bitter, self-pitying individual that had been sitting opposite them wasn't the real thing at all. Well, they sort of knew that. It just meant that they were dealing with someone highly duplicitous and probably very dangerous.

Good.

Phillipa had mentioned fishing, Margaret too. Why? How had they known? Perhaps the man calling himself Diarmuid Geraghty had mentioned it when he'd first arrived. Or was it possible that Phillipa already knew who he was? Knew he was a fisherman. Michael couldn't discount the possibility. People in the Intelligence Service lied to each other explicitly, implicitly, and by omission every day. Even when there was no reason. It was just a reflexive instinct. It occurred to Michael that the whole event might be an elaborate training exercise. Or an assessment. In which case, whose? His? Richard's? Both of them?

Three days of interrogating Geraghty. And what did he have to show for it? A lot of off-the-shelf republican grievances and some allegations about a geriatric fag smuggler from County Armagh. If this was an assessment, he was in danger of failing it. The grandfather clock struck five. Richard and Geraghty were talking about reels now, or something. Michael brought his thumb and index finger to the bridge of his nose and closed his eyes. He felt a headache coming on.

*

Nobody had explicitly set out what Diarmuid Geraghty's exact status was. Was he free to leave? He'd never asked. And he'd never been told. If he'd been forced to guess, he would have said that he didn't have the option of just declaring that he'd told them everything he wished to, and he'd like to go home now.

For the time being, he had no wish to leave. He still had more information that he wanted to feed into the British state apparatus, and he knew that if he were to rush it, he risked damaging his credibility. So, he had to go slowly for now. But he knew that there would be a time when he would have to vanish. When that time came, he needed a foolproof escape option. He had a few ideas.

*

Michael spent Saturday morning writing a report for Phillipa Templeton. She would already have read the transcripts of the interviews themselves, so he focussed instead on his impressions. In particular, he recounted the evening at the pub quiz and his sense that it revealed a small window into the real man and the implication that the public face of Diarmuid Geraghty, or whoever he was, might be an elaborate act.

It was necessary to be comprehensive when drafting these reports and so, erring on the side of caution, he described in detail the Irishman's expert knowledge of nineteenth century literature and enthusiasm for fly-fishing. He even felt bold enough to request that Phillipa, or more realistically one of her underlings, check out a theory of his.

He didn't know whether Phillipa was aware of Geraghty's true identity, but it couldn't hurt to document these clues. If that's what they were. It occurred to Michael that perhaps even these apparent slips might be a deliberate red herring planted to mislead him as to the Irishman's identity.

He was starting to think like a real spook, distrusting everything he was told and even everything that he thought he'd deduced by himself. He imagined his grandfather sitting in his favourite armchair and nodding approvingly.

*

Heather hadn't phoned. What did he expect? She probably thought he was a weirdo. Who pushed hand-written notes through letter boxes in 1999? She probably wouldn't be at the pub quiz on Thursday, either. Wouldn't want to risk running into him again. Wouldn't want to risk being dragooned into Ron's Team alongside him. It didn't matter. She was just a girl. Just a girl who he'd known for a couple of hours. Didn't matter at all. He checked his phone. No missed calls. It didn't matter at all.

Chapter 10

Heather had had a difficult day too. Mrs Bell, who usually taught Year Six had phoned in sick. Mrs Bell was always phoning in sick, often on Fridays. Normally, the teaching assistant would manage things and Heather only had to look in from time to time but today had been different. Some sort of dispute seemed to have been simmering in the class for a few days and today it spilled over in to a full-scale civil war.

The exact grievances involved were hard to determine, but the consequences were all too obvious. Pencil case mutilation featured quite a bit. There had been some sort of upturned drawing pin on the chair incident. Honestly, it was almost the twenty-first century! Could nothing more original be found?

When responding to what seemed to be a medium scale riot Heather walked in to discover three children in tears, one in a rage that rendered him incapable of speech and on the brink of hyperventilation and Jameson Roche – who names their child Jameson? – trying just a little too hard to play the role of innocent bystander.

On a different day of the week Heather might have been tempted to hold a full court of inquiry with testimony, advocacy, and no doubt at the end a phone call to someone's, let's be realistic, Jameson's, parents. But it was Friday and Heather had plans. She was visiting friends in London for the first time in months and she wasn't going to have the weekend spoilt by the nagging prospect of a Monday morning interview with Mr and Mrs Roche.

*

The echo of the final bell of the day had barely ceased but Heather was already halfway across the car park. Within an hour she was on the platform at Peterborough station awaiting the half-past four train to London and clutching a large bottle of water. She thought that with the evening likely in prospect it would be wise to hydrate early.

Her first stop would be the house that she'd once shared with Louise and Lucy. There she would cast off her schoolmistress clothes and change into something more suitable for an evening that was scheduled to start at a tequila bar somewhere near Drury Lane. She, like her friends, had no idea where the evening might end. But she needed this. She spent her working life surrounded by people old enough to be her parents and most of the inhabitants of Leighton Parva could have been her grandparents. She needed to remind herself that she was young, free, and single.

Actually, she didn't need reminding of that last part. She was only too aware that for the first time in many years she wasn't part of a couple. Some of the relationships had been short, barely meriting the description. One or two had been measured in months and the last, no, not the last she told herself, the most recent, well, at the time she'd thought that that one would be the last.

But perhaps she'd meet the love of her life this weekend. Were Prince Charmings found in tequila bars? Perhaps they were. It seemed likelier than in Leighton Parva, anyway.

Her thoughts turned to the young man at the pub quiz. He wasn't her type at all. He was roughly the right age. He wasn't actually ugly, but he wasn't Pierce Brosnan. That wasn't the problem. Heather was used to more of the Alpha male type, you know, confident, assured.

Michael, his name was Michael. She smiled to herself as she remembered how he had managed to say so three times in the first ten seconds. Michael was more diffident, shy, a little bit awkward. Actually, he'd been rather sweet. Perhaps that was her type. He hadn't even told her what he did for a living. In London that was almost the first thing anybody said. Perhaps he didn't have an impressive occupation. Anyway, it didn't matter.

But why had she kissed him? She'd definitely initiated it. Because they'd won a pub quiz in the middle of nowhere? That was absurd. But there wasn't any other reason. He'd been there. A man of roughly the right age in a social setting. When had she last even been in that position? That was why she needed this weekend in London.

*

Louise had a new boyfriend, Harry. Harry was a barrister. Heather just knew that this information had been vouchsafed in the first thirty seconds wherever they'd met.

'But you won't meet him tonight. Tonight is just us girls.'

'I don't suppose he has a friend.'

Louise and Lucy exchanged a look, 'Well, actually...'

'It was a joke. Just a joke. I'm not looking for anything right now.'

Why had she said that? That was a downright lie. She was definitely looking for something. She wasn't exactly sure what, a steady boyfriend? A reckless fling? Perhaps it didn't matter. Tonight was just about blowing a few cobwebs away. Hitting the town. Visiting a few bars that didn't look like they belonged in time capsules. Going somewhere with no horse brasses. And if she did meet someone, what would she say?

'Oh, you must come back to mine. It's only a hundred miles away in the land that time forgot.'

In fact, that particular dilemma didn't arise. Lucy had come home with the numbers of three different men. Tom, the other Tom, and the one with the eyebrows who claimed to be something in publishing. But that was only par for the course for Lucy. Heather had spent a little while dancing with a very tall man with startling green eyes, but when he'd mentioned that his name was Julian, for some reason, she went right off him.

*

When Heather awoke, she was still tired. When had she last been out until three in the morning? She was badly out of practice. Not just at late nights and tequila, but at the whole exercise. She'd almost forgotten how to scan a crowded bar looking for eligible men, how to make eye contact apparently by accident, how to flirt.

Perhaps she needed a refresher course. For some reason Michael popped into her head. Why on earth was she thinking about him? She'd only met him once. And she probably wouldn't see him again. She was pretty confident he didn't live in Leighton Parva. Surely, she would have noticed.

Louise was busy making, well, it was a bit too late to be called breakfast, so brunch, when Heather went downstairs.

'What's the plan for today?'

'Well, we'll take it easy for a bit and then this afternoon, we're off to Richmond.'

'Richmond?'

'Yes, Harry's playing rugby. But I have an ulterior motive.'

'Oh! I thought you might. What's his name?'

'He's called Mark. He's a university friend of Harry's. You'll like him.'

'Is he a rugby player too?'

'Oh no, he's much more...cerebral.'

'You mean he's a geek?'

'No, no, no, no. Not at all. He's quite dishy actually. But he is an absolute brain on legs. He's studying for a PhD.'

'So, he's a penniless student?'

'Darling, why are you determined to be so negative? You'll like him, I promise. And he's far from penniless.'

*

Heather was more of a football fan. Manchester United since you ask. But it's okay, she came from Sale. She had nothing against rugby per se, but she hadn't expected to spend two hours standing on a windy terrace in horizontal sleet when she'd packed for the weekend. She was therefore very grateful when Mark, rather gallantly, lent her his coat. But within fifteen minutes it was quite clear that the poor man was going to perish of hypothermia and so, having adjourned to the bar at half time, Heather suggested that perhaps they should remain there for the second half.

As well as being gallant Mark did his best to be charming, but unwittingly his conversation set off a number of what Heather considered to be warning flares. For a start he referred to rugby as 'rugger'. When he heard that she was living in Rutland he mentioned that 'his people' owned a holiday cottage there.

Once those flares were visible, she began to look for further warning signs. Mark's brown brogues were highly polished. There was no reason why that should have been a point against him but somehow it was. She'd glanced at the tailor's label in his overcoat. Yes, a tailor's label. Not a shop. And it had what she assumed were his initials too. There were four.

Heather couldn't have told you why she'd had a prejudice against men with two middle names, couldn't have told herself, but she did. She couldn't help it. But perhaps she was doing him an injustice. Perhaps he had a double-barrelled surname. Was that better? Or worse?

She decided that since she was running the rule over him in the way that Sherlock Holmes might have she might as well do the job properly.

'So, Mark, tell me a little about yourself.'

He'd been to school at Rugby – was that why he called it rugger? He had read history at Cambridge and then spent a year in the army. 'Coldstream Guards,' he'd said casually. Heather didn't know what that signified. She knew nothing about the military, but she was vaguely aware that there were such things as elite or prestigious regiments. She was willing to bet that this was one of them.

And now? Now he was studying for a doctorate at Oxford, military history, something to do with railway lines in the Crimean War. Heather was finding it difficult to follow, and her attention started to drift. Perhaps he still had a batman to polish those brown brogues. Was he a trained killer? Well, yes, technically, she supposed he was. She'd always imagined that trained killers didn't wear horn-rimmed glasses.

She became aware that behind the glasses Mark's eyes were looking at her in an expectant manner. Oh, God! He'd asked her a question, hadn't he? Heather opened her mouth, as though that might make an intelligent response pop into it. As though that might mean that she would know what on earth Mark had been talking about? But she was spared. At that moment, the crowd made a noise.

It wasn't a cheer. Nor was it a roar of support. Not the sound made when people collectively witness something astonishing. A different noise. A noise with which Heather wasn't familiar. Not her fault. She hadn't been to many rugby matches.

The noise was the one that's made when fifteen hundred people simultaneously realise that a player has suffered a sickening injury. It is a sort of chord, the top note being a sharp crack, the bulk of the sound provided by a collective oral flinch and finished off with a gasp-like scream from Louise.

It wasn't anybody's fault really. If you were determined to apportion blame you might criticise Harry himself for not taking the option of the inside pass to his teammate. But most of the crowd would have attributed it to sheer bad luck. Harry had elected to sidestep to his right placing his entire weight on his left leg just as two opponents, arriving simultaneously from East, and West, hit that leg just above and just below his knee. Heather turned, but from her position all she could see was a crowd of heads some of which were turned away from the pitch with expressions ranging from horror to nausea.

The thing about a rugby crowd is that even at small local club match there is likely to be a doctor in attendance, together with various solicitors, accountants, bankers, brokers, and the type of person who would probably describe themselves as an entrepreneur. Frank McBride would have called such people well-heeled spivs. However, a solicitor is rarely called upon to do a bit of urgent conveyancing or a broker to hedge a position on Patagonian wombat futures. A doctor, however...

Chris Phillips, a gynaecologist from the West Middlesex Hospital, was on the scene in seconds. Although this particular incident wasn't at the very centre of his field of expertise, he was still confident in his diagnosis and prescription. An ambulance was sent for immediately.

Louise insisted on riding along, holding Harry's hand, generally getting in the way and fantasising about a hospital bed proposal. All of which left Heather and Mark alone, and with a reservation for a table for four at the tapas bar next to Richmond station.

*

Mark proved an agreeable companion. It seemed to Heather that he'd only deduced that Heather and he were being set up when he asked for the menu. So much for being a brain on legs. Heather started compiling a mental balance sheet of the man opposite who, she supposed, she now had to regard as what? Her date, her suitor, or just a friend of a friend whom fate had cast in the role of her Saturday night companion.

He wasn't bad looking. He was obviously very clever and probably very rich. He was polite and attentive. He seemed to know a surprising amount about Spanish food. And Spanish wine. And, well, just about everything really. Heather didn't think for a moment that she was sitting opposite her soulmate, but it had been six months since Julian. She had to get back on the horse sometime. And Mark might be fun for a while. He was in Oxford. She was in Rutland. It didn't need to be too intense. It would give her somewhere to go, something to do at weekends. And the wine he'd chosen was really excellent. She decided that she'd let him know she was interested. If she could remember how it was that she used to do that.

'It's Mark.'

'I beg your pardon.'

'It's Mark. You called me Michael.'

'I'm so sorry. Did I? Are you sure?'

'Quite sure. Four times actually.'

Why had she done that?

*

Heather spent most of her journey home the following day asking herself the same question. She eventually decided that it wasn't about Michael. It was her subconscious telling her that Mark wasn't for her. It wasn't about Michael. He was just the pretext, or rather his name had been.

After all, who was Michael? Some guy she'd bumped into at a quiz in a pub she'd never visited before and might never visit again. She knew nothing about him. She didn't even know where he lived, or what he was doing in Leighton Parva. It was very likely that she'd never see him again. No, it wasn't about Michael.

It was starting to get dark when Heather got home, despite the clocks having gone forward. She was tired, and a little hungry. A quick audit of her fridge revealed nothing that tempted her and despite having had quite an indulgent weekend she decided that perhaps she might treat herself to a pizza. There had been a leaflet a few days ago. Perhaps she'd left it on the little table by the front door. No, no leaflet, she must have thrown it out. But there was an envelope, still wedged in the letter box.

Plain white, good quality, addressed simply to Heather, in the sort of handwriting that people with poor penmanship use when they're trying to be more legible than usual. Heather frowned. She turned it over. Nothing. She heard the faint click that indicated that the kettle had boiled and returned to the kitchen still holding the mysterious correspondence.

*

It had been Tony's turn to cook. Perhaps it was because it was the weekend but for some reason, he'd decided to extend himself beyond the beans on toast or bangers and mash that were his best known, if not his best loved, dishes. He attempted something ambitious. Michael just wasn't sure what it was. Well, he knew what it was. It was a sort of tepid beige slush. He just wasn't sure what it was supposed to be. And he daren't ask. Was it paella? Or some sort of risotto? He was fairly confident that there was rice involved somewhere.

He briefly considered the possibility that it was rice pudding and that he was considering his two-course dinner in the wrong order. But that couldn't be correct because the second dish was clearly intended to be some sort of dessert. It had a scoop of ice cream on the side. A risotto then, possibly.

And then his phone rang.

Chapter 11

There was a pile of advertising leaflets on the little table by the hall where the house's main telephone had been. The previous occupants were obviously the type of people who still had their telephone just inside the front door. Michael flicked through them. There were three advertising takeaway pizzas. One of them offered a delivery service but he doubted that that would apply to Leighton Parva. The second was from one of those national chains. The third leaflet made no mention of delivery, or even of takeaway. But it was a small independent restaurant, which claimed to be family run.

Michael had forgotten to ask what she'd have liked and so he decided to play it safe. This is why he hated improvising. Perhaps she was vegetarian, or allergic to capers, or something. Could you be allergic to capers? Probably, well, possibly at least. I mean, people are allergic to all sorts for things. Giles was allergic to pineapple for example.

One margherita, one pepperoni. That was safe. Unless she'd be appalled at him munching animal flesh, right in front of her. No, no she would have said something. And some garlic bread. Now he realised that he had a further unanticipated dilemma. Should he bring two litres of cola, or a bottle of Chianti? Was that presumptuous? Could you just turn up at a girl's front door with booze? What message did that send? Was it the equivalent of having a toothbrush in his breast pocket? Michael didn't know. His dating history was liberally sprinkled with faux pas. He glanced at his watch. There was probably nowhere in Oakham selling wine at this time on a Sunday anyway.

*

Heather was also conscious that she was in uncharted waters in terms of etiquette. The whole scenario was very odd and part of her already regretted making the phone call. I mean, when you looked at it, really stood back, and looked at it, it was very odd.

'Hello. I got your note – which you delivered two days ago. Please come round immediately and bring me food.'

That wasn't what she'd said, of course, well, not in so many words, but that was the essence of it. And what was a young man supposed to think when he got a message like that? He'd seemed pleased, a little surprised, certainly, but pleased. He'd suggested that he pick her up and take her into Oakham for a pizza. But she'd plead tiredness. That was true, of course, but why had she said it. Was it rude? On balance, she thought it probably was. And now that she'd suggested he pick up a takeaway, what was he thinking? You just didn't do that sort of thing.

'Pick up a takeaway and come to my house.'

That was something you said to your best friend, or to somebody you had known for years, at least. It wasn't what you said when you were arranging a first date. Was that what she was doing? Arranging a first date? She picked up the note again.

Dear Heather,

I really enjoyed meeting you last night and I'd love to see you again. But perhaps not at a pub quiz.

Michael.

And then a mobile telephone number. And she'd called it. She didn't weigh her options. She didn't devise a plan, or a strategy. She didn't even know what she wanted. Or what she was hoping to achieve. And she didn't know what she was going to wear, or anything.

Should she lay a table? With cutlery? For a pizza? And what about wine glasses? Was that presumptuous? Yes, it was. Unless she had some wine. She didn't. She knew she hadn't. A single woman, living on her own in the middle of nowhere didn't need wine in the house. That way led disaster.

Perhaps they should just eat it out of the box in front of the fire. No, that was far too informal. But the fire was a good idea. Yes. She should light the fire. She could do that. It would be cosy...and romantic. But was that what she was aiming for? No. No, not at all. That would make her look like, well, she wasn't sure, but she knew she didn't want to look like that. But she would light the fire. It would take a few minutes, give her time to think.

Since moving to the country, Heather had embraced what her younger self would have called, 'country ways'. She had a pair of green wellies and one of those quilted jackets without sleeves. She could differentiate cock and hen pheasants. She could identify several different breeds of dog, although the Weimaraner had initially puzzled her. And she could make an open fire.

Lots of people, okay, lots of men, think that lighting a fire is straightforward. A lot of men, the ones who think that a barbecue requires a Y chromosome, think that they can call upon some ancient palaeolithic memory and have a roaring fire blazing in the hearth in five minutes.

Heather knew better. Her grandmother had taught her how to do this properly. The secret was to work methodically, as though following a recipe. She made a little nest of medium size logs and filled it with kindling. Then she placed a pair of thin pieces of wood the size of envelopes on top. Finally, she fished two firelighters out of the box. Danish firelighters. Not the rubbish you buy in Sainsbury's. Those Vikings knew a thing or two about wood fires.

She pushed the first deep into the nest of kindling. She posted the second like a letter half exposed from a letter box. Then she lit it and sat back on her heels to admire her work, and to ensure that the fire properly caught. There was always a little feeling of satisfaction when it worked the first time.

'If you lay a fire properly, one box of matches should last all year.'

She missed Nana.

Heather's methodology and technique were flawless. But it wasn't swift. She'd just satisfied herself that the fire was well set when she heard the knocker on the front door.

Primrose Cottage was a small dwelling. Everything seemed to be at about seven-eighths of the size that it ought to be. The rooms were small, the ceilings were low, and the front door was so tiny that many people had to crouch to enter the house. The one thing that wasn't small and to scale was the door knocker. It seemed to have been salvaged from a cathedral, or a larger than usual castle. It crashed down like a sledgehammer.

Heather realised that by spending so much time laying the fire that she'd spared herself the agony of deciding what she ought to be wearing. She hadn't had time to change and so she was clad in jeans and a rather baggy, but very comfortable, jumper. She hastened to her feet and hurried to the front door lest Michael try the knocker again and risk sending the door off its hinges. She needn't have worried. Michael was mortified, and for a moment, considered just fleeing in shame. When the door opened, his first words were,

'I'm so sorry. The knocker just sort of slipped.'

Heather smiled and brushed her hair back from her forehead, leaving a broad dark grey stripe of soot running from her left eyebrow to the top of her right ear.

'Don't worry. Don't worry, come in, please. I've lit a fire.'

She was immediately angry with herself. Why did she say that? Why shouldn't she light a fire? Did she want congratulations? Was she expecting him to be impressed? What sort of mating ritual was this? Woman make fire. Man bring pizza from hunting grounds.

'You've got a tiny smudge...' He brought his hand up, semi apologetically to his own eyebrow.

She glanced at the mirror in the hall. Oh no. She looked like a chimney sweep or a survivor of a mining disaster.

*

They sat on cushions in front of the fire eating pizza and drinking Valpolicella from Heather's only two wine glasses.

'This is very nice,' said Heather, sipping from her second-best glass.

'Well, the chief sommelier at the Oakham Co-op said it was the ideal vintage to go with pepperoni.'

She liked him. He was polite. He was attentive. He was a little self-effacing, but not too much. Most importantly of all, he was interested in her. Most of the men that Heather met were chiefly interested in themselves and thought that everybody else ought to be, too. They'd finished the pizza and were on their second glass of wine when she realised that she knew almost nothing about him.

She was a little nervous about asking. What if he turned out to be some sort of under-achieving loser? Heather didn't think of herself as a snob, but she was used to bankers and barristers and people who were 'something in the City'. She'd chosen to make a career teaching primary school children in the public sector, but that didn't mean that she'd a principled objection to marrying a millionaire.

Why was she thinking in those terms? This was just a nice man she'd met at a pub quiz and now they were sharing a pizza. But she would quite like it if he were some sort of high achiever, or even someone with high aspirations. A would-be novelist or musician or inventor.

He said that he was a civil servant with a role too menial and too tedious to be worth discussing further. He lived and worked in London, but he was spending a couple of weeks locally on a training course. Heather couldn't help it. She was just a tiny, tiny bit disappointed. A civil servant! But there were all sorts of civil servants, weren't there? After all, James Bond was a civil servant. Michael didn't look much like James Bond. But, probably, in real life, they never did. But somewhere, in the back of her mind she'd a vague idea that spies, real proper spies always said that they worked for the Foreign Office, didn't they?

'Which government department did you say you worked for?'

'The Foreign Office.'

Oh well, another theory shot down in flames. Michael was quite sweet; he wasn't actually ugly, but there was no way on earth that he was a secret agent. The wine was quite nice, though. Heather was just thinking about what would happen, what she wanted to happen, when the bottle was finished when she heard a low buzzing sound.

'I'm so sorry. That's me. Do you mind if I just quickly...'

Michael fished in his pocket for his mobile telephone. He had a text message.

MY OFFICE 0900 TOMORROW – TEMPLETON

'Anything serious?'

'No, no, nothing like that. Early start tomorrow, that's all. I probably ought to be going, anyway.'

He rose from the cushions in a single smooth movement. Heather was slightly less graceful. She was tired and her second-best glass was slightly bigger than her best.

'Well, thank you so much. How much do I owe you for the pizza?'

'Will I see you at the quiz on Thursday?'

'I don't know. I hadn't thought...'

'Perhaps I could pick you up here at seven?'

'Okay.'

That had been well done. Smooth even. He sidestepped the issue of paying for the pizza and made a date without her really having the opportunity to demur. Smooth. Not James Bond. But smooth. Last time they'd parted she'd kissed him. This time, he kissed her. But only on the cheek. She felt the hard bulge under his left armpit and thought again of 007, then remembered that she'd seen him put his mobile phone in that pocket.

*

When Michael returned to Windmill Cottage, the man calling himself Diarmuid Geraghty had retired to his room. Richard was in the living room thumbing through a magazine called *Fly-fishing* or something similar.

'Have you had a message from Phillipa?'

Richard looked up from his magazine with a slightly puzzled expression.

'Templeton. Phillipa Templeton?'

'Oh, yes, I see. Or, rather, no. No, I haven't. Why do you ask?'

'I've had a text. She wants to see me tomorrow at nine. Or us. I don't know, actually.'

'Might consider asking her, old boy.'

'What's happened? Do you think we've done anything wrong?'

'Well, it doesn't look like I have, since I haven't had a message. Still, I'm sure she'll understand. After all, you've been doing your best.'

Michael considered and discounted half a dozen responses, some verbal, some percussive, and some involving borrowing Big Chris' gun. Instead, he said nothing, but he made a mental note to drop in on Margaret and ask her what she'd meant by her 'Perceval' remark.

*

Michael had a naturally inquiring mind, but his curiosity didn't extend so far as discovering what the consequences would be for being late for a meeting with Phillipa Templeton. Consequently, he boarded the 06:41 just as the sun was climbing above the south spire of Peterborough Cathedral. He'd spent a restless night trying to imagine what had prompted the summons. Had he committed some terrible error in his questioning of Geraghty? He didn't think so. Had he broached some protocol by taking him to the pub quiz? That didn't seem likely, but it might be possible. Was he being taken off the assignment all together? Or was it something else entirely? He had no answers. He decided that he would spend the next forty-five minutes thinking through the various possible permutations so that he could approach the meeting with a fresh perspective and a clear head. But instead, he spent the journey to Kings Cross daydreaming about Heather.

At five to nine, he was sitting on an exceptionally uncomfortable chair outside Phillipa's office. Was it just an example of the type of furniture supplied when government contracts were always awarded to the lowest bidder, or had Templeton deliberately sought out furniture designed to make her visitors uncomfortable? Both seemed equally likely. He'd already straightened his tie three times and was considering doing it again when Margaret sailed into view a little like a man-o'-war with all its gun ports open, but slightly more intimidating.

'Michael! How are you? She won't keep you a minute. She's on a call to the minister at the moment. I'm afraid I can't guarantee that it will put her in a good mood. How are you getting on with the Perceval Pup?'

'It takes all sorts.'

Margaret pursed her lips. 'So, he's a little shit like all the others then! I can't say I'm surprised. Watch your back, Michael.'

'The others?'

But Margaret gave him a look that said more plainly than words that she considered she'd provided him with all the information he needed. She pushed open the door to the office, poked her head inside for something less than a second and immediately withdrew it. 'In you go!'

Phillipa Templeton had probably been at her desk before Michael had left Windmill Cottage, but she still looked like she was midway through a *Vogue* cover shoot. She gave a tiny nod, and Michael sat down. He could feel his pulse rate climbing as Phillipa pulled a manilla folder from a desk drawer.

'We have identified your Mr Geraghty.' She pushed the folder towards him. 'James Christopher McKenna. He has been known to use a number of different names, but we think that they're all temporary, used for a single mission only and then discarded forever. But he's known in republican circles as the Scholar.'

'Ah, so I was right?' Michael regretted it immediately.

'Yes, Michael, you were right. Well done. I expect the Queen will want to give you a medal.'

Michael inwardly vowed not to utter another word unless he absolutely had to.

'He's clever. He's dangerous. And he's a nasty piece of work. Spent some time on the Nutting Squad...'

Michael's face must have betrayed his confusion.

'IRA internal disciplinary team. Punishment beatings, kneecapping, the occasional execution. Some people think he may have carried out an assassination or two, but that hasn't been verified. That's the problem when someone has a catchy *nom de guerre*. He becomes a sort of bogeyman. People ascribe all sorts of things to them.'

'A sort of Keyser Söze?' What had made him said that? Why had he said anything? Keep your bloody mouth shut, Michael.

But Phillipa smiled. 'Yes, a little bit I suppose.'

Michael tried to imagine Phillipa Templeton going to the cinema to watch *The Usual Suspects*. He couldn't. Was it a date? Did Phillipa have a boyfriend? Or perhaps a girlfriend? It seemed impossible. I mean where would you find someone with the courage to ask Phillipa Templeton on a date?

'The point is that there is nothing in his record that suggests that he'd suddenly had a fit of conscience, become disaffected, or had some sort of epiphany. He's sitting in Rutland because he wants something from us. Well? Read the file!'

It was a pretty thin file. Michael was trying to reconcile that man he'd known for a week with the man described, mostly through his actions. He had a terrible feeling that he was badly out of his depth. Perhaps that was why he was here. Was he going to be told that he was off the case and the matter was going to be passed to somebody more experienced? If so, why wasn't Richard Perceval here too? Surely, she couldn't be considering taking him off the case and leaving Perceval in place? He reached the end of the file. Phillipa extended her hand, and he passed it over.

'So?'

'You've interrogated him. You've read the file. What do you think?'

Michael paused. He didn't normally mind thinking aloud, allowing a theory to be formed by mulling the facts around. But he was distinctly uncomfortable about doing this in front of Phillipa Templeton. But she'd basically ordered him to do so.

'So far most of what he has told us is about republicans in places outside Derry. People who might be rivals, subjects of a feud, political or ideological opponents, or...' He hesitated. 'Or business rivals. I mean, he's mostly told us about cigarette smugglers. Perhaps he just wants them taken off the board to leave the field clear for himself.'

Phillipa nodded. 'Yes. That is a viable theory. And it means that while he is providing us with the information he wants us to have, he has an incentive to behave. Once he's has scattered all the breadcrumbs he has...well that might be different. So, make sure that you recognise the signs that he is reaching the end of his mission. When he starts to dry up, we'll need to be very, very careful. So, I think we'd better have daily reports from now on. Keep up the good work. And, Michael, don't trust him an inch!'

Chapter 12

Unusually, the man that everyone pretended to believe was called Diarmuid Geraghty had gone down to eat his breakfast in the kitchen. He was pushing it around his plate and trying to decide if it was porridge or scrambled eggs when Richard came in.

'Enjoying your omelette? It's okay. I had to ask what it was. Tony's on kitchen duty today.'

Geraghty's eyes returned to his plate. It could have been an omelette he supposed.

'Listen, Michael's had to pop back to London this morning, so I thought that you and I might take a little trip down to Rutland Water and see what the lie of the land is with respect to a spot of fly-fishing.'

Geraghty nodded slowly. He was wondering what might have required half of his interviewing team, the senior half if his instinct was right, to race back to London.

'Sure.'

'Be ready to go in, what, say...twenty minutes?'

'Sure.'

*

Tony had insisted on frisking Geraghty before they left the house. Richard met the Irishman's eyes with a look that seemed to say something like, 'Sorry about this.'

When he was satisfied, the former soldier, realistically, could he possibly be anything else, led the way to the Land Rover. Tony drove. Richard sat in the front and Big Chris sat beside Geraghty in the back. The Scholar took the opportunity to examine the two large men closely. He was looking for the bulge of an automatic pistol under the left armpit, but such was their size it was impossible to tell. It didn't matter. He knew what gun oil smelt like.

Tony parked, and Richard and the Scholar walked towards the shore. They were followed at a discreet distance by Big Chris and Tony. It was the distance that was discreet, not the two men. Big Chris and Tony would find it hard to blend in anywhere except at a giant convention or a bodybuilding competition.

*

If you didn't know Big Chris very well, you might have described him as a gentle giant. Certainly, he had an outwardly placid nature. And he didn't rile easily. But it hadn't been easy. He'd done two tours of Northern Ireland, South Armagh, and Londonderry. Twenty-two years in the army, most of it in the Royal Green Jackets. But it wasn't Northern Ireland that lay at the root of Big Chris's hatred. Well, not directly. 20th July 1982. Regents Park. The IRA bomb that killed seven, including Stephen, Big Chris's little brother, a trumpet player in the Royal Green Jackets band.

Big Chris hated the man called Diarmuid. Hated him, his organisation, whatever it was, his political beliefs, whatever they were, hated everything about the man. And if Diarmuid Geraghty gave him the slightest excuse...if he raised his hand or quickened his pace...if he posed any threat at all...to anyone at all...Big Chris would drop him. Unless Tony did it first, of course.

*

Richard Perceval had done a fair bit of fly-fishing. But actually, he knew very little about it. He was technically accomplished. He could cast accurately. He could play a fish, even a big salmon like those on the River Tweed where his uncle had an estate.

But Richard had just wandered into the river where the ghillie had told him and used the rod, line, and fly that he'd been given. He'd picked up enough knowledge and jargon to hold an intelligent conversation on the subject, but strictly speaking he wasn't really a fly fisherman. He didn't know how to read the water, to interpret the little ripples and waves. He had only the most basic understanding of which fly to use and when.

The Scholar most definitely was a fly fisherman. But he hadn't decided yet whether, or to what extent Diarmuid Geraghty was going to be.

Rutland Water was big. It was difficult to estimate exactly how big. Its horseshoe shape made it difficult to judge. Bigger than Lough Anure anyway. There were a handful of anglers in waders standing a few yards out in the water. The Scholar stood on the bank with his hands in his pockets, watching. Richard did the same for a while, but not knowing what he was supposed to be observing. He soon grew bored. Shortly after that, he grew restless.

He glanced around. Tony and Big Chris were about thirty yards away. Big Chris was eating an ice cream cone. But he was eating it with his left hand. His right hand was at his side. His jacket was half unzipped. His right hand could be inside it and under his left armpit in a second. He was staring at the back of the Irishman's head. Tony had his hands in his pocket. But his jacket was half unzipped too.

Richard turned back towards the water. An angler was wading back to shore. He'd caught something, a little brown trout, perhaps two or three pounds. Richard glanced again at Tony and Big Chris. They were alert. It was okay.

The Scholar was now in conversation with the angler. He was pointing out features on the far shore, or perhaps something else. The breeze carried his words away. After a few minutes, the two parted. The angler returned to the water. The Scholar returned to Richard.

'Learn anything?'

'A little. Your man says that there are guides at the centre just down the shore.'

'You don't have enough faith in your own ability to sniff out a fish?'

The Scholar gave him a look of pure scorn. 'Your man said that there is tackle and boats to hire too. At the centre. Shall we maybe have a wee look?'

Richard shrugged. He glanced towards his bodyguards. Big Chris had finished his ice cream. 'Is it far?'

'I don't think so.' And the Scholar began walking.

*

Michael had found a seat in a near deserted carriage and mulled over the events of the morning and the hours and days ahead of him.

On the positive side, he'd survived a meeting with Philippa Templeton without aggravating her, disgracing himself, or providing her with irrefutable evidence that he was a half-witted moron. That was definitely a plus.

His little chat with Margaret had been less successful. She seemed to express herself as obliquely as everyone else in that building. He would have to mull over everything she said, weigh every word, measure every pause, inflexion, and sniff, especially the sniffs. If he was lucky her true meaning would come to him in a day or two's time. Why was everyone like this? Would he become the same one day? Was he starting already?

The only thing he could be sure of, or thought he could be sure of, was that sometime in the dim and distant past some Perceval or other had let his grandfather down very badly. Of course, that didn't tell him very much. It might have been anything. An overly aggressive bid at the bridge table or leaving him stranded in East Berlin. There was absolutely no point in asking the old man. The best way was to provoke him into bursting out with it in a fit of temper.

Oh, God! He was becoming like the rest of them. Devising strategies to trick an old man into revealing decades old secrets!

But he needed to decide how much he was going to tell Richard Perceval. Everything? Well, why not? They were supposed to be on the same side, after all. But maybe keep just a little back. Richard would know, but that was the point. Just let him realise who the senior hand was here. I am the one being briefed by Templeton, and I choose how much to share with you.

He really was turning into one of them.

*

The Rutland Fishing Centre was part tackle shop, part café, part boat hire facility, and about a dozen other things besides. The Scholar was clearly in his element. He chatted to staff; he chatted to customers; he studied the noticeboards. And then he did it all again. Richard was starting to lose interest.

Big Chris and Tony had not come in. There were very few spaces that didn't instantly become rather crowded when either crossed the threshold. The pair of them in here would have been like trying to insert an inconspicuous hippopotamus in a telephone kiosk.

Instead, Tony was watching the main entrance while Big Chris surveyed the area more widely. There were a few tables and chairs outside for the café's customers. But none were occupied today. It was still a little chilly. Along one wall were a dozen pairs of oars chained and padlocked.

A path led down to the waterside and to a little wooden jetty about twenty yards away with a slipway beside it. A pair of hardy anglers were launching a boat from a trailer attached to the back of some sort of Japanese jeep. Big Chris, who was an unrepentant landlubber, found the whole scene vaguely comical.

Surely, he thought, the idea of a boat was to avoid getting your feet wet, but this fool was standing almost knee deep in water as he manhandled the vessel off the back of the trailer. His mate, clearly the more sensible of the pair, was standing at the prow. Is that what you were supposed to call the pointy end and trying to bounce the craft down the length of the trailer?

Big Chris watched in amused silence for a minute or two before 'wet ankles' hopped into the boat and pulled it close to the jetty. His friend, 'dry feet' then got into his car. It was a Mitsubishi, Big Chris noted, and drove away behind the fishing centre and out of his sight. He decided that he might as well follow. He needed to see if the fishing centre had a rear exit.

Behind the centre, there were half a dozen fibreglass boats each with a small outboard motor. They clearly belonged to the centre. Each was an identical model, so far as he could see, and each bore a Barnsdale Boats logo and a unique number.

Behind all this was what could only be described as a boat park. A couple of dozen of various sizes and designs, all on trailers. Almost all of them were covered in tarpaulins. Blue seemed to be a popular colour. Some had outboards fitted, others didn't. One or two had tiny wheelhouses. A modicum of shelter in the event of a shower. A few had names proudly painted on the side: *On the Rocks, Chicka-Dee, Escapist, Half Pint.*

There was no rear exit.

Big Chris completed his circumnavigation to find Tony nursing a polystyrene cup. 'Got you a tea, one sugar.'

Big Chris nodded his thanks and gave his whole concentration to the task of peeling the plastic lid off without spilling most of the scalding hot brew all over himself.

*

When Michael returned to Windmill Cottage, he found Richard in the garden, smoking a cigarette.

'How's your day been?'

'Well, I know a great deal more about flies and trout than I did before. But it would take a year or two before I know half what our Mr Geraghty knows.'

Michael walked half past him. Richard turned and now both men had their backs to the house. 'I don't suppose our friend would be able to lipread through the window, but there's no point in giving him the chance.'

'What have we learnt?'

'Well, we know who he is. And he's not the minnow he would have us believe. He's pretty senior and pretty serious. Used to be in the Nutting Squad.'

Michael really hoped that Richard wouldn't know what that was. Maybe he didn't, but he wouldn't give Michael the satisfaction of asking.

'Traced him through fingerprints?'

'No. No, he made a slip. We traced him via his nickname.'

'Which is?'

'He's known as the Scholar. Obviously, he's not to know that we know that.'

Richard drew on his cigarette.

'So, he's a big fish. A serious player. And he has chosen not to tell us. He's chosen to play the part of a small fry.'

'Do you think we could dispense with the piscine references, old boy? I've had quite enough or our be-finned friends for one day.'

'Now if he was here, talking to us, for any of the reasons he's given, or hinted at, wouldn't he emphasise how important and knowledgeable he is?'

This was obviously astute, but Richard wasn't going to acknowledge the fact. 'So?'

'So, here's here on some mission. He's using us for something or trying to. And when his mission is complete...'

'We sort of knew that. Does it really change anything?'

'He is a very dangerous man. And we don't know what he's up to.'

'I don't know if you'd noticed, old thing, but we have three pretty dangerous men ourselves. And you and I are scarcely amateurs, at least I'm not.'

Michael was privately hoping that the Scholar would make a break for it and maim Richard Perceval in the attempt.

Chapter 13

Andy Bishop's alarm went off at eleven thirty. Eleven thirty PM. He groaned, rolled over, and reached for his Camels. Empty packet. Probably just as well. He needed to get up. He wanted to be on the road by midnight. It was 900 kilometres to Santander, and he planned to be there by midday.

Downstairs he could hear Selena and her parents eating their evening meal. Bishop had made a lot of adjustments since coming to Spain, coffee instead of tea, lager instead of bitter, wine even. But he didn't think he would ever get used to having his tea at nearly midnight. And he certainly would never get used to sort of living with his in-laws.

He'd assumed, wrongly, as events revealed, that he and Selena would find their own place when they moved in together. Or at least when they got married. Or at least when little Pepe had arrived. But his father-in-law always had a reason why they should continue living under his roof, even if that roof had to be made bigger.

When they'd announced that Selena was pregnant, one of Javier's friends had been in the kitchen the following morning with a tape measure. There was a certain amount of pursing of lips. That seemed to be part of a universal language of builders the world over.

Then there was a brief but fierce debate, too fast and passionate for Bishop to follow. There were mentions of dates and pesetas and cots. Bishop's heart sank. He knew that another escape route had been closed off. Suddenly, all was broad smiles, and handshakes, and a bottle was produced, glasses clinked. This was eight thirty in the morning. One more adjustment that Bishop needed to make.

Bishop showered and shaved, selected a clean shirt, one washed and ironed by his mother-in-law, and went downstairs. It was five minutes to midnight. If he could catch the lunchtime ferry, he could have a meal, sleep in a cabin and would arrive in Plymouth at ten o'clock the following morning with the benefit of a good night's rest.

He would need it because he had to travel to Exeter and then Sheffield before picking up a groupage load in Doncaster the next day and heading back to Spain. He would be home for the weekend. It didn't occur to him that anything might happen to jeopardise those plans.

He knew very well what was in his trailer behind the two pallets of increasingly unappealing looking onions, but nobody could prove he knew. He was just a lorry driver. He never touched the fags, never signed any paperwork. He was just an innocent bystander on wheels.

And he didn't expect ever to have to plead that case. He'd made this trip, or one very like it, more than a dozen times. The first couple of times he'd been slightly nervous as he passed through the docks at Portsmouth or Plymouth, not anymore. Usually, he never even saw a customs officer. Even when he did, they seemed bored and uninterested. The risk seemed minimal, but he was paid a premium for taking it. A trip on behalf of this customer paid twice as well as any other. He was building up quite a nice little nest egg.

Ideally, he would have preferred to have been away over the weekend. Sunday lunch with his in-laws was the highlight of their week, but not of his. In particular, Javier enjoyed sitting at the head of his table on a chair slightly larger than all the others. Bishop always thought of it as a throne and perhaps Javier did, too. He seemed to think that it imbued him with the authority to make unarguable pronouncements on matters of family policy and express opinions that Bishop disputed at his peril.

The fact that these opinions changed from week to week made no impression on Javier's sense of infallibility when he sat on his throne. Politics, football, the history of Anglo-Spanish relations and Bishop's career were all the subjects of opinions that were often inconsistent, incoherent, or just irrational. But the confidence with which they were expressed never varied.

On balance, Sunday lunchtimes were the low point of Bishop's week. But that might change soon too. For six months he'd been pursuing a subtle campaign to persuade Selena to move out of her parents' house, move out of Cartagena all together.

It would be nice for the children to be raised by the seaside he'd told her. He'd seen a few properties a few miles down the coast on the Mar de Cristal. If the well-paid trips continued, he might be able to afford quite a nice villa in about a year. And who knew what business opportunities might be presented by his proximity to the wealthy English tourists who visited the La Manga resort nearby?

He would prefer to be working for Englishmen. The Irish had been good to him. Regular well-paid trips running cigarettes to England. But they were disorganised. And unreliable. Sometimes he didn't hear from Dominic for days, and then everything was urgent. Could he go to England tomorrow? Drop everything, just like that?

And there were other things he didn't like. Dominic wasn't an Irishman like Terry Wogan or David O'Leary. He had the harsh accent of Ulster, not the gentle lilt of the republic. He was probably being unfair, but Bishop always associated that accent with the voices on the television news after a bomb had gone off somewhere. He was probably being unfair. It wasn't right to hold a man's birthplace against him...but all the same.

Realistically, Bishop didn't think that Dominic could really be a terrorist. He was too comical, too absurd, and far, far too indiscreet. He could be found in Molly Malone's almost every night and by about eleven o'clock he was telling anyone and everyone he met his business. That was how Bishop had learnt about the trips to England in the first place. And he'd been pleased. The money was very welcome.

That was another reason to move out of Cartagena, as if he needed one. To avoid bumping into Dominic and his friends at The Molly Malone. When he'd made enough money and bought his place out in Mar de Cristal or perhaps Los Nietos. He would just drift quietly away, change his phone, and disappear. A few more of these trips, maybe ten, maybe twenty. That was his plan.

*

Bishop made Santander in good time. He boarded and made his way immediately to the drivers' lounge. His cabin wouldn't yet be ready. The lounge was about half full. There was a group of four Spaniards playing Cuarenta noisily, another cursing softly but fluently at the coffee machine, and one or two others reading *El Correo*, the Basque newspaper.

Nobody was reading *La Verdad* or *La Opinion de Murcia*. That was good. He didn't want to see anybody from home. He now thought of Cartagena, Murcia, as home. Perhaps that's why he didn't immediately register the man in the corner reading yesterday's *Daily Express*.

He threw himself into a club chair and attempted to snooze, but it wasn't very comfortable, and the card players were making too much noise. He decided that if he was going to be awake, he may as well be properly awake and he walked over towards the coffee machine just as the ferry's hooter sounded and the vessel began, almost imperceptibly, to move.

'*Creo que está...roto? Kaput. Mierda?*'

The Spanish was so halting and the accent so atrocious that the speaker could only be an Englishman.

Bishop peered behind the machine where it was plugged into the wall. He flicked the switch to 'on'.

'Might take a minute or two to warm-up.' He wished he hadn't spoken in English. He wished he hadn't spoken at all. But he was tired. And it probably didn't matter. He wasn't a spy undercover. He was just a slightly anti-social cigarette smuggler, not that he would have thought of himself in those terms.

'English?'

There was no sense in denying it.

'Going to Plymouth?'

The speaker immediately realised what a stupid question that was. Everyone was going to Plymouth unless they planned to jump overboard in the Bay of Biscay and swim to France. He decided to start again.

'Bryan Sharpe.'

'Andy.'

The coffee machine signalled it was ready. 'What would you like?'

'Milk and as much sugar as they'll give me.'

Bishop jabbed a couple of buttons and nodded towards the nearest table where, as on all the other tables, there was a little cup filled with sachets of sugar or sweetener.

'Do you use this route often?'

Oh, good! He was a talker, Bishop inwardly sighed. 'Quite often.'

'First time for me. I usually go through France. Pick up in Seville like, then all the way up through France to St Malo...or Caen sometimes, sometimes Cherbourg, varies really but always through France. This is better. Chance for a bit of kip. Are the cabins good?'

'They're all right.' Bishop didn't want to get drawn into a conversation, and he certainly didn't want to discuss his travel itinerary, particularly not with a garrulous Englishman.

'Never been in to Plymouth either. What's it like?'

Bishop shrugged. What sort of question was that?

'Any bother with Customs? Anything like that?'

Bishop turned to the machine and selected a café cortado. 'Never had any bother.'

'What's your load?'

'Onions.'

'Mine too, taking it to Leicester.'

'My home town or used to be.' Why had he said that? Why had he got himself into a conversation at all?

*

Joe Lake and Monster were in their shared office, taking stock. It wasn't just that fact that it was now dual occupancy that indicated that this was no longer Andi's office. The desks were littered with empty and half empty coffee mugs. The bin was overflowing. Four pot plants, now in the very last stages of their lives, had been pushed to the end of the window ledge, which now served as an additional filing facility. If the haphazard collection of documents, radio batteries, and old newspapers could be said to be filed.

In a pile midway between them was a stack of forms that both were ignoring. Each was wrestling with a similar dilemma. Lake was wondering whether he ought to propose dividing the pile between them. Monster was inwardly debating whether he could delegate the whole task to somebody else. Independently and simultaneously, each decided to postpone the decision.

The presence of the teetering tower of forms was a testament to the success of Operation Bridegroom so far. Nine separate premises had been visited by customs, not by Lake's team of investigators, by local officers, but the results had been highly satisfactory. Over six million cigarettes had been seized. Now the details had to be entered into ten sets of forms for inputting into the central computer system.

The one premises that had not been visited was The Walnut Tree. And this was the topic of Lake's and Monster's case conference.

'Do we think he still has some fags?'

'Very likely, but we're not completely sure.'

'And the Other Office?'

'Nothing. They don't know.'

'So, we could just go and raid him. Or get the locals to do it.'

'It's an option,' conceded Lake.

'I mean, he must have heard about all his customers being raided. I mean, visited.'

'Must have.'

'So, he must be expecting it.'

'Must he? I don't know. I don't know what he's thinking. That's what the Other Office is for.'

'Supposing he decided to lie low for a while. Or give up all together. And his customers. Will they want to re-stock?'

'Some will. According to the Other Office, they're already asking about it. And some of them have only paid for half and are refusing to pay for the other half. One of them wants a full refund.'

'And there are possibly other customers, ones who didn't have a piece of this particular load. What are they going to do?'

Lake shrugged. 'I'm not really concerned about them. It's the people further up the supply chain that I'm worried about. How are we going to get to them?'

It was Monster's turn to shrug. And then the phone rang.

*

Lake told Nick Harper to assemble a surveillance team.

'And tell everyone to pack for two nights, just in case.'

'Where are we going?'

'Portsmouth, to begin with, we think. Then Sheffield.'

Harper nodded and started mentally composing his to-do list: charge radio batteries, camera kits, films of different speeds, check on hotels. Sledgehammers.

'Wait, what are you doing?'

'Monster and I are going to spin the possible slaughter.' He waggled a set of car keys. Monster came down the stairs like an elephant that had decided to attempt the record for descending the Eiffel Tower. A glimpse of the old Monster, the pre-Amy Monster.

*

'What's a Christy Ring?'

'It's not a what. It's a who. Christy Ring was a hurler.'

'A what?'

'A hurler, played hurling. Ireland's national sport.'

'Another Irish connection?'

'Possibly.'

'There it is.'

Intake isn't Sheffield's most salubrious district, and The Christy Ring wasn't Intake's most salubrious pub. But at least it was easy to find on the Mansfield Road. Lake parked diagonally opposite and surveyed the scene. Monster produced a Scotch egg.

Lake's first thought was that The Christy Ring was the very antithesis of The Old Volunteer. Lake would have been offended if you had suggested that he was a 'pub snob' but, in fact, he was. The Christy Ring was very much not his sort of boozer. For a start, it had a flat roof. Lake had a deep held loathing of pubs with flat roofs, or anything built after the death of Queen Victoria for that matter.

The windows were full of posters advertising forthcoming televisual sporting attractions. At least somebody must have thought that they were attractions. Ipswich Town v Port Vale! Really? Other posters advertised nasty mass-produced lagers at suspiciously low prices. Lake knew without crossing the threshold that there would be far too many fruit machines and double measures of improbably coloured shots available at happy hour. Lake could never have been happy at The Christy Ring, unless perhaps he had a search warrant.

Lake thought that The Christy Ring looked like it was very much a locals' pub and not the place where a stranger could pop in for a pint without attracting attention. Lake had no intention of putting this assessment to the test. In any event it was what was outside the pub that commanded his attention. Monster had noticed them too, three lock-up garages secured with padlocks of a size that might have seemed overcautious at Fort Knox at the back of the car park. Lake nodded in their direction and Monster would have responded in kind if it were not for the fact that his head was tipped back as he attempted to pour the last few breadcrumbs from the cellophane wrapper into his gaping maw.

'Do you think you could get an articulated lorry in that car park?'

'Probably. But the place is overlooked. I wouldn't want to unload millions of fags in broad daylight.'

'After closing?'

'Might be worse. Early in the morning would be my guess.'

'Ferry arrives at seven. Be here by lunchtime.'

'If he comes here directly. If he comes here first. We're assuming it's one load one destination because it was last time. But what if he's dropping off at multiple locations?'

'I'm going to have to call the Other Office.'

But he didn't. Because they called him.

*

'He's going to bloody Exeter first.'

'Bloody hell! Still Portsmouth?'

'Plymouth.'

'So, Exeter, not Sheffield. Plymouth not Portsmouth? What are they playing at down there?'

'There's something else.'

'What?'

'The Other Office. The intel. There was something slightly different about the way Jack said it.'

'Different how?'

'I don't know. I can't quite put my finger on it. But it was different.'

'Too right, it was different! Different destination. Different port of entry.'

'Yeah, but also it was like perhaps they'd a different source of intelligence.'

'What makes you say that?'

'I don't know. It was just something. I don't know.'

'Well, we've had two different stories in two hours.'

'Which makes me wonder.'

'There's only one source of intelligence from the Other Office.'
'Is there? I wonder?'
'You're thinking Box? For fag smugglers! It's not very likely, is it?'
'Irish fag smugglers.'
'Oh, come on! They're not really Irish fag smugglers are they? The driver wasn't Irish. That bloke who runs The Walnut Tree is a plastic paddy at best.'
'So was Seán Mac Stíofáin, and he was the leader of the IRA.'
'Who?'
'Doesn't matter. It's probably nothing.'

Lake turned the key in the ignition, took one more glance at The Christy Ring, and swung out into traffic. Neither said anything until they reached the M1.

'You know, we might have to knock it in Exeter.'

Lake had already reached this conclusion, but he wanted to hear Monster say it first. Wanted to hear him explain his reasoning. It was the sort of thing Frank McBride used to do.

'I see it this way. If he unloads at Exeter. It might be the full load. It might be partial. And we probably won't be able to see which.'

Lake nodded and indicated to move into the fast lane.

'And if it is a partial drop off who knows where he may be going next?'

Lake didn't even have to nod this time.

'He might be going to Sheffield, or somewhere else, or Sheffield and then somewhere else.'

'And if he does that, we have an unknown number of smuggled fags sitting in Exeter, probably waiting for customers. They could be gone in a day or two.'

'They could be gone in an hour or two. We don't know. If we knock it in Exeter, we get all the fags and at least one customer.'

'We could sit on it for an hour or two, see if anybody turns up to collect.'

'Could do. Could do. But I think we need to be ready to knock it in Exeter.'

'Agreed. Call the office. Get the whole team ready to go. Find a hotel in Plymouth. Find out what time the ferries arrive. Do you want to call Amy?'

Calling Amy to explain that he was heading for the south coast and that he didn't know when he would be back was the last thing Monster wanted to do. But he did it just the same. A little bit of the new Monster.

Chapter 14

Heather had had a particularly busy day. It had begun with an incident involving crayons. Those were common. And a nosebleed, less common, but not an exactly unprecedented. At lunchtime, she'd somehow found herself forced to settle a dispute about a penalty decision in the playground. The afternoon had been little better.

On the positive side, she'd had almost no time to think about Michael. She was congratulating herself on this silver lining as she drove home when she realised that she probably ought to think about him just a little. He was quite sweet, and she wanted to let him down gently.

He seemed very nice. And it was to his credit that she knew very little about him. Men of her acquaintance usually liked to talk more than they listened. And their favourite subject was usually themselves. Michael wasn't like that.

But he wasn't tall. He wasn't dark. He wasn't handsome. He wasn't rich. She told herself that didn't matter. Of course, it didn't. But he wasn't rich. And he wasn't her type. Her type was bold and ambitious.

Her type were barristers and bankers. They drove flashy cars and knew the right wine to order in restaurants.

But she didn't want to hurt him. He was obviously keen. He'd rushed around with pizza and Valpolicella at the drop of a hat last night. Better to let him down gently. And before Thursday's pub quiz.

It was only a few minutes past four when she got home. She decided to take advantage of the spring evening to take a little walk across the fields.

*

Heather began to feel slightly breathless as she climbed Beacon Hill. She should probably take a little more exercise. Do this more often, now that the weather was improving. What were those birds? If I'm going to live in the country, I should know this sort of thing. No need to go overboard. No need to join the Young Farmers or anything. Were you supposed to actually be a farmer to be in the Young Farmers? She didn't know. Anyway, she wasn't going to do that. What was she going to do? She couldn't stay here. She would end up a wizened old spinster, surrounded by cats. She was a city girl, really.

She paused for a second to regain her breath. It was beautiful, though. There were sheep in that field. She was pretty sure that she could recognise sheep. One or two lambs too. Quite a lot now that she looked carefully. It was beautiful. If circumstances were different. If she had a boyfriend, or even, well, you know. Because she would get married one day, wouldn't she? Most people did. And maybe her children (there were going to be three, two boys and a girl) maybe her children would know what those birds were. Maybe they would know when lambs were born and calves and piglets. They would be able to tell the difference between wheat and barley and all those other things that she assumed were lying beneath those green shoots.

Lost in her thoughts and taking in the panorama she didn't notice Rocky until he was almost upon her scampering around her feet, his tongue at its usual four o'clock. She immediately looked up the hill and saw Brunhilde galloping towards her at a speed that meant she couldn't possibly stop and on a course that looked certain to catch Heather around about the knees and possibly send her cartwheeling all the way to the bottom of the hill.

Rocky was giving little yelps of joy. Brunhilde diverted her course by a fraction and shot past with an inch to spare and then pulled the canine equivalent of a handbrake turn to join in with Rocky in the general gambolling. Or was it lambs that gambolled?

Breasting the hill were the three old men, whose names Heather had still not learnt. Actually, she knew one, or thought she did. He was her quiz teammate, Ron. At least she assumed so. The team, which at the time of arrival had comprised only him had been called 'Ron's Team'. So, he must be Ron.

Ron was talking to the quizmaster himself, a tall assemblage of waxed cotton and tweed. When you thought of an English country gent, this was the image that came to mind. He might have been a minor member of the aristocracy, or a retired colonel, or possibly a classics professor. He was talking animatedly to Ron and hadn't noticed her yet. The third man was the landlord of the pub. He hadn't noticed her either. He was puffing away at a pipe, which seemed to transport him away to some distant land of contentment.

At this point, the quizmaster noticed her. His face broke into a broad smile. The ends of his silver moustache twitched up and his eyes seemed to twinkle.

'Hello again!' Was everyone in the country so delighted to bump into a minor acquaintance? She rather hoped so.

The landlord returned to the real world. 'Rocky! Stop bothering her.'

'Oh, I don't mind...'

'Frank.'

'Heather.'

'Heather is Sid Hobday's granddaughter, Frank.'

Heather was slightly puzzled. Her grandfather had been called Harold.

'A lovely man, your grandfather. Of course, I didn't know him well. Ron knew him better, didn't you, Ron?'

'Arr!' This seemed to be Ron's stock reply, but unusually for him he added a further unsolicited comment, 'Good man, Sid, a real gent, decent bowler...and a very brave man.'

She didn't quite know how to reply. Before she'd framed what she hoped was a suitable response, Ron had turned his attention to Brunhilde, who seemed to have found something particularly horrible at the bottom of a ditch.

'Leave it! Leave it, Gurn, fezzit gerkermitt!' He growled, or something of that order anyway, 'Come arrn, levvit, levvit! Assa good gurll. Good Gurll!'

Ron strode towards the errant dog. His vocabulary was largely unintelligible, but his meaning was very clear. Brunhilde, rather sheepishly abandoned whatever it was she had in her mouth, Heather didn't want to speculate, and trotted over, her tongue at eight o'clock.

'And that, young lady, is the opinion of the bravest man you're ever likely to meet,' murmured the quizmaster. 'We've not been formally introduced. I'm Bernard Taylor. This is Frank McBride. I hope we'll be seeing you at the quiz again on Thursday. Defending your title, so to speak.'

This was a bit awkward. 'Well, I'm not sure I'll be able to...I'm very busy at the moment.'

The old man met her eyes. He evidently considered this a very poor excuse.

'Oh, but you absolutely must. Ron and Michael will be counting on you.'

'Arr.' Ron had rejoined them. He seemed to agree.

*

Heather had been puzzling about what Bernard had said. She was absolutely sure that her grandfather had been called Harold, not Sid. She knew that he'd been in the RAF. Did that make him a brave man? She supposed it must do, in a way.

More puzzling still was what Bernard had said about Ron. The bravest man she was ever likely to meet? How could he possibly justify a statement like that? He had no idea who she might meet. And Ron? Really? She supposed he might be of Second World War vintage like her grandfather. She wasn't very good at estimating the ages of anyone over about forty-five. And with Ron it was even harder. If you had told her that he'd been wandering these fields issuing incomprehensible commands to dogs since Roman times, she would have had no difficulty believing it.

As she turned to follow the track down into Leighton Magna, Leighton Parva's slightly smaller twin village, a third puzzle had occurred to her. How had Bernard known Michael's name? They hadn't spoken to each other at the pub quiz. Perhaps Ron had mentioned it. She liked Ron. It was impossible not to. The elderly, passive, almost mute countryman was a gentleman. Not in the socio-economic sense, but according to the much more important criterion of character. A brave man, though? A war hero? That seemed a little unlikely.

It was starting to get dark as she reached Leighton Parva again. The lights were just being switched on at The Old Volunteer. One by one the windows lit up. Finally, the little light above the inn sign flickered into life, illuminating the picture of the soldier in khaki. Just for a second, as the light warmed, the soldier looked like Ron. Then, for a far shorter period, a fraction of a fraction of a second, it looked like Michael.

Heather shook her head. She wasn't going to fall into the trap of imagining omens and portents. Too many of her friends had bored her for hours with lengthy and improbable explanations about how they just knew that their current beau was 'the one'. She certainly wasn't going to indulge herself in any nonsense like that. But perhaps she would go to the pub quiz after all. For Ron.

*

Little Chris was on kitchen duties that day. He'd served up gammon and eggs with new potatoes and greens. It was actually pretty good. The Scholar retired early with a book he'd bought in Walkers of Oakham. Richard hadn't mentioned that.

Michael decided that he would make a social call on his grandfather and gently probe him on the subject of the Clan Perceval. He had already decided that Richard was at least as treacherous and slippery as the Scholar but conversations with the old man were seldom completely fruitless even if it sometimes took up to forty-eight hours to understand what you had been told.

He was met at the kitchen door by Brunhilde, who seemed to see her role as some sort of canine butler. She barked once, as if to announce his arrival, and then scampered off to notify his grandfather in person. She might have been regretting that she wasn't able to take him a calling card on a silver tray.

THE RUTLAND VOLUNTEER

His grandfather was in his drawing room, always a drawing room, never a sitting room, or lounge, reading a book about the Peloponnesian War. He was in his favourite armchair beside a log fire. Even in the spring weather, the old man seemed to feel the cold. A function of his age, Michael supposed.

The room was decorated in a style that you might have called 'Rutland Chintz'. There was a mantle clock that ticked steadily. If you listened carefully, you could hear the grandfather clock in the hall working in quiet harmony. Both armchairs had embroidered antimacassars (was that the word?) and the walls were decorated with watercolours of pastoral scenes. Even the television set looked like it belonged on the set of a period drama.

This wasn't the lair of a devious, manipulative scoundrel who meddled and provoked, interfered, and influenced for the sheer mischief of it. No, that was the old man's study. He called it 'the library', just along the hall, beyond the grandfather clock.

'Hello, Mikey, had a good day?'

Michael decided that he would take the initiative. 'Yes, been to the office. Margaret sends her best.'

'Is she really still there? She must be about a hundred.'

'Remembers you very well.'

'Well, her memory was always among her greatest assets.'

'She seems to have a soft spot for you.'

Michael didn't know his grandfather well, not like that. There probably wasn't a man alive who did. But he would have been willing to bet that he would now try to change the subject.

'I saw that young lady of yours this afternoon, Heather.'

Michael was prepared to count this as a private victory.

'She's not my young lady.'

'I was forecasting, not commentating. She seemed reluctant to come to the quiz on Thursday. But I twisted her arm. Now, you mustn't expect to win this time. It'll do you both good for her to see you in triumph and defeat.'

'No questions on the Peloponnesian War then?'

'Good Lord, no. No, I read this for pleasure. That Lysander was a bit of a scamp, wasn't he? Makes me chuckle.'

'Listen, Grandpa, I know you enjoy little more than a bit of meddling and manipulation, but would you mind laying off the matchmaking?'

'By all means, if that's what you want.'

'It is what I want. And no nudging, hinting, sowing of seeds, or contriving serendipitous circumstances either.'

'Very well. But perhaps there is something else I can help you with.'

This was his chance. 'Perceval, or rather, the Percevals.'

'Ah, yes, I thought we might get to that subject. Better make yourself comfortable.'

Chapter 15

Someone in the management at Brittany Ferries was clearly paranoid about drivers oversleeping. Bishop was roused by a gentle ascending arpeggio of bongs, followed a few seconds later by a slightly louder one. After that the volume, and it seemed to Bishop, the insistency, increased. There then followed announcements in three languages. Why three? The ferry had left Spain and was arriving in England. Why did he need to hear an invocation to rise in French? Perhaps the clue was in the name. Perhaps he should be grateful that there wasn't an announcement in Breton too.

He'd stayed up later than he intended to. Bryan Sharpe just wouldn't shut up and let him go to his cabin. Worse still, the more he drank the louder and less discreet he'd been. Bishop had found himself glancing nervously around to see if there were any attentive witnesses to their conversation. Or rather, any witnesses to Sharpe's self-pitying whine. If Bishop had been the praying type, he would have offered up an invocation that he didn't meet him again at breakfast.

In fact, there was no sign of him. Perhaps he'd drunkenly slept through the trilingual bonging. Bishop didn't care, just so long as his rig wasn't prevented from disembarking.

It may have been his imagination, but there seemed to be one or two more customs officers than usual at the port. It didn't matter, while one or two seemed to be studying him none invited him to pull over into the examination bay. In a little over five minutes, he was out of the port and heading for the A38 towards Exeter. He glanced in his mirrors to make sure that there were no police cars, reached into his breast pocket and fished out his phone.

*

Gerard Duffy was sitting at his desk in the small booth cum cupboard that served as his office and trying to do his accounts. It was a struggle. Not just because he found accounts difficult and boring, but because he had to do three sets. First, there were the books and records that showed the true trading position of St Anselm's Roman Catholic Social Club. Second, there were the books that mitigated the club's VAT position (a VAT inspector would probably have used a different word). Finally, there were the records of Duffy's own private enterprise.

Duffy was the club's steward and only employee. He'd been a bar steward all his life, or at least since he'd arrived at Fishguard as a young man nearly forty years ago. He'd started his career, if you could call it that, at the British Legion. The institution had been in decline from the day he joined. A combination of an ageing customer base and the competing attractions of television had finished it off in the early seventies. Then there had been the Labour Club. Margaret Thatcher's trade union policies had done for that. And a combination of these two factors, ageing customers and Mrs Thatcher's policies, had led to the closure of the Conservative Club.

Duffy knew a thing or two about failing social clubs. He didn't need to pore over books and records, calculate the stock take, or estimate revenue forecasts. He could tell by smell alone, or feel, or osmosis, or something. Perhaps it was osmosis. It didn't matter. St Anselm's was failing. And it would fail, probably in a year or two despite him fiddling everything that could be fiddled.

He considered himself an honest man. He'd never stolen so much as a shilling from the Legion, the Labour Club, not even from the Tories. And he certainly wasn't going to steal from St Anselm's. That would be tantamount to stealing from God, or from the church at least.

But St Anselm's was going to fail in a year, or two at most. And Duffy didn't think that he would find another job easily. He was almost sixty-three. That was why he had a third set of books. That was why he was distributing smuggled cigarettes throughout Devon and Cornwall.

Duffy knew who his suppliers were. Not specifically, but he knew. He'd been born and raised in County Cork, the Rebel County. He could smell a Provo as easily as he could smell a pint of bitter that was three days past its sell-by-date or an unprofitable fruit machine. As a young man, well, a child really, he'd sat in the corner of McCarthy's Lounge in Fermoy and listened to stories of the Tan War. His father had been too young, but Uncle Des and Uncle Gerry had played their part. And Uncle Tom, his mother's eldest brother. Uncle Tom was a hero, a legend, a martyr.

Duffy had no sympathy for the IRA. Any politics he may once have had were diluted and eventually evaporated by years of pulling pints at the Labour Club or pouring Scotch at the Con Club. This was strictly business. It was his pension.

He glanced at his watch. As if on cue, the telephone on his desk rang. The conversation was very short. He glanced at his watch again, closed the books, picked up the keys to the lock-up garage and rose.

*

'From Pisa, X-ray Twenty, leaving the port area.'

'Madrid acknowledge.'

'Venice acknowledge.'

'Zebedee acknowledge.' Kevin Cleary on the motorcycle always sounded a little crackly and indistinct.

'Geneva acknowledge. Geneva has eyeball on X-ray Twenty. Approaching the roundabout.'

'From Geneva. He's taken the third, taken the third, A38 towards Exeter.'

In the Mondeo driven by Lake, Monster's phone rang.

*

Andy Bishop didn't see the surveillance team behind him. In truth, mobile surveillance on a forty-foot lorry isn't especially difficult. And it's even easier when you know where it's going.

'The customer is St Anselm's Social Club. But that's not where the slaughter will take place. He's headed for a lock-up. Possibly near the football club.'

'St James Park.'

'What?'

'Exeter City play at St James Park.'

'I doubt it'll be there.'

'From Venice. He's indicating nearside, indicating nearside...Onto the slip road. He's at the roundabout. Indicating inside. Madrid, can you take it?'

'Madrid, yes, yes.' Monster shifted forward in his seat. Lake's grip on the steering wheel tightened slightly.

'He's taken the first, taken the first. Eyeball to you, Madrid.'

'Madrid has eyeball on X-ray Twenty. Convoy close up. We're expecting a slaughter somewhere near here.'

Nine pulses increased slightly. Officers felt for their handcuffs or for binoculars. Earpieces were put in. Personal radios were checked. Minutes passed. Miles passed. Mouths dried.

'From Madrid, X-ray Twenty. Indicating nearside. Sports and playing fields...He's into the car park. We're overshooting. Nobody follow him in. I want some footmen out. Get some eyes on that wagon.'

'Venice. There's an old man waiting by the pavilion.'

'Nick's on foot. Moving to eyeball.'

'Julia's on foot.'

Cars ducked into side streets. Monster and Lake in the Mondeo, code named Madrid, shot off looking for somewhere to turn round.

'Nick has eyeball. X-ray is a stop, stop, stop in the car park.'

'From Julia. Old man walking. He's got keys. I've got a good position.'

'Car park has only one exit.'

'Brown Allegro in the car park, wait for index.'

'Brown Allegro! I don't think it's the godfather of south Devon!' muttered Lake as he spun his car round at the entrance to a cul-de-sac.

'Driver getting out of the cab.'

Andy Bishop yawned and stretched himself. He reached up to his sun visor and withdrew a sheet of paper. The man he knew as 'Gerry' was already waiting by his cab door. Bishop hopped down. He looked around. Nothing.

'Alright, Gerry?'

'Grand.'

Bishop consulted the piece of paper. 'Twenty Embassy, twenty Lambert & Butler, twenty Silk Cut, ten Marlboro, forty Benson & Hedges, and forty JPS. Is that right?'

Gerry nodded. The two men walked to the back of the trailer and Bishop looked around again. He saw nothing untoward. There was a young man walking on the far side of the nearest football pitch, but he seemed to be alone and was showing no interest in him, or his lorry.

He opened the back doors. The lorry was about three-quarters full. A casual observer, and all the actual observers were far from casual, would only have seen two pallets of onions, a folding ramp, and two trollies.

'Rear doors open. Onions.' Julia was in a telephone kiosk on the opposite side of the road. It might have been designed to serve as an observation post.

Gerry Duffy selected a key and opened the doors of a large metal shed at the end of the main pavilion. A corner flag fell out. Duffy picked it up and carried it inside. Despite a dozen sets of goal nets, a hundred corner flags and a selection of rollers and lawnmowers there was still plenty of room.

Bishop had climbed into the back of the trailer. He freed the pallet trolley from its securing harness and began to wheel one of the pallets of onions to a spot out of the way of the shed doors.

'He's moving the onions.'

Julia wondered where Nick Harper had found to give himself that view. She couldn't see him anywhere. Harper adjusted the focus on his binoculars slightly. He was leaning against the side of a ride-on roller, the type used at the more serious types of cricket clubs, some two hundred yards away.

'Pallets behind, wrapped in blue shrink-wrap.'

Bishop drew a Stanley knife from his pocket and extended the blade an inch or so. He grew it diagonally across the shrink-wrap. He retracted the blade and started to tear away the polythene.

'Silk Cut first, Gerry, twenty master cases, wasn't it?'

Duffy grunted, whether in agreement, or from the effort of fixing the ramp to the back of the lorry wasn't clear. When he was satisfied, he walked up the ramp and freed the second trolley from its fixings against the side of the trailer.

'From Nick. Unloading. Four boxes to a trolley.'

'Make sure you count them.'

The whole exercise took nearly half an hour. Bishop had to move and open half a dozen different pallets. Duffy had to make nearly forty journeys up and down the ramp with the pallet trolley.

'Looks like they've finished.'

'How many?'

'Thirty-seven times, four plus two.'

'That's not a lorry load.' It wasn't clear if Monster was talking to himself or to Lake.

'More customers. More drop-offs.'

Monster looked at Lake.

'You're the case officer. Your call.' He'd never felt more like Frank McBride.

Monster thought for a moment. Any decision was always better than none. He pressed the transmit button.

'All units from commander. When the doors are closed but before anyone leaves...'

'Lorry driver back to his cab. The old man is locking up.'

That was Julia. Decision time.

'All units from commander. Knock, knock, knock.'

*

Their sessions in the interview room at Windmill Cottage were now taking on a sort of routine. Michael and Richard would be in place. Michael with a mug of coffee, Richard with a cup of tea, when the Scholar arrived. He would raise his eyebrows slightly. Michael or Richard, or both would give a tiny nod and the Irishman would flick the switch marked 'record', the little light would come on and he would sit placing the demitasse of espresso in front of him and sit back in a kind of, 'And how may I assist you gentlemen' manner.

'You said that Mr Higgins is mostly concerned with his cigarette smuggling business these days. But that he still makes regular and substantial financial contributions...'

The Scholar nodded, so this was going to be this morning's topic, was it?

'Are you able to tell us to whom? And more importantly, what are these funds later used for?'

The Scholar had nodded again. He ostentatiously collected his thoughts. 'Have you heard of a man named Samuel Dunne, sometimes called Newry Sam?'

Richard hadn't. Michael had.

'So, it's a bit of a long story but we should probably start with him.'

The Scholar spoke for almost two hours. They didn't even break for biscuits. And that was the only departure from the normal routine, albeit a significant one. Eventually they came to what seemed a natural pause and Michael suggested a short break.

Richard and Michael withdrew to the garden.

'Extraordinary! Show the man a few fish, or a few fishermen at least and he starts to sing like a canary.'

'Maybe you softened him up yesterday.'

Michael might have imagined it but it did look a little like Richard Perceval had puffed just a little with pride.

'Possibly, possibly. You shouldn't be too hard on yourself though, Michael. We can't all charm the birds from the trees.'

Twenty-four hours earlier Michael would have resented the conceited, preening little fop. But, armed with the information from his grandfather's lecture of the professional and personal history of the Perceval family it didn't bother him at all.

'Of course, the other possibility is that he has decided, for whatever reason, that he wants to strengthen his bona fides.'

'Churlish, Michael!'

God, the man was exasperating! 'Let's see what volume two has in store shall we?'

The flow of information was so incessant and so valuable that they almost regretted stopping for lunch. Little Chris was back on galley duties and he'd knocked up a very respectable spaghetti carbonara.

'All it's missing is a decent Chianti,' mused Richard.

'Oh, I don't think so. A Gavi di Gavi or a nice Soave. I suppose if you absolutely had to have a red, I might risk a Teroldego.'

Richard looked as if he was about to enter into a spirited debate on the subject, but Michael silenced him with a look. The Scholar hadn't learnt about that on the Bogside. Was it another slip? Was he starting to feel a little pressure? Or was it the opposite? That was the trouble with this game. It was like a hall of mirrors. Literally, anything might mean the exact opposite.

By the end of the day, Richard and Michael had heard almost the whole history of the South Armagh IRA for the past thirty years. It was a lot to take in. At one point the Scholar had resorted to drawing diagrams of organisational structures, family trees, and had provided a sort of three-cornered glossary of names in English, their corresponding Gaelic versions and, in many cases, nicknames, or *noms de guerre*.

Michael was exhausted, and he actually felt relieved when the grandfather clock struck five. He glanced across at Richard, who seemed to have abandoned all hope of keeping up sometime around mid-afternoon.

He was going to have his work cut out, compiling his daily report for Phillipa Templeton.

*

Richard was writing a report too, but not for Phillipa. He'd been asked, strictly informally you understand, to keep William Fielding in the picture. He'd been pleasantly surprised to have been entrusted with this task. He wouldn't have expected Fielding even to know who he was. But of course, he was a Perceval, not quite Service royalty perhaps, but certainly aristocracy. So perhaps it wasn't such a surprise. And Bill Fielding, not that Richard would have dared call him Bill, was rumoured to be a leading candidate to become the chief when the old man retired.

He frowned and sucked hard at the end of his pencil. These things were tricky to draft. Perfectly easy after the event, of course, when one could bring the full weight of hindsight to bear, but difficult when providing a live update, particularly when the end result was uncertain.

He decided that it would be best to sow just the gentlest of hints that Michael Butcher was slightly out of his depth and that he was having to try to steer him in the right direction. That way a failure was Butcher's fault, in spite of his best efforts, but a success may have been due to Michael being lucky to have a highly competent partner. Yes, that was it.

*

The next day, if anything, was even more intense. The scene had moved from South Armagh to West Belfast (at one point they'd had to gather around a large-scale map of the city). The morning was spent on a sort of clan history. It was very difficult to follow. As soon as you really understood where some individual fitted in, he suddenly disappeared. It was like *Coronation Street* except that instead of moving to a neighbouring town, characters went to prison, or blew themselves up, or sometimes just disappeared. Only to reappear later in Boston or Tripoli.

Michael had to insist upon regular breaks just to clear his head and to attempt to digest what he'd just heard. And for biscuits, naturally. On one of these breaks, Michael and Richard were again in the garden, backs to the house, of course.

'What do you think?' asked Richard with what he doubtless imagined was studied indifference.

'I don't like it. He's gone from being cagey and non-committal to dictating a PhD thesis on the history of the republican movement. It's far too easy. I don't understand what's caused it.'

'Might it just be that he and I have established a rapport? A budding relationship nurtured in the fertiliser of our mutual love of the rod and line?'

Michael thought this unlikely. It was true, however, that the Scholar had been directing more and more of his attention to Richard. Was it possible that they had a rapport? It seemed improbable that anyone could actually form any attachment to Richard Perceval. But perhaps he was allowing his personal antipathy to cloud his judgement. Or was the Scholar doing it on purpose to drive a wedge between his interrogators? Or just for the sheer hell of it?

But everything he'd learnt led him to suspect that Geraghty, or 'the Scholar' as he now privately thought of him, was playing some game. Michael wasn't jealous of Richard's newfound sympatico with the Irishman. He was suspicious of it.

Chapter 16

There was only one exit from the car park. One of the targets was an old man. An old man who drove an Allegro. Nobody was going to flee. Nobody was going to escape. There was no urgency and no need for drama. Everyone on the team was an experienced investigator. They all appreciated this.

But it's not like that. When you've made the journey from Nottingham to Plymouth, stayed in a hotel, got up earlier than you wished and sat around in a parked car in Plymouth backstreets for an hour, smoking, fidgeting, rehearsing ever more unlikely scenarios in your head, it isn't like that. When you've followed a lorry across Devon, the adrenaline slowly accumulating in your system, when you've experienced the quickening of the pulse as the target approaches the slaughter point, your rationality starts to subside. They're unloading the boxes. This is going to be it. Any second now, the commander will call it. The tension will be released. Action will replace waiting.

'*Knock, knock, knock!*'

If there had been a textbook, and there wasn't, it would probably have stated that the knock is the moment at which an investigation moves from being covert to being overt. I suppose that would have earned you a mark in an examination. At a push, it might even be considered an adequate response at a promotion interview. But to an investigator it would be a woefully inadequate description.

The knock, a knock, was the climax of an investigation. The fulcrum about which everything turned. Call a knock too early and valuable evidence could be lost. Call it too late...well that didn't bear thinking about. The commander called the knock, well, except *in extremis*, but in the seconds or minutes that preceded that moment every member of the team would be muttering under their breath, 'Call it! Call it now! What are you waiting for? Knock it!'

And even if a situation was under control. Even if the call was made in the stark tones of a speak your weight machine or a platform announcer regretting the necessity for a replacement bus service, it didn't matter. It was always a war cry. A starting pistol. The tension could be realised. The agony of decision making extinguished. The die cast. Really, you might just as well have cried 'Havoc' or 'Strike' as the Old Bill did. The reaction was always the same.

The Volkswagen, Geneva, was the first on the scene, screeching through the open gate to the car park just a little too fast, spraying loose gravel in twin arcs from the front wheels. The Peugeot, Pisa, lacking its passenger was next. Julia was running across the road. The Vauxhall was next, also missing its passenger. Nick Harper was striding across the playing fields, torn between the desire to sprint and the knowledge that he could only be last on the scene and wanting to preserve a little dignity.

Only Lake and Monster, in the Mondeo, Madrid arrived at a normal pace, like the wise old bull who had noticed the gate left open.

Kevin Cleary on the Suzuki, Zebedee remained out of sight mentally debating whether he could remove his helmet and have a cigarette.

*

Gerard Duffy's first thought was that he was being robbed. His second thought was that he was going to be robbed and beaten. Realistically, he couldn't expect to outrun anyone. He was sixty-two and had spent almost his entire working life standing behind bars. His feet were flatter than the beer at the Con Club and he had varicose veins that looked like a relief map of the Andes. He couldn't remember the last time he'd moved at more than a slow walk or lifted anything heavier than a crate of light ales.

He dropped the keys and set off across the playing fields in that manner that people use when apologetically they break into a high-speed shuffle crossing a road.

He didn't have a plan beyond putting distance between himself and the cigarettes that were surely the target of this raid. After all, what would they want with him? And if he had his back to them, they need not even fear his identifying them later. But one of them was coming towards him. Coming from the direction in which he was fleeing. He didn't look like a robber. He had a pair of binoculars around his neck.

*

Andy Bishop's first thoughts were also of a hijack, but he didn't entertain those thoughts for long. The word 'Customs' kept being shouted. He stood still and raised his hands above his head. Nobody had asked him to, but he'd seen a lot of American films.

When Lake and Monster arrived, Bishop was being searched. He was relieved of his Stanley knife, his keys, his wallet, and finally the piece of paper that had been in his breast pocket.

'Good morning, Mr Bishop.'

How had they known his name?

'Would you mind telling me where you were planning to go next?'

Bishop had been cautioned. He didn't have to say anything, something, something, used in evidence. He offered no reply.

'It's like this, Mr Bishop. You are under arrest. You can either go to the police station, or you can continue your journey with one of my officers beside you, and make your next delivery.'

'And then you'll let me go?'

'No. You will remain under arrest. You will just be cooperating with us. Helping us.'

'I know nothing about any of this.'

'We can discuss that later, in Exeter police station, or somewhere else later on. Where are you going next?'

To refuse to cooperate would be an admission of guilt. But hadn't he been caught red-handed, anyway? But if he cooperated, would they perhaps let him go? Let him off with a warning? It didn't seem likely. But he didn't want to go to prison. Is that what happened to cigarette smugglers? And he didn't want to act as an informant against Dominic and his friends. Realistically he wasn't afraid of Dominic, but, you know, Northern Ireland accent, who knew who his friends might be?

The man opposite him wanted an answer. He thought of Selena, of Pepe, of Carla, of a little house on the coast.

'Sheffield. Somewhere near Sheffield.'

The man opposite nodded.

*

Gerard Duffy hadn't even been given the opportunity to cooperate. The man with the binoculars had arrested him. Harper, he said his name was, a customs officer. That hadn't even occurred to him. He'd been marched back to the pavilion and searched. They'd taken his keys, his wallet, even his rosary beads. He'd had to ask for the caution to be repeated twice. It was confusing. He was confused.

The young man who said that he was a customs officer man was very patient, very polite. In different circumstances Duffy might have thought him a fine young man. Not like that wastrel that his daughter had ended up with.

He thought customs officers wore navy blazers with gold buttons. When he'd arrived at Fishguard all those years ago, one of them had asked him if he had anything to declare. He'd scribbled something in chalk on the side of his little suitcase. His only suitcase. Now this man was patiently explaining to him that he was under arrest.

'Mind your head, Mr Duffy.' The hand on the back of his head was almost gentle as he was guided into the back of the Vauxhall Vectra. There was a young woman in the driver's seat. He glanced over his shoulder. Somebody was taking photographs of the shed. The shed that contained one and a half million cigarettes.

'Excuse me, miss. Do you think it would be all right if I spoke to my priest?'

*

Steve Moore was selected to play the role of driver's mate. He'd agreed with Bishop that if challenged they would say that he was his nephew. Having been photographed the cigarettes were loaded back on the lorry. The shed attached to the pavilion was hardly secure and there was nowhere else to put them.

Bishop was already starting to worry whether he'd made the right choice.

Lake was treading a fine line between legal questioning, intending to identify others involved, and illegal questioning, gathering evidence about Bishop himself.

'So, where are we going?'

'A transport firm, just off Junction 30. Sort of a depot.'

'Who will be there?'

'The customer, I think his name is Patrick, a few others.'

'How many?'

'Maybe four or five.'

'Vehicles?'

'I don't know.'

'I don't believe you.'

'I don't remember.'

'What do you do with the load?'

'He has a forklift, Patrick's son. I don't know his name. He unloads it, and puts it in a shed. I don't think it stays there very long. There's usually a couple of vans, you know, transits.'

'What time are they expecting you?'

'About seven. I'm to call them when I'm an hour away.'

Lake nodded. He turned and walked over to the pavilion where Monster was supervising the re-loading.

'We're going to need back-up. We're looking at maybe half a dozen targets, plus we need to keep Bishop under control. We have to leave two people here with the old man. We can't manage it with just us. That would be dangerously close to fair sides.'

'The Old Bill?'

'Might have to be, unless we can get some more troops from the office, or from Birmingham. You call the Other Office and bring them up to date. I'll call Brum.'

*

Steve Moore was trying to decide why he'd been chosen to play the role of 'Driver's Mate'. Perhaps it was a compliment. You might even describe it as going undercover. Although when customs officers used that term, they meant something else entirely. But it was an important role. He would be the team's eyes and ears. His information would determine when the knock was called. He might even call it himself.

Or perhaps he was chosen because he most fitted the role of lorry driver, or because he could most convincingly pass as Bishop's nephew. Or maybe it was because he happened to be standing beside the lorry when the idea occurred to Lake.

It had been Lake's decision. Moore had seen him turn towards Monster to give him right of refusal so to speak, but it had been Lake's decision. Strictly speaking, Monster was the case officer. Strictly speaking it should have been his call. Senior Investigation Officers were rarely out on the ground. Andi Woodman was almost always content to remain at her desk on the end of a phone. And before her, Howard Spencer had never come out to play. Not that he would have been the slightest use. But Lake was only temporary SIO, and the team was an officer light, so perhaps it didn't represent a breach of protocol.

*

The team, minus Julia, and Nick who had taken Duffy to Exeter police station, decided to treat the journey to Sheffield as though they didn't have a spy in the cab. They conducted surveillance exactly as normal, albeit in a more relaxed frame of mind. If they somehow lost the lorry, they could call Moore and ask him to stop and tell them where he was. But it wasn't necessary. They didn't have to hang back for fear of being spotted. The driver knew they were there. Everything went smoothly until Bishop announced that he needed to stop at the services on the M42 at Tamworth.

'Commander, Commander, Steve.'

'Madrid'

'We need to stop at the services. Junction ten.'

'Yes, yes. Don't let him out of the cab until I say so.'

*

Bishop climbed down from his cab and headed for the main building. Steve Moore accompanied him, trying to appear casual. The surveillance team divided its time between watching Bishop, watching his lorry and looking for anyone else who might be watching Bishop, or looking for a surveillance team. All except Monster, who was still in the Mondeo, on his telephone.

Bishop bought a sandwich and a can of Coke. If he could see or hear the frantic activity that surrounded this short journey he might even have been amused. Officers variously alerted their colleagues to suspicious looking vehicles and individuals in between soliciting and specifying preferred sandwich fillings. They were all quite relieved when Bishop, with Moore on-board, pulled out onto the motorway again.

Bishop stopped again at Trowell Services at four thirty. This time, he didn't leave the cab. He made his call to his contact in Sheffield. A man he knew as 'Pat'. Moore insisted he use the speakerphone. He depressed the transmit button in his trouser pocket so that the call was broadcast to the surveillance team.

'It's me, Andy. I'm at Trowell Services. Maybe forty-five minutes away.'

'Okay, come to the usual place. Wait until after five.'

'Will do. See you in a bit.'

Bishop hung up. And looked across at his driver's mate. Steve Moore said nothing. He was listening to his orders from Monster. Bishop could just hear a tint crackle from Moore's earpiece.

'Okay, let's go. What do you usually do when you get there?'

'Nothing much. I get out, open the doors, and have a fag while they empty the trailer.'

'Empty?'

'Yeah, this is my last drop off.'

'Okay, let's go.'

Behind them, the surveillance team closed up, pulses quickened, mouths dried, and Monster called the Birmingham team.

*

Amy had persuaded Monster. On good days, she almost convinced him. If he was going to be a family man, and he was, he couldn't continue to play cops and robbers for a living. She was right. Of course, she was right. And although he would never, ever admit it to his teammates, he actually enjoyed studying the law. But he would miss it. Playing cops and robbers was fun, if childish. Putting bad guys away was satisfying. And being part of a team...well now that his rugby days were behind him, work filled that gap. It also filled another little gap. Because one of the things that Chris 'Monster' Bolton enjoyed and one that he would miss most, was a really good punch-up.

*

'*Approaching the slaughter. Blue and white sign. Armstrong Haulage. Gates are closed...wait.*'

Anil Sharma, from the Birmingham team had had a chance to inspect the gates earlier. Even if they were closed and fastened, they didn't look robust. He was pretty sure that if he rammed them, they would burst open. He really, really hoped he would have a chance to do that.

'*Gates being opened, white male, jean jacket, red baseball. He's going into the yard.*'

So, they didn't intend to close the gates behind them.

'I usually just drive around the back.'

'Do that then.'

Bishop's lorry cruised past the young man in the baseball cap and swung right behind the large corrugated iron building. Steve Moore was able to see what awaited them a fraction of a second before the driver.

'*Three transits, four, no, five men. Earpiece out.*'

'*Commentate when you can.*'

But Moore had already slipped the earpiece from his ear and put it in his pocket.

Bishop slowed to a halt and wound down his window as a middle-aged man approached him.

'Hello, Andy.'

'Pat. Where do you want me?'

'Just here is grand. Who's your friend?'

'My nephew. Don't worry. He's sound.'

'He can give us a hand, then.'

Bishop opened the driver's door and climbed down. On the passenger side, Moore did the same. Now was the period of maximum danger. He couldn't see Bishop and the Irishman who had greeted them. More importantly, he couldn't hear what they might say. If Bishop had decided to blow the whistle, this would be the moment.

Bishop had been having similar thoughts for the past three hours. And he hadn't arrived at a decision. Until now.

Chapter 17

It said Patrick Wilson on his birth certificate, but he preferred Padraig Mac Liam. However, for the purpose of this mission, he was Patrick Wilson again.

Padraig had been born on the Bogside on Bloody Sunday. Not literally. He'd been born six days earlier. But the Brits told so many lies, why couldn't he discard that inconvenient date for a broader, deeper, more poetic truth?

Padraig needed all the help that he could get. He wasn't from Republican Royalty. Well, Republicans don't have royalty, obviously, the clue's in the name. He wasn't from one of the established families with a history of nationalist activism.

The Wilsons voted for the Social Democratic and Labour Party. The constitutional nationalists. They were suspicious and fearful of the IRA. Not Padraig, though. He'd wanted to be a volunteer from the age of nine. Not because he had a personal tragedy to avenge. Not because he was won over to the ideology that determined that a united

Ireland could only be achieved by physical force. Not because he felt a duty to defend his community. Padraig just wanted to be somebody.

It was hard to be somebody growing up on the Bogside in the eighties. The traditional routes out of the Bogside weren't available. He couldn't sing or play the guitar. He was a long way from the top of the class at school, and he definitely, definitely wasn't going to become a priest.

Padraig was only average at sport. He'd pestered, persuaded, and cajoled an uncle to take him to a boxing club, but quickly realised he'd made a dreadful mistake. The coaches worked him till he dropped. An old man, who looked about a hundred, made him skip till the sweat was running down his face, then put him on the heavy bag. But worst of all, people kept punching him in the face.

Having made such a fuss to be allowed to join he had to stick it out for a few months but after that he quietly drifted away.

So that left the Provos. Everybody knew who was a member of the Provisional IRA. They were, if not actual celebrities, people of consequence. They were shown respect, allowed first on the bus, seldom had to buy their own drinks. Padraig wanted to be somebody, and that meant becoming a volunteer.

He joined on his eighteenth birthday. Swore the oath. Started to learn Irish properly, started to call himself Padraig. For the first few months, nothing seemed to happen. Worse still, nobody seemed to know who he was. He still had to queue at the bus stop like everyone else. But by the end of the summer of 1990, he started to notice a difference in the way people treated him.

When the Good Friday Agreement was ratified, it threatened to take all that away. He was twenty-six, had never had a job, no qualifications, and now his status as a volunteer, instead of being a source of respect and fear, was a disadvantage. People mocked him behind his back. He never heard them. But he was sure. So, when Paschal Carty asked him if he wanted to continue the struggle, of course he said, 'Yes.' What other choice did he have?

And now he'd been given a mission. In England. He was given a mobile telephone and a thousand pounds in cash. Bank of England notes, not Ulster Bank. He was told to pack a bag, two weeks' worth of clothes.

'And don't carry anything, anything at all that might identify you. You'll be given your new identity when the time comes. Until then, await instructions. But be ready to go at a moment's notice.'

*

He got the call just before midnight. A minute later, there was a car at his door. He didn't know the driver, didn't know the car. A red Ford, Dublin registration. They crossed the border at Aughnacloy. The driver never said a word. Not a single word. It was nearly two when they reached Monaghan. They pulled into a yard belonging to a small haulage company. There were three or four lorries, but only one had its lights on and its engine running. His driver spoke for the first time. 'This is you.'

Padraig got out, retrieved his holdall from the back seat and was about to lean in and say thanks to the driver, but his engine had started already. The lorry blinked its headlights twice. He hurried over and hopped into the cab.

The driver was a middle-aged man with thin sandy hair scraped across his scalp in a manner that Bobby Charlton would have dismissed as absurd and with a bushy light brown moustache highlighted with streaks of nicotine yellow. He wore a yellow and orange coat that had been designed to be high visibility and probably had been before years of grease, dirt, and God knows what had transformed it.

'I don't want to know who you are, your name, where you come from, what you're doing, or where. If you need the jacks, go now. We're not stopping until Dun Laoghaire ferry port and that's at least two hours even at this time of night.'

Padraig fished a packet of Major King Size out of his breast pocket and offered the pack to the driver. The man's hostility reduced fractionally. He took two cigarettes, pushed one into an invisible hole beneath his moustache and the other behind his ear.

'I mean it about the jacks, though. Heater's busted. It'll be cold in this cab.' He lit the cigarette from a cheap disposable lighter and nodded in the general direction of the building to their left as if to emphasise the wisdom of his advice.

*

Two hours and five minutes later they drew into Dun Laoghaire and joined a queue of parked lorries. A light rain began to fall.

'Got another of those cigarettes?'

Padraig decided not to mention that the driver still had one behind his ear. He took one himself and passed the pack to the driver. One cigarette disappeared beneath the moustache; the pack went into the breast pocket of a checked shirt beneath the once high visibility coat.

'Be about half an hour. Just need to show the ticket. No other formalities. You're a driver's mate, so you come with me into the drivers' lounge on the boat. Don't talk to anybody, right?'

Padraig had only been on a ferry a couple of times. A holiday on the Isle of Man when he was a small child and a trip to the Arran Islands. He'd been as sick as a dog on both occasions. He planned to spend the crossing standing by the rail, hoping that the chill and the sea breeze might ward off seasickness. He wished he'd brought a warmer jacket.

By the time they arrived at Holyhead, as dawn was rising over the Welsh hills he was freezing. But he hadn't been sick, although he had come close a couple of times. There was the promise of a few more formalities as they entered the United Kingdom, a handful of customs officers standing around with their hands in their pockets or clamped around steaming mugs. Nobody bothered them. As they crossed the Menai Bridge connecting Anglesey to mainland Wales, the driver told them their destination.

'I'm dropping you at Hartshead Moor.'

A blank look in response.

'Motorway services, near Leeds. You go to the café, get a cup of coffee, a copy of *The Mirror,* and a copy of *What Car?* And put them both where they can easily be seen.'

Padraig nodded. 'And you?'

'You don't need to worry about me. You don't know me. I don't know you.'

*

In the event, Padraig had three coffees. And a bacon sandwich, and then another one. He was starting to wonder what he would do if nobody came. He'd bought two hundred Marlboro on the ferry. He preferred Majors but there was no point in advertising himself as an Irishman unnecessarily. If he had to, he thought he could fake an English accent.

It was almost three o'clock when the woman arrived. He didn't know why, but it simply hadn't occurred to him that his contact might be female, so he hadn't paid much attention when the young woman weaved her way through the table towards him. She was dressed like a student, or perhaps a mature student. She was a few years older than Padraig; he judged. But attractive.

'Padraig?'

He nodded.

'*Tar liom.*'

THE RUTLAND VOLUNTEER

Even Padraig's Irish was good enough to understand such a simple instruction. He rose, gathering the newspaper and magazine.

'You won't need those.' The accent was pure Derry.

He followed the woman as she wove between the tables towards the exit. The jeans were admirably tight. Was she swinging her hips just a little bit? Padraig chose to believe that she was.

He hadn't had a great deal of success with women as a rule. And when he had it was largely due to the certain cachet that came with being a known Volunteer. Terrorists have groupies too. But that was unlikely to be such a powerful draw here. But, if, if they were on a dangerous mission together, behind enemy lines, in England...well, who knows, perhaps they would be thrown together by their mutual reliance in the face of danger. Padraig was sure he had seen lots of films where that happened.

They passed through the double sliding doors and across the little concourse towards the car park.

'I'm Padraig.' He regretted it as soon as he said it. Stupid.

She turned and looked at him. 'I know.'

There was no scorn in it, no exasperation. It was much worse than that. It was...what was the word? Indulgent, it was indulgent, the way she said it, indulgent, and condescending and patronising. She stopped.

'Blue Mondeo.'

Padraig looked a little to his right. There was a blue Ford Mondeo parked between an empty grey Volkswagen and a Vauxhall Vectra. Sitting in the driver's seat was a man wearing a dark grey suit and a purple tie.

Dr Niamh Clarke née McKenna nodded, turned, and walked across the car park, not back towards the services, just away. She had to give a lecture back at the university.

Padraig walked over to the Mondeo, opened the passenger door, and climbed in.

The man in the suit passed him a road atlas, new, by the look of it.

'Page forty-seven.'

Padraig turned to the page. Somewhere in England. He wasn't familiar with most of the place names. He only recognised one.

'Leighton Parva. Here. Tiny place, just outside Oakham, place called Rutland. Know it?'

Padraig shook his head. He was trying to place the accent. Dublin? Further south than that? Not Cork. He could recognise Cork. Wicklow perhaps, or Wexford.

'Here's Leicester. East of there is Melton Mowbray, there's Oakham and follow this tiny road…Leighton Parva. Got it?'

Padraig nodded.

'You're Patrick Hickey. You've got a reservation at the Harboro Hotel, Melton Mowbray. In an emergency, you call this number, and you ask for Brendan. Got it? Now here's what we want you to do…'

When he was sure that Padraig had fully understood his orders, the man handed him a credit card in the name P T Hickey. He opened the car door. 'Oh, you'll need some petrol. Petrol, not diesel, use the card. Practise the signature. Only use it for a week, then bin it, okay?'

The man, who may or may not have been 'Brendan' walked off towards the services. Padraig walked around to the driver's door, looking in all directions. He got in and adjusted the seat, adjusted the mirror, then did both again. He took a deep breath and turned the key. The bastard hadn't been kidding. The tank was almost empty.

*

Padraig decided that he would take a look at Leighton Parva first and then check in to his hotel. It took two hours to get as far as Oakham, but it was the last five or six miles of the journey that was memorable. That morning, Padraig had never even heard of Rutland. Now he was struggling to believe it was even real.

Volunteer Mac Liam, while a city boy, was familiar with the countryside. He'd spent plenty of early mornings crouching in a ditch in County Fermanagh waiting for the British Army, usually futilely.

On the one occasion his Active Service Unit had managed to ambush a patrol, Padraig had been absolutely disorientated and terrified. The sounds! The smell of cordite! The utter, utter confusion, and then the stinging pain in his shoulder, the hurried journey across the border to the house of a sympathetic doctor, might have been a vet, actually. The blood. Gallons of the stuff. And then the realisation that he was going to live. The realisation that he was now a wounded hero. And the prospect of letting Erin McCrory see his scars.

Rutland was nothing like County Fermanagh. The whole place was like an American's idea of what 'Little ole England' was like. Padraig was expecting to see a helmeted policeman on a bicycle, or possibly Miss Marple. And Leighton Parva was the apogee.

He cruised through the village at thirty miles an hour. Slower would have been suspicious, faster would have attracted attention. There was nothing there. No shop, no petrol station, nothing. Except the pub, of course. It seemed to be the only commercial premises in the entire place.

A mile past the village he reached Leighton Magna, which seemed to be even smaller. He spun the car round and returned to Leighton Parva. He found a little car park and set off to examine the place on foot.

The pub was closed. The trading hours were posted outside the door. It opened at six. There were a handful of side streets and an Anglican church. He didn't see a single person in the village. The only signs of humanity were a pair of old men walking a dog along the ridgeline behind the church and a green tractor bouncing down a distant lane.

He returned to his Mondeo, drove slowly out of the car park turned right and left the village, forcing himself not to slow down as he passed Windmill Cottage. An hour later, he was in the bar of the Harboro Hotel, sipping a pint. He would have preferred Guinness, but he was undercover, on a mission, lager then.

*

Padraig didn't need to rise early the following day. He'd been told to make his phone call from a public phone at exactly a quarter past ten. He made the call from a telephone kiosk just around the corner from premises calling itself, 'Ye Olde Pork Pie Shoppe'. Now he remembered where he'd heard the name Melton Mowbray. He gave a brief report of his movements over the past thirty-six hours and received some very detailed instructions.

Padraig returned to the Harboro Hotel and collected his car. An hour later, he was in an independent mobile phone shop in Leicester's Belgrave Road under a sign erected by the city council that announced that he was at the start of Leicester's Golden Mile.

Fifteen minutes later he bought a second phone in a similar shop three doors down. He followed Belgrave Road north for a mile, examining the Asian jewellers, the Indian cafés, and the sari shops. There was nothing like this in Derry.

After twenty minutes, he turned south again, back towards the city centre. He decided to count how many white faces he saw on his return journey. It was three. He'd expected England to be similar to Ireland. He'd been watching English television his whole life, but he was still wrestling with the idea that Leighton Parva and the golden mile could be in the same country just twenty miles apart. Truly, he was deep behind enemy lines.

Padraig started to play the part. He slowed his pace, then sped up. He waited at a pelican crossing until the lights had changed again to red and then scurried across. He doubled back. He entered a furniture store and then immediately left through a different door.

He bought a baseball cap and pulled it down over his eyes and headed for the city centre, noting the location of security cameras. After an hour, he was bored and hungry. He ate at McDonald's, returned to his car, and drove back to Melton Mowbray. His actual mission, well that might be overstating it a bit, his actual tasks, were scheduled for tomorrow.

Chapter 18

Bishop had been out of sight only for a couple of seconds, the amount of time it took Steve Moore to walk around the front of the cab. It was obvious immediately that something had gone badly wrong. There was something in the body language. Exactly what had gone wrong became obvious pretty soon too.

'Police! Customs!'

'Run!'

Harper reached for his right pocket. *'Knock, knock, knock!'*

Seven cars filled with an outpouring of frustration and profanity.

'From commander, Knock! Knock! KNOCK!'

Anil's car was the first to reach the gates. Disappointingly, they were open. He roared through, forgetting about second and third gears. Carl Sanders was next, then two more Birmingham cars, followed by Lake and Monster.

For five minutes, all was chaos. Smugglers ran in all directions heedless of calls to surrender. A man in a Sheffield United padded coat ran towards the gate, dodged the cars, and headed for the street. A

Birmingham car skidded to a halt. Its passenger leapt out and set off in pursuit. The Blades fan had shown an impressive level of acceleration over the first thirty yards, but he was very much a sprinter and his talents didn't extend to longer distances. Alan Mancini caught up with him before he reached the corner of the street.

Another smuggler, even less well suited for hasty flight, although he may have held his own in the twenty stones and upwards category, waddled away towards the back of the yard. Anil and his passenger, Dave Gillard, set off in pursuit. Initially, at a jog trot, which quickly slowed to a walk. The man had run into a dead end facing a chain-link fence.

'Wait, wait. I want to see him try to climb it.'

The man surveyed the fence, which was ten feet high. He glanced over his shoulder and seemed to weigh his options. He turned back and looked at the fence again before turning a final time. He held his hands out in front of him in a gesture that seemed to say: It's a fair cop. Slap on the bracelets!

Others were less inclined to come quietly. It took three officers to wrestle one of them to the ground.

One young man had taken up a boxer's stance. He'd done it before. He felled Carl Sanders with a left-right combination, and a Birmingham officer walked directly into a straight right. He heard the bones in his nose crunch like an overladen Range Rover on the gravel drive of a Surrey mansion.

The man's next opponent was Julia Hayes. Mrs O'Connor hadn't raised her sons to hit women. He hesitated slightly. He later conceded that this might have been a mistake.

Like all her colleagues, Julia received regular arrest and restraint training. Every couple of months in a school gymnasium or a village hall, she was coached in arrest grips and compliance holds. She'd been taught to bend her knees, transfer her weight, exactly where to put her thumb. Everyone agreed that it was all very well in theory.

She stepped forward and kicked O'Connor exactly where she'd been aiming, a couple of inches south of the belt buckle. He crumpled to the ground tears pouring from his eyes.

'You're nicked, dick-head,' said Julia, complying with the spirit of the Police and Criminal Evidence Act, if not the exact letter. O'Connor vomited.

Lake arrested, or re-arrested, or confirmed the ongoing arrest. The details could be worked out later, of Bishop himself. When he'd cuffed the man, none too gently, he noticed Monster. Monster was leading a handcuffed young man who had a dazed expression and his nose somewhere just under his left ear.

'This little twat tried to hit me with this!' He was genuinely affronted. 'What is it anyway?'

'It's a hurl, a hurley. I'll explain later.'

The chaos seemed to have abated somewhat. Lake couldn't tell if anyone had got away. It seemed unlikely. The adrenaline slowly subsided. He was the SIO. He needed to take charge. What a bloody mess! What would Frank McBride do?

He decided that his first task was to talk to Steve Moore. It wasn't his fault. He'd done nothing wrong. No blame attached to him. If anyone was at fault, it was Lake himself. He looked around. Steve was nowhere to be seen. Oh no!

Stephen William Moore was lying where he'd fallen, under the front bumper of Bishop's lorry. He wasn't moving, but a puddle of dark red framed his head and was slowly growing.

*

'Monster, you're in charge.'

Lake climbed into the back of the ambulance. Steve's face was obscured by an oxygen mask. He was, at least, still breathing. The paramedics were working with quiet and efficient professionalism. That was what really scared Lake. He recognised the behaviour. He'd done it himself when under extreme stress, when less than one hundred per cent wasn't an option.

Steve was single. He had a girlfriend, but Lake didn't know how serious it was or whether it elevated her to the status of next of kin. Probably not. He called the office and asked them to contact whoever was in the file and get them to call him.

One of the paramedics had a radio. He was calling ahead to the Northern General Hospital. It was mostly code and jargon. Lake understood very little, except the word 'critical'.

*

He'd expected to find the office empty when he arrived at five to midnight, but it wasn't.

Monster was there and Alan Hawkins too.

'Sit down, Joe. Take your time.' Hawkins poured a measure of Scotch into a coffee mug. It was Steve's. He wasn't to know. 'Take your time.'

'He's stable. Two skull fractures. He lost a bit of blood, but they don't seem worried about that. They were talking about maybe an induced coma. You can't get anything sensible out of these people. They won't offer any opinion at all. They're going to decide whether to operate in the morning.'

'And his folks?'

'They arrived just as I was leaving.'

'How are they taking it?'

'They looked terrified. I wanted to say something to them. But I didn't know what to say.'

'I've booked you a room at the Moat House, Joe. Chris here has phoned your wife. Didn't give her too many details. I've spoken to the Chief. He's asked me to tell you that there might have to be an inquiry, but not to worry. You did nothing wrong, Joe.'

Lake reached for the mug, then withdrew his hand. 'What's the score?'

'You don't need to worry about that. Everything's under control.'

'I'm the SIO. I have a right to know. It's my bloody operation.' Even he recognised the near hysteria in his voice.

'We'll talk about it in the morning. They're all tucked up, Sheffield nick. Nobody's been interviewed yet.'

Lake reached for the mug again. This time he emptied it. 'What the hell is that muck?'

'It's Lagavulin, ten-year-old.'

'It tastes like shit! I'm going to bed.'

*

Lake knew that there was nothing he could do. Steve's life was in the hands of others, and no amount of self-recrimination on his part would make any difference. And he didn't waste his time or any emotional energy of that 'what would Steve want?' rubbish.

He would do his job. Not because it offered any catharsis or because he somehow imagined that bringing a crowd of Sheffield low-lifes to justice would somehow give Steve's injury meaning. Please God let it just be an injury, some validity, or purpose. He would do it because he couldn't think of anything else. And he would do it as well as he could. He would pour the anxiety, the horror and, yes, the guilt into it.

He arrived at Sheffield police station full of drive and determination and all those other qualities that people only usually possess in their imaginations, or on job applications.

Even people who had known him for years said that they'd never witnessed this version of Joseph Lake. He was horrible...and terrifying...and something else besides, something hard to define. He seemed to be possessed.

Strong men turned and fled when he approached. Police officers of all ranks, solicitors, and sizeable outbuildings quaked in fear as he hove into view. And when he appeared dissatisfied with a sausage roll from the canteen, the chef threw himself in the deep-fat fryer.

Well, possibly not. But it was very close.

*

Patrick O'Connor, the publican, had refused to answer questions. That didn't matter. A search of the three lock-up garages behind The Christy Ring revealed a couple of thousand cigarettes and more importantly the cardboard boxes that had once contained tens of thousands more. Careless. The decision to charge him was an easy one.

He'd also had a list of customers on his person when he'd been arrested. Bad news for him, but equally bad for the names on the list, particularly if they'd been present at Armstrong Haulage as two of them had.

*

The first of these was a Sheffield lad called who liked to be known as Ricky Ward, although it said Ambrose Richard Ward on his birth certificate and Carl called him 'Ambrose' throughout the interview, just for fun.

He'd been the one who had required three officers to wrestle him to the ground. He was cocky and liked to remind the interviewing officer that it had taken three to arrest him.

He claimed that he'd been an innocent bystander who had been offered fifty pounds to unload a lorry. He claimed that he hadn't asked and hadn't been told what the lorry contained. Unfortunately for

Ricky, he wasn't able satisfactorily to explain the piece of paper in his pocket.

'Five Thousand Silk Cut, Bob T, four hundred, and fifty pounds. What does that mean, Ambrose?'

'Silk Cut is a mate of mine. We call him Silk Cut 'cause he smokes 'em. He owes me four hundred and fifty quid for a poker game.'

Ricky/Ambrose leant back evidently satisfied that he'd played an ace.

'Excellent. What's his name? What's his address? When did this game take place? Where? Who else was present? Did you win any other sums? From whom? What are their names, addresses, how much money?'

'No comment.' He still smirked, but even he must have realised that this was a deuce.

'Five Thousand Marlboro Light, five hundred pounds. Bob T? What does that mean?'

'No comment.' The smirk was still there, but his solicitor shifted nervously in his chair and focussed his attention on his notepad.

'Who or what is Bob T?'

Ambrose looked at his brief who continued to stare at his notepad as though it held all the secrets of the universe.

'Can't remember.'

By the time they'd reached the end of the first interview tape, Ambrose Richard Ward had talked himself onto the charge sheet.

*

The second unfortunate was Martin Byrne. His position was almost identical to Ward's, but he at least bright enough had the wit to realise the hopelessness of his position. He refused to answer questions. Didn't matter, he went on the sheet too.

*

Sean O'Connor refused to answer questions, like his father. He didn't have a scrap of paper on his person and because he no longer lived at the family home in the accommodation above The Christy Ring, the evidence there didn't relate to him directly. It was debatable whether his presence at the scene was enough to charge him with cigarette smuggling. But he had other problems.

*

The real breakthrough came from the least promising source.

Martin Clarke had no documentation on him and nothing incriminating was found at his home either. If he'd had the wit to keep his mouth shut, he would have walked. But he didn't. He, or more likely his solicitor, had heard of the duress defence. But whichever of them it was they didn't understand it properly. Clarke told Julia Hayes and Kevin Cleary that he had plenty to tell, but feared for his life.

He was invited to disclose why he was frightened and of whom. But he made a bit of a mess of things. Within five minutes he'd conceded that nobody had threatened him and that none of the people of whom he claimed to be in mortal terror had, to his knowledge, ever injured or even threatened to injure anyone. Neither had anybody insisted that he be at Armstrong Haulage or that he involve himself in any way.

Julia suggested that they take a short break while Martin consulted his solicitor (or his solicitor consult a textbook). Fifteen minutes later they were back. Either he would refuse to answer further questions or he would have to spill the beans on a grand scale. Both Julia and Kevin were confident that he would go 'no comment'. They were both wrong.

*

Most of the team were in the police station canteen. They were enjoying the traditional investigators' banquet. Bad coffee, indifferent sandwiches, and KitKats a la vending machine. Everyone was tired except Joe Lake. His body language looked like he was going to suggest that everybody spend a relaxing half hour wresting crocodiles or bears before returning to work.

He was currently standing in the corner on his telephone, head cocked, half hunched over the way people do when there was a lot of background noise, or the call was especially important.

'What did your boy say?'

'Plenty. Let's wait until Joe's off the phone. I don't want to do this twice.'

Lake's call ended, and he rejoined the group, beckoning everyone over to a single table in the middle of the room. In the corner, a uniformed police officer was considering his options very carefully, very, very carefully.

'I've bought a house in less time than he's taking.'

'Clearly an important decision.'

The police constable finally made his mind up. Quavers. He left and the Customs officers had the canteen to themselves.

'All that time, and the wrong decision.'

'Frazzles are two pence more.'

'Yes, but worth it, it's a false economy to compromise on the quality of maize-based snack. Everyone knows that.'

'Well, I wouldn't argue with a gourmet expert like you.' Julia glanced at the table in front of Monster. There was an empty packet of Frazzles, and another of Quavers.

'What?' He sounded affronted. 'I was hungry.'

Joe Lake gave an exasperated cough. And if you think it's not possible to convey indulgent amusement, mild exasperation, and an impending conversational gear change in a cough, well, you're wrong.

'I hate to break-up this episode of *Master Chef*, but that was Nick. The little Irishman, Duffy, has spilled his guts. Confessed everything.

He says that he gets one or two deliveries a month. It's always Bishop who makes them and that there's always more on the lorry, but he doesn't know where it goes.'

'Ze case, she is soll-ved,' Kevin offered in his best Poirot.

'It's better than that. Duffy says that his supplier is a man called Dominic Higgins...'

'Is that an Irish name?!'

'Oh, it's better than that. He's from Crossmaglen.'

'Oh shit! IRA?'

'Well, Duffy seems to think so. But if I wanted to frighten people, I'd emphasise the accent, and tell people I was from South Armagh, so he might not be.'

'Where will we find this Higgins?'

'Cartagena.'

'I'll go!' said six people simultaneously.

'Which one?' said Kevin, who had been on a specialist cocaine team and knew a bit about Colombia.

'The Spanish one. Now, tell me about Clarke... Hang on I'd better take this.'

*

A Sheffield number. One of those with a few noughts on the end. The kind that indicated that the call had come through a switchboard. The call he'd been dreading. Was it too early for good news? Probably. Was it too early for bad news? Definitely not, or too late either.

'Just a second. Let me find somewhere quiet.'

He felt sick, he sweated, and shivered. He could hear the blood pumping in his ears. He ran to the staircase and down the first half flight where he stopped. There was a large window looking out onto the street below. A street filled with people going about their business, walking, talking, breathing.

He hadn't heard from the hospital since that morning. There had been no news. He didn't know if they'd decided to operate. Didn't know what he wanted that decision to be. To have been.

Now there was news. But was he ready for it? The image of the blood puddle inexorably growing, the grey face behind the oxygen mask, the expressions of the paramedics. The rush, no, the charge, through the hospital corridors, the swing doors closing in his face. 'We'll take it from here. He's in the best possible hands.'

His breathing slowed. He forced himself to be calm. He realised he was crying. The tears were rolling down his cheeks. He took a breath, tried to arrest his silent sobbing. But until he answered, it hadn't happened. Steve was still alive. Until he uttered the words,

'Joe Lake.'

'Ah, hello, yes.' An accent, West African probably. 'Is that Mr Joseph Lake?'

'Yes.'

'My name is Blessing Ikande. I am a nurse in the Intensive Care Unit at the Northern General. We are the hospital.'

'Yes.' It seemed so inadequate, but what else could he say?

'I have somebody here who wants to talk to you.'

'Hello, guv, it's Steve.'

Lake slid down the wall. He was sitting on the floor among the fag butts, the empty crisp packets, and the dirt. The sobbing had started again. He couldn't stop it, and it wasn't silent anymore. He tried to speak, but the words wouldn't come. He was drenched by a tidal wave of relief, swept away from the horror. He still couldn't speak. Finally, he composed himself. It took two attempts.

'Don't call me, guv. We're not bloody coppers!'

And then the sobbing started again.

Chapter 19

It was a golden rule of investigation: it didn't matter how much or how little you had to do. It didn't matter how early you started or how late. You were always, always, always standing in a police charge room at midnight. Always.

It had been a quarter past one when the last suspect had been charged. They were all bedded down in cells and would be in court in the morning. All except Sean O'Connor.

Sean had been arrested wearing a red, gold, and green football shirt. Most Englishmen would have assumed it was the national kit of Ethiopia, or another African nation, or some sort of Rastafarian statement. Lake knew better. He'd seen fifteen just like it at Croke Park once.

None of that mattered. The key thing about O'Connor's Carlow shirt was that it was striking, unique, and memorable. Steve Moore had remembered it. And that was why, after he had been charged with smuggling, Sean Patrick O'Connor was re-arrested by South Yorkshire Police on suspicion of attempted murder.

Lake decided to spend a further night in a Sheffield hotel. He didn't think that Bella would appreciate him arriving home at two o'clock in the morning. He rose early and was home instead at ten to seven.

Bella was being violently and operatically sick. Perhaps that meant it was a boy. Lake had read that somewhere once. He decided not to share this speculation with his wife. Perhaps he could do something useful, like get Caroline dressed.

This proved much more difficult than usual. She wouldn't stay still. She wanted to tell him everything that had happened at nursery for the past two days. And that's a tricky thing to do when you have a vocabulary of about fifty words. All those pop fasteners were also pop un-fasteners. He was just congratulating himself on a job half done when he noticed that her dress was on backwards.

When he came downstairs carrying his still struggling daughter, Bella had recovered and was sitting at the kitchen table taking alternate sips of peppermint tea and mouthwash.

'How did it go?'

'Successful.'

That was it. She didn't need to hear the details. She wouldn't have cared about most of them. And she definitely didn't need to hear about the ones that she would have cared about. Steve lying in a pool of blood, the distinct possibility that his operation's targets were recently retired violent terrorists. Assuming they were retired, of course.

*

None of the team was in the office. They were either still in bed at home, or in Exeter. Monster was in Sheffield, managing the court hearing. Perhaps that was just as well. Lake didn't want him to hear even half of the conversation with the other office that he knew he had to have. And that he was dreading.

He was taking stock, mentally composing a balance sheet. He wanted to be sure of the situation before he updated the Other Office.

So, on the positive side:

Six million cigarettes seized from the lorry, plus a few found at The Christy Ring.

Seven arrests. Six charged with smuggling and Sean O'Connor was likely to be charged with attempted murder although they would probably knock it down to Grievous Bodily Harm by the time it reached court.

And the name Dominic Higgins, which might be false, from Crossmaglen, which might be false too.

But what looked at first like as operational success was, viewed from another angle, actually a setback.

And then there was the debit side. Well, Steve Moore had almost been killed for a start.

Bishop wouldn't be making any more trips. His lorry couldn't be followed. The customers would all be lying low for a while. Anyone involved would be dumping their phones if they had any sense. And if they were too stupid to do that, then they weren't worthy targets, anyway. By the time they resumed operations, if they did, they might have a new and entirely different supplier.

So where did that leave Operation Bridegroom? He'd given the Other Office only the briefest of updates yesterday. He owed them a call now to put them in the picture fully. What would their response be?

It was entirely possible that they would decide that they'd expended enough of their precious resources on a cigarette job and simply pull the plug.

'You've seized a lot of fags, felt a lot of collars. Well done, that's it. We have bigger fish to fry.'

Lake would have understood. But it would have felt like a failure. This was his first target operation, his first case as an SIO. It could easily be his last too, depending on how Alan Hawkins assessed things. Despite what he'd told Bella that morning, he felt like he'd failed.

Everybody failed occasionally. Everybody who actually tried to do something difficult, anyway. There were some, blowhards from the public bar who mistook hindsight for wisdom, who never failed.

Lake didn't have much time for them, or their opinions. But he'd been in this job long enough to understand the damage that pernicious criticisms could do. And when they were amplified via the Nottingham and Birmingham rivalry, well that made it even worse. It might not be accurate or fair, but for all he knew Operation Bridegroom was widely viewed as a fiasco.

But you were supposed to learn from mistakes, weren't you? What had he done wrong? What could he have done differently? In different circumstances, the team would have gathered, on licensed premises almost certainly, and conducted a postmortem. But the thing was, the SIO was never at these gatherings. And Lake was the SIO. Temporary. Possibly very temporary.

He wouldn't let Monster take the blame. That would have been easy. Monster was probably going to be Christopher Bolton QC or something soon anyway, so arguably it didn't matter. But he wouldn't let Monster take the blame. And not just because managers shouldn't do that.

He'd probably taken too many decisions himself. He'd probably interfered too much. It was his fault. He was to blame. He would face the consequences. Alone. That loneliness of command nonsense, it turned out it was true.

Lake picked up the phone to call the Other Office. He put it down again. It was times like these when he missed cigarettes. But he hadn't any. And he wasn't going to ask. But he had his pipe. He hadn't touched it for well over a year. Bella used to tease him about it. And then when she'd learnt she was pregnant she'd banned it all together.

He told himself that he'd kept it for emergencies. And if this wasn't an emergency... Strictly speaking smoking was banned in the office. But what was the point of being a temporary Senior Investigation Officer if you couldn't break that rule? And who knew how long he would have that status, anyway?

He filled the bowl. The tobacco was probably a little dry, but did that really matter? It was just something comforting to do. Frank McBride used to say that it contributed to zen. He used to talk a lot of old rubbish sometimes. Lake struck a match, put it to the bowl and drew lightly on the stem. He did feel a little better. He picked up the phone.

*

What an anti-climax! It was just like any other call to the Other Office. There was no suggestion that they were going to pull the plug. It was all very routine. The only time they reacted at all was when he'd told them what Duffy had said about Dominic Higgins.

*

Thursday lunchtimes were quiet at The Old Volunteer. None of the various village groups gathered on a Thursday. The evening quiz, which was growing in popularity every week, meant that very few made two trips to the pub on the same day. Frank McBride didn't even bother hiring bar staff for Thursday lunchtimes. Sometimes nobody came in at all.

Volunteer Mac Liam cruised past the pub. He couldn't fail to notice that the car park was empty. The pub itself was likely to be empty, too. That wasn't ideal. He didn't want to be engaged in conversation by a chatty barman. He didn't think that he could disguise his accent long enough for that. But it had to be done.

And it had to be done now.

The orders had been explicit. He pulled into the car park and found a spot where his car was least visible from the road. He picked up the newspaper that had been lying on the passenger seat. If he had to, he could pretend to be engrossed in the previous day's events, or, if absolutely necessary, pretend to do the crossword. He took a deep breath, reminded himself he was a soldier of the republic, and headed for the pub.

Before he had reached the door, a second vehicle pulled into the car park, a Mondeo like his own, but a newer model. He hesitated. If he allowed the other customer in first, he might strike up a conversation with the barman. Mac Liam could be a minor interruption and retreat into a corner. But he was five paces from the door. How could he let the other man in first? Ah! Wasn't there a second door just around the corner?

*

Lake entered via the first door, the one into the lounge bar. McBride was sitting at a table just inside the door. He seemed to have abandoned his accounts in favour of *The Guardian* crossword.

'Good morning, Joseph.'

Somewhere unseen, Rocky gave a little bark of welcome.

'Two customers at once. Let me just see to that and I'll be right back.'

McBride rose, was Lake imagining it, or was he a little more sprightly these days? Not so many hours in parked cars. Not so many meals eaten at fast food takeaways and from the chilled cabinets of petrol stations. And there was Rocky of course. Frank was probably walking for miles each day. Lake wondered how he was going to raise the subject.

*

Mac Liam's plan had worked. He entered the side door into the saloon bar, which was entirely unoccupied. Somewhere a dog gave a little yip. It didn't sound threatening, and in any case, Mac Liam was sure that whatever had made the noise couldn't get to him. He didn't like dogs.

A moment or two later, possibly alerted by the unseen canine alarm, a man appeared at the bar. In his sixties, Mac Liam judged. He had a full white beard and thinning hair that might have once been sandy, but was no more. He greeted his customer by raising his eyebrow a quarter inch.

'Pint of lager please, chief.'

McBride reached up to the shelf for a glass. Who was this Ulsterman trying to sound like a Londoner? McBride poured a pint of Carlsberg. The young man hadn't specified, and he wasn't prepared to torture his ears again by subjecting them to the absurd faux Cockney nonsense. It was as if Dick Van Dyke had come from Donegal.

'One ninety, please.'

The young man pushed a five-pound note across the corner, new, clean, and crisp. McBride turned and rang the transaction up on the till, giving himself the opportunity to view the man via the mirror behind the bar. He looked nervous...and shifty.

McBride turned. 'Three ten.'

'Ta.'

How was it possible to get the accent so badly wrong in a single syllable word? McBride turned for a last time and went back through to the other bar.

'Pint?'

'Please.'

McBride drew a pint of bitter and poured himself a slimline tonic.

'Still not drinking.'

'Not when I'm working.'

'Isn't a publican always working?'

'Not on Sunday nights. That's my stool at the end of the bar on Sundays. Now, I hope you're here to ask for advice and not to force me to listen to you whining and lamenting your ill fortune. If that's what you're here for you can talk to Rocky. He's more empathetic than I am. Rocky!'

McBride's Springer spaniel bounded out from behind the bar. *It must be wonderful*, thought Lake, *for every single thing in your life to be such a source of unalloyed joy*. Rocky was always happy, always pleased to make or renew any acquaintance. He was the very essence of sociability and affability. The ying to McBride's yang, or something like that.

'You've spoken to Hawkins?' That was a foolish question. 'I suppose he's given you the highlights?'

'Why don't I hear your version?' McBride sipped his tonic water and made a slight grimace.

*

Mac Liam could hear the faint murmur of voices in the other bar. There really wasn't any reason to delay. He doubted it, but somebody else might arrive. Or that barman, the one who looked like Captain Birdseye, might be back. He headed for the door in the corner, turned right, and immediately left into a little corridor and then pushed open the door to the gents.

Although the little public bar looked like it might have done a hundred years ago, the toilets at The Old Volunteer were modern and sparkling clean. Mac Liam didn't take the opportunity to note this. He headed straight for the single cubicle.

This had worked fine in *The Godfather*. Al Pacino had come out and slotted that policeman, hadn't he? He lifted the lid of the cistern and carefully inspected the underside. Bone dry. He checked the water level. It was sufficiently low. He rested the cistern lid on the toilet seat.

Mac Liam paused, listening, nothing. He took the package from his inside pocket, wrapped in cellophane triple wrapped in polythene bags. From his jacket pocket he took a roll of gaffer tape. Tearing gaffer tape from a roll was a much noisier process than he'd expected. He paused and listened again. Again, nothing.

Mac Liam secured his package to the underside of the cistern lid. Three separate bands of tape. A fourth for luck. He replaced the lid, put the gaffer tape in his pocket and had one last look round to ensure that he'd left no trace.

As he left the cubicle, he realised that he'd been holding his breath. When he saw his reflection in the mirror, he saw that he was sweating, too. Silly really, he'd undertaken much more hazardous missions than this. But this one was for Commandant Carty. And it was behind enemy lines.

He washed his face and hands, took a deep breath, and returned to the bar. Don't panic now. Don't rush. No need to throw the rest of that pint down your neck and flee. Finish it slowly, read your paper. Then leave quietly, say, in about ten minutes.

He lasted five.

Chapter 20

Michael and Richard had agreed that today would be 'Derry Day'. They'd discussed Mr Higgins of South Armagh and his cigarette smuggling. They'd discussed the complicated history and organisation of the Belfast Brigades. Now it was time to discuss Derry. They were both pretty confident that the Scholar was from Derry. Would he be as loquacious on the subject of his home city and people he personally knew?

He certainly appeared to be. He spoke about the history of republicanism in the city. He spoke about the split between the Official and the Provisional IRAs in the early seventies. He spoke about Martin McGuinness, although he had to admit that he'd been too young to know him when he'd been running around the Bogside with a tommy gun.

By lunchtime, Michael felt able to ask him the question that he'd been preparing all morning.

'Are there any dissident factions in Derry? If so, who leads them, and what are they up to?'

The Scholar leant back in his chair. For some reason the image came to Michael of a gifted student who had just been asked a question in a Cambridge supervision. Or an Oxford tutorial, same thing really. Richard had been to Durham. Who knew what they called them up there?

Not just a gifted student, thought Michael, one who had just been asked a question on his favourite subject.

'What you have to remember is that Derry is Martin's city. Martin McGuinness.'

Michael and Richard did their best to probe, but from whichever angle they approached the subject they got a similar answer. Anyone in the Derry republican movement who might have misgivings about the Good Friday Agreement, or the ceasefire, or the order to put arms beyond use would be not just a dissident. They would be an opponent of Martin McGuinness. And that meant that theirs wouldn't merely be a different point of view, it would be heresy.

'But surely there must be dissidents. Or some with dissident sympathies.'

The Scholar leant back again and allowed himself a little smile.

'There were probably people in sixteenth century Spain who had misgivings about transubstantiation. But they kept pretty quiet about it.'

Michael nodded. 'But the Inquisition found them, anyway. If you had to guess, who do you think the likeliest dissidents might be?'

'You want me to guess?'

'We want you to make an educated guess.'

The Scholar paused, as if collecting his thoughts. But he wasn't. He couldn't be. He must have anticipated this question. Anticipated it from the very beginning. He must have an answer prepared.

'Well, since you ask me to speculate, I would think that the likeliest people are those who were most recently in prison.'

Richard couldn't keep the incredulity from his voice. 'You mean the very people who owe their freedom to the Good Friday Agreement?'

'Yes, exactly those people. They went to prison for a united Ireland. They might feel that their sacrifice...I'm putting it in the terms that they would use. You understand, their sacrifice was wasted. And of course, you have to consider their status.'

'Their status?'

'Of course. They went to prison as heroes and as people of standing and authority in their communities. Now, what are they? Yesterday's men. An embarrassment. It's like all those Americans after Vietnam. Nobody wanted to know them.'

Even Richard could recognise the wisdom in this analysis.

'And of course, the peace dividend. Everyone's making money. They're not. Old men, or men old before their time. No education beyond republican polemic and fourth rate Irish. No skills, well, no skills that can be peacefully employed. It's not much of a CV is it? Good at identifying ambush sites and improvising bombs.'

Michael consulted a notebook. 'Joe Quinlan? Pat Carty? Alec Lavin?'

'It's Paschal Carty, not Pat.'

The smoke alarm went off in the kitchen. Tony was on galley duties, and it was time for lunch.

*

As five o'clock approached, the Scholar raised the subject of that evening's pub quiz.

'We are the defending champions, after all.'

Michael was confident that his grandfather wouldn't permit that to happen twice in a row. 'I seriously doubt that we'd do as well again tonight.'

'Perhaps if we strengthened the team. You know, brought in a star signing.' The presumption of that lanky idiot!

Michael quite liked the idea that a team without Richard Perceval had won and that, knowing his grandfather, very likely a team with him would finish dead last. Childish, he knew, but the prospect was oddly satisfying. And it would free him up to collect Heather at seven o'clock. He'd been wondering how he was going to do that without the Scholar in tow.

'By all means but try not to be too disappointed if we do not earn the coveted laurels.'

'Well, let's make it interesting.' This was from the Scholar' 'If we win, we can reward ourselves with a day's fishing tomorrow. It's likely to be far less busy than at the weekend. And if you don't fancy it, Michael, I'm sure you have a long report to make about our discussions this week.'

Michael shrugged. He was confident they wouldn't win.

*

There had been a Perceval in the service since before there had even been a service. The family claimed that one of their ancestors had played a part in exposing the gunpowder plot. It might even have been true. Richard's father had been 'Our man in Istanbul', and in Vienna, and in a couple of other slightly less agreeable places.

His grandfather had worked mostly in London, during the war of course, and for a few years afterwards. He'd entertained high hopes. Whatever their collective and individual weaknesses nobody ever accused the Percevals of a lack or self-belief, or ambition.

Confidence and pedigree counted for a lot. And those were qualities shared by a great many of those at the top of the service. They shared other things too, school, university (and that meant Oxford or Cambridge, fashionable colleges only), Pall Mall clubs and a sense of Britain's place in the world, the service's place in Britain and their place in the service.

These things counted for a lot and would carry you a long way. Minor indiscretions or errors of judgement would be overlooked. Well, usually. After all, there were lots of people who were willing to swear that Kim Philby was a jolly good chap, one of us, and absolutely to be trusted. One or two even said something similar about Donald Maclean. But only one person was prepared to vouch for all three: Burgess, Philby, and Maclean. Archibald Perceval had the full trifecta. In 1952, he was given a knighthood and told to retire.

*

Richard Dunstan Howard Perceval hadn't applied to join the Secret Intelligence Service. He simply waited to be invited. He'd expected to have been quietly approached while at university. But then he'd expected to go to a different university. An unfortunate B in Latin had doomed him to the wretched weather of the north-east. He was forced to spend a year or two teaching at a minor public school before finally the tap on the shoulder arrived.

He was a year, possibly two, older than Michael Butcher, and deeply resented having to play the role of the junior partner in this interrogation. It was perfectly clear to him that the Scholar regarded Butcher as a humble functionary. It was he who had established the rapport. It was he who had manoeuvred the Irishman into trading fishing for information. Richard was determined that by the end of this assignment it would be he who was regarded as the senior partner.

He was also pretty confident that he would be seen by the new chief as just the right sort of officer, sound, reliable, one of us.

*

Mac Liam was on his second mission of the day. He now considered himself an expert at working deep undercover. He was like your man, Ronnie Brasco, was it?

Being a dissident republican was actually even cooler than just being a Provo when you thought about it. I mean, it wasn't cool now. The people in Derry were actually scornful of those who refused to sell out to the Brits. But that would change. The heroes of the Easter Rising were scorned at first, weren't they? And now they're heroes. Padraig Mac Liam would be a hero, like the men of 1916. He tried not to dwell on the fact that it was being executed that had turned those men into heroes.

He'd overestimated how long it took to drive from Rutland to Leicester and arrived almost half an hour early. No matter, he would profitably use the extra time to conduct a reconnaissance. He walked past The Walnut Tree, reached the end of the road and walked past it again. Still twenty minutes early. He would check to see if there was a back entrance.

He took the first left after the pub and then turned left again and walked on a parallel street. It was all rear entrances. But he couldn't tell which rear entrance corresponded with which front entrance. This was proving more difficult than he'd expected. Then he had a brainwave. He continued to the end of the road, turned left, and then turned left again. He was back where he started and if anybody had been watching him (they weren't) they would have thought that he was either up to no good or not very bright. Or both.

This time, he counted the chimney pots. He followed the same route, but this time he was able to orientate himself. The twin blue gates were directly behind The Walnut Tree. They were about seven feet tall but if he took a bit of a run up, he could probably grab the top, pull himself up, and get a look at whatever lay beyond.

Okay, perhaps they were eight feet tall. And perhaps he wasn't quite as athletic as he thought. It didn't matter. He could stand on this bin.

*

The Walnut Tree opened at six. The first hour was usually quiet so the bar staff started at seven and Eamonn Walsh opened up himself. Mac Liam walked in thirty seconds later.

He'd been rehearsing his lines ever since he left The Old Volunteer. Just a hint of menace was needed, not too much. He knew that he wasn't a physically imposing man. He used to insist he was of average height. All men of slightly less than average height do. That hadn't mattered in Derry. People knew who he was, or rather, what he was. Here, he would be going in cold. The first impression was crucial.

He hadn't been given a description of Eamonn Walsh, but he didn't need one. The man had the map of Ireland painted on his face, as they say. The accent might have been English, but the man was as Irish as a greyhound under a false name. Mac Liam had tried to disguise his accent in Rutland. Here, he dialled it up a notch. Derry accents frightened English people. They just did.

'Mr Walsh, my name is Patrick, I represent a group of businessmen, may I have a few moments of your time?'

That was good. Derry accent! Very polite! A group of businessmen! That should scare the crap out of him! Anybody who describes themselves as representing a group of businessmen should be taken seriously. A group of businessmen always meant a group of very violent men. Everyone knew that.

Apparently Eamonn Walsh didn't. And a Derry accent didn't frighten him, either. He wasn't that sort of Englishman.

So, not a great start. But it did get better.

'I understand that your current cigarette provider has run into some legal problems.'

That was nice, straight to the point, barely oblique. No nonsense. Now he had the man's attention. He could see it in his face. He decided to dial up the Derry another notch.

Walsh was paying attention now. Who was this man? How did he know? The *Leicester Mercury* had carried a few stories about his customers being raided, corner shops, and so on. So far, his name, and The Walnut Tree, had been kept out of it. He suggested that they continue their discussion in the office.

Eamonn Walsh had a bit of a dilemma. On the one hand, his existing suppliers had let him down. Let him down in two ways. Firstly, this week's delivery had not arrived. Secondly, there was obviously some sort of security problem. It couldn't be a coincidence that all his customers had been visited by Customs and Excise. And yet, he hadn't. So perhaps it was. Except that he wasn't aware of anybody who wasn't one of his customers being raided. So, back to where he started. Two problems. Plus, a third. He couldn't contact his suppliers. All their phones were dead.

Now here was a man offering to solve his problems. A man from Northern Ireland, well, the last one had been too. But this one was slightly more frightening. Eamonn Walsh wasn't actually scared, but he was able to appreciate the differing levels of menace. Who would be the more upset if he switched suppliers? And which group was it most unwise to upset?

And then the dilemma resolved itself.

Mac Liam pushed a sheet of A4 paper across the desk. It had a list of brands. And a list of prices. Walsh didn't react, not outwardly. He was a fairly good card player. Twenty-Five, not poker, but it was the same skill set.

'Per master case?'

'Ten thousand cigarettes, packs of twenty, sleeves of two hundred.'

The prices were low.

'And are they genuine, or snides?'

The Ulsterman looked puzzled.

'Knock offs, counterfeits.'

'My associates stand behind the quality of our product.'

So, they were counterfeits, never mind. At these prices, well, dilemma solved.

'Let's talk about delivery schedules.'

Chapter 21

For the second week in a row, Heather was standing in front of the mirror deciding what to wear for a pub quiz in Rutland. This was simply ridiculous!

She shouldn't be attending at all. But it had been hard to refuse the old man with the Weimaraner. At least she thought that the dog was his. He looked so hurt at the prospect that she wouldn't be there. And you couldn't go around breaking the hearts of old men like that, not anywhere, but for some reason especially not in Rutland.

It was silly, but half an hour later she had a slight feeling that somehow the old man had manipulated her.

So, here she was preparing for an evening that shouldn't be taking place at all. Michael was perfectly nice of course, quite sweet in a way. But he wasn't her type. He wasn't anyone's type, really. He was sort of like the best friend character in a Richard Curtis film. Hugh Grant's wing man. But a sweet one.

No, this wasn't the plan at all. She wasn't exactly sure what the plan was, but this wasn't it. Either she would eschew the company of all men for at least a year, no better make that six months actually, or she would get herself organised, move back to London, and get back in the game. Find an actual Hugh Grant, although she was more of a Colin Firth type of girl.

But if a girl was going to get back in the game, shouldn't she have a couple of warm-up fixtures? Keep the old repartee muscles in shape, give the tinkling laugh a bit of a road test? She selected a pair of jeans. Just at random, no special reason, could have been any pair, really. But they were the tightest.

*

As he pushed open the gate to Primrose Cottage, Michael wondered whether he ought to have brought a bunch of flowers. By the time he reached the front door, three seconds later, he was glad that he hadn't. How on earth would that be interpreted? He was walking a woman about a hundred yards to a pub quiz on a Thursday. It wasn't prom night.

Michael wasn't exactly sure what a prom night was. Was it an American only thing? He'd attended a single sex boarding school. Sometimes he attributed his lack of success with the gentler sex to this, but in his heart, he knew it wasn't so. He knew he wasn't the matinee idol type. In the highly unlikely event of a film of his life, he would be played by James Stewart.

Well, obviously not him. The man must be about a hundred if he was still alive. And not in one of his square-jawed hero roles like *The Spirit of St Louis* or even *Rear Window*. No, he would be played by the awkward, gawky Stewart of *It's a Wonderful Life* or *Harvey*, the one with the rabbit.

So, no flowers.

He reached up and rang the bell (he'd learnt his lesson with respect to the knocker). It was one of those very old-fashioned ones where you pulled a handle down and hoped that a bell rang somewhere within. He stood back to inspect the little cottage and noticed that one of Heather's neighbours was surveying him through her front window.

There had been neighbours like that in the Sussex village where Michael had been raised. Always on the lookout for cars parked overnight or suitors leaving a house quietly in the early dawn. His sister, Emma, had regularly scandalised the neighbourhood. She did it deliberately. She thought it was funny. He often wished that he was a bit more like his younger sister.

Heather heard the bell. She inspected herself in the mirror. She'd selected the expensive lipstick. She didn't really like it. The colour was a little tarty. But that didn't matter. She wasn't trying to impress anyone. It was only Michael. But if she was going to treat the evening as a warm-up for other more serious dates, she had to do it properly, hence the lipstick, and the jeans, and the scent.

'You look lovely.' That was a bloody stupid thing to say, a stupid way to start the evening. He just couldn't help it. She did. And the words were past his teeth before the emergency brakes could engage. Try not to be a total arse! Don't, for example, offer her your arm. That would be ridiculous.

When she took it, he felt unimaginably happy. He felt like the better, bolder version of James Stewart, from one of the westerns perhaps.

*

The Old Volunteer had barely begun to fill up when they arrived. Ron wasn't there, but they decided to sit at the table that they'd shared with the old man the week before.

In fact, he arrived just as Michael was being served at the bar. Some people have the knack for that. Michael ordered three pints of bitter, and Ron went to sit beside Heather. He was a sweet old man, she thought. She reminded him of one of those actors from the black-and-white films that were sometimes shown on television on Sunday afternoons.

'Is your friend Diarmuid joining us?' Heather couldn't decide what she hoped the answer would be.

'Arr,' said Ron. And he nodded towards the door.

*

It had been at least four years ago, maybe five, at a party at a student house in Newcastle. Lucy's brother had come up with half a dozen of his friends from Durham. They were rugby players, or rowers, or something. Posh, brash, noisy, entitled, Heather could probably list a hundred unattractive adjectives.

They'd all arrived at least half drunk and it hadn't taken them long to achieve the second half. Lucy was clearly deeply embarrassed and out of loyalty to her friend Heather had tried to speak to one or two of the more sober ones. It was no use. They were all awful, even Lucy's brother, who was perfectly pleasant when not in the company of this assortment of toff-yobs.

She hadn't actually spoken to him herself and so it was very unlikely that he would remember her, but everyone had agreed that even among this puddle of self-regarding dick-heads one had stood out. The very tall one. She couldn't remember his name. Everyone had called him 'James Bond'. He'd spent the evening trying without success to persuade various women that he was about to be recruited into MI6. As if that would actually impress anyone.

Well, he obviously hadn't because here he was stooping to enter through the door of a pub in Rutland.

The first round had been science. Ron's Team scored six out of ten. Five of those were due solely to Heather. Richard, his name was Richard, had tried to talk her out of one of them. He was definitely the same guy. Six out of ten was normally a good score at The Old

Volunteer but one of the teams, 'They don't like it Uppingham', contained the head of science at Uppingham School and they scored ten.

The second round was popular culture. Ron managed to get a question about *Gardeners' Question Time* right. And Heather was able to guess a couple of others. She also knew the answer to a question about *Neighbours* but she was embarrassed to say so. Ron's Team finished the second round in joint last place.

'Our fishing trip is in jeopardy here, Diarmuid, need to pull our fingers out. Tell you what, I'll get some more thinking fuel, same again for everybody is it?'

Richard relied quite a lot on lazy stereotypes in his analysis. The Scholar was an Irish terrorist; therefore, he must be a hard drinker. It followed that he would admire and seek the company of other hard drinkers. They would be kindred souls to him. Richard already imagined that he'd established a rapport with him and now here was an opportunity to reinforce that.

'And two large Jameson's please.'

The Scholar left his untouched.

The next round was art and literature. This was where the Scholar could get Ron's Team back in contention.

Percy Bysshe Shelley, Jack Butler Yeats, Samuel Langhorne Clemens, Cubism, The Medici Family, Dimitri Shostakovich, Antonio Salieri, George Eliot, The Quarrymen, Marcel Proust. Ten out of ten. Ron's Team was now in second place, behind Shake Rutland Roll. Diarmuid excused himself to visit the gents.

'Well, well, well.'

'He was like that last week as well.'

'Arr.'

'Well, the land of saints, and scholars, I suppose.'

'Exactly.'

'I'll just polish off his whiskey. He doesn't seem to want it.'

*

The Scholar wasn't the only person to decide to visit the toilets at the end of round three. He waited until everybody had left before going into the cubicle and locking the door. He paused, listening. Nothing. He put down the seat and then gently lifted the lid of the cistern, spun it in his hands so that it was upside down and placed it down gently on the seat. He paused again. Nothing.

There it was, exactly as ordered, triple wrapped in clear plastic bags and fixed to the lid with far too much gaffer tape. Still, better too much than too little. He gently peeled away the tape, except for one length, folded it as neatly as he could and put it in the back pocket of his jeans. Then he did the same with the polythene bags, different pocket. Finally, he used the last piece of tape to secure it to the inside of his left thigh and returned to the bar.

The fourth round was geography. Nobody was very confident.

'Question one, in which German city was Ludwig van Beethoven born?'

'Pretty confident that's Salzburg, actually.'

Well, he would be. Richard was pretty confident about everything.

'That's Mozart! And Salzburg is in Austria.'

Heather, Michael imagined, was using the tone that she must reserve for her most exasperatingly stupid pupils. This was definitely the girl for him.

Michael knew the answer. Bonn. Beethoven was born in Bonn. He'd spent six months studying at the university there and you couldn't move for statues of the man. They were bloody everywhere. It was pretty much the first thing that everybody told you when you arrived. This is Beethoven's birthplace you know? And by the way, it's also the capital of Europe's leading economy.

But the thing was Michael's grandfather knew all that too. It was a question maybe half of those present would know, but with Michael it was guaranteed. So why had the old man included it? He certainly wasn't giving Michael's team a free point. He wouldn't do that. And he didn't do it for no reason at all. Brigadier Bernard Taylor never did anything without a reason. And the reason was almost always sneaky, duplicitous, or mischievous. Which was it this time?

'It's Bonn.'

'Yes, I think that's right.'

'Arr.'

The Scholar pulled the answer sheet towards himself and wrote it down.

An answer that Michael was sure to know. An answer his grandfather would know that he would know. And he would know that he would know that he would... Oh for God's sake what... Ah! It was a sign, like a codeword, or a secret handshake. It meant...actually he'd no idea what it meant, except, be alert. Battle stations!

'Question two, in which modern country is the ancient city of Sabratha?'

'Come on, Richard, you're supposed to be the classicist. Where is it?'

'Ah, umm, I think it's probably near Carthage, so that would make it...Tunisia?'

'It's in Libya.' The Scholar had written it down before Richard could argue.

'What is the state capital of Illinois?'

At half a dozen tables, a very similar discussion was taking place, sotto voce.

'I think that's Chicago.'

'State capitals are tricky. It's never the one you think.'

'That's right, the capital of New York is Albany.'

'And California's is Sacramento or something.'

'Well, what other cities do you know in Illinois?'

And so, at every table, in the confidence that they were wrong, everybody wrote, 'Chicago'.

Except at Ron's table. Where the Scholar, without a word, clearly printed, 'Springfield'.

'What is the third largest town or village in Rutland?' Ron knew that.

'In which country are seventy-five per cent of the world's pineapples grown?'

The Scholar shrugged, Michael shrugged, Ron finished his pint, and looked around expectantly. Richard started naming countries with warm climates more or less at random. Heather drew the answer sheet to herself and wrote, 'USA'.

'If a Spaniard calls you *Gomia*, what does he mean?'

Michael frowned. Richard saw an opportunity for revenge.

'Come on, Michael, you studied Spanish at Cambridge. Surely you must know this? Or did you spend all your time punting and swotting for *University Challenge*?'

Michael hadn't mentioned he'd been to Cambridge. In Heather's experience, it was this first thing that Cambridge graduates told her, or certainly in the top three. Some of them wouldn't just boldly state it outright, but you could be sure they found an opportunity to drop it into conversation pretty early on. But Michael hadn't said a thing.

'It means friend. It's back slang, *amigo, Gomia*,' the Scholar said.

He nodded at Heather, who still had the answer sheet.

Richard knew the answers to the remaining questions, but to be fair, they all did. At least Michael assumed that Ron did. He nodded and said 'Arr' emphatically.

*

Bernard, as quizmaster, announced the correct answers at the end of each round.

'Question five: in which country are seventy-five per cent of all pineapples grown? Well, three-quarters of the world's pineapples are grown in Hawaii, which of course is in the United States of America. Very well done if you got that one.'

Under the table, Michael gave Heather's hand a congratulatory squeeze. Hang on! How long had he been holding her hand? Had he initiated it? Or had she? She squeezed him back. Was it possible to be happier than this? In a funny little pub in a funny little village in a funny little county? At a Thursday night pub quiz sitting opposite a terrorist and a twenty-four-carat arse? All pretty unpromising and yet, here he was, absolutely filled to the brim with excitement and contentment and perhaps just a tiny dash of lust.

*

And then his grandfather spoilt it all. That was unfair. What spoilt it was that it dawned on him what his grandfather was up to. This was an exercise in testing the depth and breadth of the Scholar's knowledge. What did he know about Chicago, about Libya? Did he understand colloquial Spanish? No, not colloquial, way beyond colloquial, back slang! Who used back slang? Criminals, mostly. Oh, you cunning old sod!

But why? He hadn't told his grandfather anything about the Scholar. He knew Michael was debriefing someone. And he couldn't believe that MI6 just happened to acquire Windmill Cottage. His grandfather had suggested it. But there was a limit to how much even he could work out on his own. He was being fed information by someone. And that was highly irregular. It was probably illegal. Unless his grandfather was still on the payroll. And he easily might be, the old goat.

Or it was Phillipa Templeton? Would she bend the rules? Yes, she bloody would. She had bent them to recruit him. She had allowed? Encouraged? Ordered? His grandfather to turn him into a drug smuggler in order to assess his suitability for intelligence work. She definitely wasn't above using the old man for her purposes.

Why did everyone in his professional life have to be so devious, oblique, and bloody dishonest all the time? And what did it say about him that he was able to identify it? What was he going to be like in twenty years?

*

They were three points clear going into the final round, which was sport. Michael was pretty confident that they could manage at least seven out of ten. They would win and Richard and the Scholar could go fishing. Fine. It was going to take him all day to write up his report of today. And he would need to parse very carefully the implication that he knew what Phillipa and his grandfather were up to.

There was even a question in the sports round designed to probe the Scholar's knowledge. Ice hockey teams from Boston, I mean, come on! Michael hoped that it wasn't too obvious. After all, he'd worked it out, and the Scholar was at least as smart as him, first class honours from Cambridge notwithstanding.

But the Irishman appeared flushed with success. There was the competitive instinct that Michael had identified last week, or course, and the prospect of a day on Rutland Water locked in a battle of wits with some brown trout. Probably provide a more stimulating intellectual opponent that Richard, he thought ungraciously. But was there something else as well? He did seem very pleased with himself.

*

'And the winner, for the second week running is Ron's Team.' There was a smattering of applause. Heather turned and kissed Ron on the cheek.

'Arr!' he said, and you could tell he meant it.

Then she turned to Michael. 'Walk me home?'

*

They left the pub hand in hand. This was the time to put Michael's carefully designed plan into operation. He had given it a lot of thought, weighed his options, considered the possible reactions, contingencies, failsafes, and alternatives. It was as foolproof as he could make it. His grandfather would have been proud of him.

Would have been if he could remember even the slightest detail of what it was.

But he couldn't and so he did the last thing that his grandfather would have advised; the two last things, actually. He improvised, and he told the truth.

'I think you're wonderful.'

'Why?'

This was easily the hardest question of the evening.

'Well... you know so much about pineapples.'

She laughed. 'I've got one in the house. Would you like to see it?'

'Have you really?'

'No.'

'Well, perhaps I should come in anyway, just to check.'

Heather thought about it for a moment. He wasn't her type. But the way he was looking at her now, those earnest, hopeful, slightly pleading eyes. He looked like Rocky when he thought that you might be going to tickle him behind the ears. He definitely wasn't her type, but what the hell? Why not?

'Why not?'

Richard had been quite drunk by the time the Scholar and he'd made it back to Windmill Cottage. He suggested a whisky or two before they retired, but the Irishman declined.

He assumed that his room was searched regularly, and he further assumed that whoever searched it would also check for his detectors. After all, anyone who had ever seen a spy movie had to be familiar with the old eyelash across the doorframe trick. So, the Scholar hadn't left any detectors. By now, he hoped, the searches would have become routine, perfunctory, if he was lucky. So, he'd left his detectors before going out to the pub that evening.

Let's start with the loose bit of skirting board. He assumed that it had been deliberately loosened by the Brits themselves to provide him with a hidey hole. It bordered on insulting, really. Detector disturbed. Okay, let's check the loose floorboard. Honestly, what did they think of him? It was all a bit Escape from Colditz wasn't it? Now, under the wardrobe. Yes, they checked there too.

The Scholar was neither disappointed nor frustrated. He expected these obvious places to have been searched. But what about the chimney? He'd worked at it for a few minutes each day, gently scraping away the mortar between the bricks and replacing a convenient spider's web. He lit a match (he'd stolen the box from Richard) and checked carefully. Yes! Or rather, no, they hadn't checked.

He removed the spider's web, placing it carefully on a tissue, and gently worked the brick free, catching the dust in his other hand. Stop. Listen. No sound. He winced as he peeled the gaffer tape from his naked thigh. That really stung.

Whoever it was had done well. The Ericsson T28 was among the smallest phones on the market. He turned it on and immediately reduced the volume to zero. Full battery. No messages. He turned it off again, wrapped it in the plastic bags and placed it in the tiny aperture behind the chimney brick. He rubbed a bit of dust and dirt around and replaced the spider's web. He damaged it slightly, but within hours, the spider would have fixed that. All he'd to do now was find a way of disposing of the gaffer tape.

Chapter 22

Things were returning to normal by Friday. Lake was in early again, back to his routine. He was waiting for the Other Office to call him at about eight. The shift changed at seven, but the proprieties had to be observed. There would be handovers and cups of coffee and bacon sandwiches.

Lake's team would be busy. Witness statements had to be written and taken. All the materials from the searches had to be sifted and sorted. Only Steve Moore was missing. He was hoping that he would be released from the hospital that afternoon.

*

Lake hadn't expected to receive any intelligence from the Other Office.

'Your friend, Mr Walsh, has found himself a new supplier.'

'Already?'

'Yep, no more details, but he must have met him personally in the last day or two.'

Lake knew what that indicated. 'So, we don't know who?'

'Not yet, but Walsh is telling his customers that happy days will be here again. Normal service will resume.'

So, the Other Office hadn't pulled the plug as Lake had feared. They were unusually cagey about their reasons. The Other Office was always slightly oblique about their intelligence sources, as if everybody didn't know. But they were even worse than usual. Perhaps there was something different this time.

So, the investigation carried on as before, except that all the known targets were now in prison awaiting trial. All the targets except Eamonn Walsh.

*

Lake had four days' worth of footage from the camera fixed outside the back of The Walnut Tree. He had nothing else to do and no other target, so he made a cup of coffee, put the tape in the machine and set it to play at five times normal speed.

Monster sat at the desk opposite, drafting his witness statement for the past few days' events. Lake was leaning back in his chair, staring at the unmoving image of a pair of blue doors.

*

'We did everything wrong.'

'What are you talking about?' Monster was glad of the distraction. He sat up and reached for his coffee, but Lake continued to stare moodily at the screen.

'Every decision we made, faced with the facts we had at the time. We made the right calls on the basis of the facts available. I don't think we did anything wrong.'

But Lake wasn't in the mood to look on the positive side.

'We did everything wrong. Not each individual decision. Those were fine. I agree with you there, but we did everything wrong. At a conceptual level.'

'Joe, if you're going to have some sort of crisis can you have it in the pub?'

But Lake was warming to his theme. 'We started in the middle. In the middle of the supply chain, I mean. The transport and the wholesalers. And we investigated downwards. Down to retailers and customers. That was wrong. We should have investigated upwards. We should have been aiming at whoever put those fags on the lorries, where they came from, who was behind that.'

'And when exactly did you have this epiphany? It wouldn't be anything to do with a grumpy old Scotsman, by any chance?'

Lake admitted that it had.

'And what was Frank's prescription? How the hell did he think that we could have done any of that?'

'I don't know.'

'Exactly, even the great Frank McBride doesn't know.'

'I didn't say he didn't know. I said I didn't. You know what he's like. He won't tell you stuff directly. He sort of sows a seed and an hour or a day or a week later you realise what he said. I think he thinks it's mentoring.'

'Oh, for God's sake! You've got to stop listening to the Yoda of Rutland.'

'You're probably right. But how could we do it?'

Monster pushed aside his witness statement. 'We'd need to turn someone. Nick them without anyone knowing and make them an informant. Even that wouldn't be enough, probably. We'd need to put an undercover officer in. There's no way the Other Office would sanction an undercover officer for a cigarette job. Just wouldn't happen.'

'You're probably right.'

'I'm definitely right. Now finish watching that vid. I'm dying for a pint.'

*

Lake pushed play. He frowned.

'That bloke. That bloke walking down the alley behind the boozer.'

He pushed pause and rewound for a few seconds. Then he pushed play again. He made a note on a pad beside him: 17:51. He pressed play again, this time at normal speed.

'What is it?'

'This guy walks down the back alley, then three minutes later he does it again.'

'So what?'

Monster was right, so what? Lake continued to gaze moodily at the screen.

'There he is again, coming out the back, through those blue doors.'

Lake paused the tape. 'How do I zoom in?'

Monster leant over and pushed a couple of buttons.

'I know him. I've seen him.' He screwed up his eyes, trying to retrieve the memory. 'Bloody hell! Still fancy that pint?'

'Now you're making sense, Limelight?'

'Nope! I fancy a game of shove ha'penny.'

'Are you sure you weren't the one who got a bang on the head?'

*

Friday lunchtimes were a lot busier than Thursdays at The Old Volunteer. It took Monster and Joe five minutes to get served and it was a further fifteen before Frank had time to speak to them. He nodded towards the other bar.

'What the...'

'It's retro chic, Monster, coveys the rustic simplicity of a gentler, simpler, bygone age.'

'Are you sure you didn't get a bang on the head?'

'Joseph is quoting *The Observer* colour supplement. They did a feature on us a month or two back.'

'Is that a spittoon? I've never seen one in real life.'

'I assume you haven't come all the way down here to make half-witted observations about my decor.'

Lake sipped his pint. Then he sipped it again. He'd been planning this for most of the journey down, but now that he was face to face with Frank McBride, it didn't seem so straightforward.

'Yesterday; young man, white, late twenties, arrived about the same time as me.'

McBride nodded. 'Never seen him before. Had one pint, left, drove a blue Mondeo, want the index?'

'Do you keep a note of all your customers' number plates?'

'No.'

'So...'

'I didn't like him. We don't get customers his age on their own at that time on a Thursday. Or any other time, really. And he was trying to disguise his accent.'

'What was the real one?'

'If I had to guess...Irish, probably northern.'

Lake and Monster exchanged glances. Lake took a coin from his pocket. 'Call.'

'Tails.'

'You lose. You're driving. Frank, we need your advice.'

'I know you do. I've been thinking about it. And I may have a solution.'

*

Richard was ever so slightly hung-over. Strangely, he didn't have a headache, but he did feel a little bit queasy. Of course, that might have been due to breakfast a la Tony. It was quite breezy and while

Rutland Water couldn't exactly be described as choppy there was a bit of a swell, which mirrored the one in Richard's guts. The boats looked very small.

The Scholar was indecently breezy too, in a way that Richard resented. He strode ahead into the tackle shop and was deeply engaged in a discussion about nymphs and buzzers when Richard arrived. Tony and Little Chris had found a bench at the edge of the car park from where they were surveying the scene.

'Your man here says that seeing as we're here for the first time, we'd benefit from a bit of local knowledge. He says that there's a local man, Robin Barnes, and that he'll take us out, take us to the good spots and provide all the tackle. But it's a hundred pounds. That's his boat over there, the *Chicka-Dee*.' He pointed to a boat on a trailer.

Richard surveyed the scene more broadly. The *Chicka-Dee* was among the largest boats. Larger was better if it was a bit windy. He was sure he was right about that. It even had a little shelter at the front. There was probably a special name for that. And it had a smallish looking outboard motor. Richard considered that important. He hadn't rowed since school, and he'd hated it then.

And if this Barnes had to be sent for that meant a slight delay. That suited him as well. As for the hundred pounds, well, the Queen could afford it. He nodded at the Scholar. The Scholar nodded at the man behind the counter. And he picked up the phone.

'We could maybe have a cup of tea while we're waiting?'

Again, Richard was inclined to agree.

*

The *Chicka-Dee* might have been a little larger than most of the boats on Rutland Water, but it was still not capacious. It was at best a three-man vessel. Or two if one of those men was either Tony or a Chris of either size. Tony was very much against the idea of Richard, the Scholar and the boat's owner setting off across the water and away from the security detail.

But Richard wanted to be in the boat with the Scholar. He saw it as an opportunity to bond. Even if it had been practical for another passenger, he would have resisted. He told Tony that it was settled and that was that. You have to keep these other ranks in order from time to time, remind them who is really the boss.

'And no hiring another boat and trying to follow us. I don't want you splashing about and frightening all the fish.'

As the *Chicka-Dee* pushed off the jetty, Tony lit a cigarette. He'd been in the Royal Marines for twenty-two years. He didn't take kindly to the implication that he couldn't handle a small boat. If the silly sod capsized, he decided that he would swim in and rescue the other two. Little Chris joined him and passed him an ice cream cone.

He was able to sum up his assessment of Richard Perceval, his professionalism, his manner, the British class system, and one or two other things in one syllable. Tony nodded, flicked his butt into the water and reached for the cone. 'No flake?'

*

It took Michael a lot less time than he expected to write his report for Phillipa Templeton. He finished just as Windmill Cottage's grandfather clock struck noon. His thoughts turned to fly-fishing. How long did that take? Was it something you did for an hour, or all day? He decided that he didn't need to worry. It was nearly lunchtime and since Tony was providing security or possibly guarding Richard and the Scholar, he was reasonably confident that lunch as prepared by Big Chris probably wouldn't kill him.

But just before he despatched his report to Phillipa perhaps he ought to drop in on his grandfather. The chances of the old man letting anything slip in an unguarded moment were zero, but he might be able to provoke him into giving something away somehow. He stuck his head around the door where Big Chris was studying the back of a box of frozen fish fingers with a puzzled expression on his face. Perhaps he could get a sandwich at the pub.

*

The wind had abated a little, and it had turned into a pleasant spring day. As he passed the village's war memorial, he saw a grey Peugeot saloon pass him and sweep into The Old Volunteer car park. He paused by the telephone kiosk from where he could observe the car's two occupants without being noticed.

The two were men he knew and men who knew him. They were customs officers, and two years before he'd been their target. He knew that his grandfather and Frank McBride had somehow reconciled themselves to their complex history, but he wasn't as sure that the same detente would apply to him and the two officers. After all, Frank had retired, and these two clearly hadn't. Perhaps they were going to seek wisdom at the feet of Frank. It might have to be Big Chris' fish finger surprise for lunch after all.

He waited until the two men had gone inside and then walked briskly through the little gate with the plate that read, 'The Old Vicarage' and down the side of his grandfather's house to the back door. As expected, he was sitting at the kitchen table studying what appeared to be a letter. On the table in front of him was an envelope of unusually high quality.

'Hello, Grandpa. Letter from the palace, is it?'

The old man looked up. 'Hello, Mikey. As a matter of fact, it is. Well, a letter from a palace, at least. Monsieur Chirac has invited me to visit Normandy this summer.'

'Really? What for?'

'Something to do with risking my life to liberate his country I expect. I know you're not an historian, but I thought that you might be vaguely aware of the second World War.'

The old man could be quite peevish on occasion, and this was delivered with enough acid to dispose of several bodies.

'Are you going to go?'

'I'm not sure. I was hoping to persuade Ron to accompany me, but he's proving reluctant.'

'Ron?'

'Oh, for goodness' sake, Mikey. Yes, Ron, obviously Ron. Are you seriously telling me you don't know who Ron Godsmark is?'

'Ron? He's just Ron, isn't he?'

'My daughter has given birth to an imbecile.' He shook his head sadly. 'Now what do you want?'

Michael was needled now. 'I'd quite like to know why you decided to use the pub quiz to test the knowledge of a man I've been interrogating for two weeks.'

'Oh that. Well, I was asked very politely, and I rather enjoyed it. I hope you've covered it in your daily report. It saves me the trouble of writing a long letter. Arthritis, you know. Where is he, by the way?'

'He's out fishing with Perceval.'

'With a bit of luck, they both might drown. I've made you some sandwiches. I assume you haven't eaten.'

And there it was again. The annoying old man was always a step ahead, always anticipating, and always so bloody sure that he was right. Which he was. And that was annoying, too.

And now he was going to have to bend the rules to look up Ron Godsmark. Why do you want to know about an old man from Rutland, Michael? Oh, because my grandfather was really annoying about it. That wouldn't work. Perhaps he could just ask Margaret.

Chapter 23

Richard Perceval counted the morning a success for a number of reasons.

First, Diarmuid Geraghty, or the Scholar, or whatever his real name was had caught a number of fish. He'd called it a 'rake' of fish. Who knew what that meant?

Second, the Scholar had been more than usually talkative. It was partly due to the circumstances. He seemed happier and more content out on the *Chicka-Dee* on Rutland Water than Richard had previously seen him. But wasn't that to Richard's credit? Hadn't it been he, Richard Perceval, who had identified this weak spot in the armour? Certainly, it was.

Michael Butcher had been indifferent to the idea. But the way Richard was going to tell it, he'd been sceptical, even hostile. The way Richard was going to tell it Michael had been hostile. Dare he say, scornful? That would probably be pushing it a bit.

Yes, Richard Perceval had good cause to congratulate himself. He'd established a rapport. He had the relationship. He was mining the deep vein of the Scholar. And the way he was going to tell it, he was going to be the hero.

And it wasn't just that the Scholar had been unusually chatty, it was what he said. With every fish he caught, and he caught plenty, he would reveal a little more about himself, about his background, about his childhood.

The only problem was that every single word of it was a lie.

The Scholar couldn't decide what he'd enjoyed more, playing the fish, or playing the Englishman. At one stage, he'd been worried that perhaps it was too easy. He'd seen all those films you see, and television programmes, the ones where the diffident, upper-class Englishman appeared to be an imbecile but was actually really shrewd. Could that be the case here? The Scholar wrestled with the question even as he landed a brown trout weighing almost five pounds.

No. He didn't think so. Richard Perceval was a bona fide eejit.

And there had been one further enjoyable element. The expression on the faces of those two goons as the *Chicka-Dee* had slipped away from the jetty and set off around the little headland. They had clearly hated it. Good.

*

When he learnt about it that afternoon, Michael had hated it too.

It had been Tony who did the talking, but Little Chris had stood behind him and slightly to one side, lending his presence as a second opinion.

'I don't like it at all, Boss. He could turf Mr Perceval and that little boatman into the oggin in a second and be away across the reservoir and gone forever.'

Michael knew that he had a point.

'Was there really no room for one of you in the boat?'

The two giants shared a look.

'Probably not. It's not very big. But, in any case, Mr Perceval ordered us.'

'Could we maybe find a larger boat?'

'We looked. There didn't seem to be one.'

'How about if you hired a second boat, and you shadowed them?'

'I suggested that, but Mr Perceval, he forbade it.'

'What about if we hired a boat without the boatman? What's his name, Barnes? There would be three of you in the boat then.'

'That would be better.'

'After all, Barnes has shown them where the fish are now. Do they really need him anymore?'

The two men exchanged glances again. Little Chris shrugged.

'There's the tackle, though. The rods and stuff. Those belong to Barnes.'

'Leave it with me. I'll speak to Mr Perceval.'

*

That conversation didn't go at all well. Richard made all the points to Michael that he'd made earlier that day. He also managed to imply that the fishing trip had been a breakthrough, and that Michael was trying to sabotage a second trip out of jealousy. Michael had had to pull rank, a rank that, strictly speaking, he didn't have.

'Right. Go fishing tomorrow. But you either find a bigger boat, persuade Barnes to let you take one of the guards, or allow them to shadow you in a second boat.'

Richard reluctantly agreed, but he was clearly sulking. This was going to feature in his report. He was only sorry that he couldn't say so, because he wasn't really supposed to be writing one. He had to content himself with a sly jibe.

'I suppose you're going to be off tonight with that popsie from the pub quiz. Takes all sorts I suppose.'

He must have seen the bunch of flowers by the front door. Yes, this time Michael had bought flowers. He was nearly sure that this had been the right thing to do. Not for the first time, Michael entertained a brief fantasy of the Scholar turfing Richard into the water.

*

Michael had spent the early part of the afternoon composing his report for Phillipa Templeton, but he had an hour to spare to go into Oakham.

Martin's Fine Wines looked exactly as he'd imagined it. It was a small shop on the High Street with about twice as much stock as it was comfortably able to accommodate. The proprietor, Martin presumably, or his son, also fitted Michael's idea of a Rutland wine merchant. He wore a waistcoat, a bow tie, and a pair of spectacles hanging from a chain around his neck.

But he was welcoming, affable, and clearly knowledgeable. He listened carefully to Michael and made a number of suggestions. Michael thought it best to play it safe. One red, one white, not too ostentatiously expensive, but better than anything found in the Co-op. French would be the best. He left with a bottle or Morgon (he'd rejected the Saint Amour as too obvious) and a Sancerre.

After his conversation with Richard, he'd gone to shower, change, and shave. He didn't have any aftershave. That was probably just as well. He never knew how much to put on.

*

Heather had left school even as the last bell was still echoing. She needed to buy ingredients, be home, and change into something suitable for cooking. Head to toe overalls would have been ideal. She never seemed to be able to boil an egg without covering herself, at least two walls, and sometimes the ceiling with various ingredients.

Heather didn't enjoy cooking. She found it difficult and stressful. The experience often reminded her of her GCSE chemistry practical when she'd allowed the time pressure to get to her and inadvertently almost created a bomb.

But she had a speciality. Was it still a speciality if it was the only dish that you could reliably produce without starting a fire or poisoning your guests? She decided it counted.

Her mother had impressed upon her that every girl had to have at least one meal that she could produce when 'entertaining a gentleman'. Heather and her mother used that phrase to describe entirely different activities. Her mother called it a go-to dish. Heather privately thought of it as her 'seduction special' although strictly speaking, it might be a bit late for that.

She also had to buy a set of wine glasses. She couldn't go on with just two, particularly since they were mismatched. It was a social and political dilemma that couldn't be resolved. If she reserved the slightly large glass for herself, she looked like a lush. If she gave it to Michael, she'd be buying into the boy gets the bigger glass, 'I'm the little woman', nonsense that she hated.

She bought a set of four. She was sure to break one.

Heather's go-to dish was spaghetti carbonara. It was easy. It seemed vaguely exotic, better than spag bol, anyway, and it had the secret ingredient. The one certain to succeed, at least according to her grandmother.

'If you can't win a man's heart with bacon, my dear, you might as well give up and join a nunnery.'

Was she trying to win a man's heart? She'd been thinking about this all day and had reached that conclusion that, yes, she was. Oh, she needed some black pepper.

*

Preparations had gone well. Heather had weighed, and put aside all the ingredients. She'd laid the table in the cottage's tiny dining room. And she'd laid the fire too. She knew she could do that competently. It was almost the first time she'd been in the room since she'd moved in. Nana used to serve tea and cake in that room.

Would she approve of what Heather was doing? Damn right she would. Anything that Heather did was all right by Nana. But there was something else. What was it Nana had said?

'Harold wasn't like the others. They were all so dashing, so devil-may-care. He wasn't like that at all.'

But the old men had called him Sid and said that he was brave. She would have to ask them about that.

Now it was time to get ready. For the third time in just over a week, she stood in front of the mirror, weighing her options. On one level, the task was easier this time, because she knew what she wanted to achieve. But it was also more complicated because there were more things to consider. The choice of underwear for a start.

*

Saturday morning dawned bright and clear. Even the most pessimistic curmudgeon would have been forced to admit that spring had arrived. Rocky and Brunhilde would have required no persuasion. They raced to and fro at breakneck speed along the path that followed the crest of ground between Leighton Parva and Leighton Magna.

The three men who followed them, combined age 215, were less energetic. Bernard was trying, again, to persuade Ron to attend the celebrations for the 55th anniversary of D-Day. It was proving hard work.

'I've been twice. First time someone tried to kill me, second time some busybody took my photograph.'

The way Ron spoke you might think that these two offences were equal in weight. And perhaps in Ron's mind they were.

'But Ron, there's only a handful of you! You can be sure that you'd be highly honoured.'

'Made a fuss of you mean. I don't want that at all.'

Frank played no part in the conversation. He'd spent a large part of the war living with an old couple who spoke almost no English in a croft in the Outer Hebrides. He'd been six years old when Ron had come ashore on Sword Beach.

It often surprised him that so few people had noticed that the inn sign at The Old Volunteer was a portrait of Lance Corporal Ron Godsmark. Of course, it had been based on a fifty-year-old photograph.

A plane flew over, a little lower than usual. Light aircraft were not exactly common, but the good weather and the clear skies seemed to bring them out. There was a little aero club a few miles away at Lynthorpe. It had been an RAF base during the war. Not a bomber base, it was far too small for that, training base or something.

'What's that, Frank?'

He took the pipe from his mouth and squinted, 'Balliol.'

Bernard had never heard of it. 'Are you sure?'

'Boulton Paul Balliol, trainer aircraft. introduced 1950, powered by a Rolls Royce Merlin 35, one thousand two hundred and forty-five horsepower, maximum speed two hundred and fifty knots. Want to know the wingspan?'

'Okay, Frank, if you say it's a Balliol we believe you.'

'Arr!'

*

Heather and Michael were walking the same path in the opposite direction, hand in hand. They saw Rocky and Brunhilde first. They tore around the couple, that's right, they were a couple now, three times, and then tore off back in the direction they'd come to where Ron, Bernard, and Frank were breasting a small rise.

'I've always wanted a dog. My mum was afraid of them, so we never could.'

'I like them too. Grandad is completely devoted to Brunhilde.'

'Wait. What? The quizmaster is your grandfather! Is that how we keep winning the pub quiz?'

The feeling returned that somehow the old man had manipulated her. That made her angry...and impressed...and grateful.

'Oh, if you knew him, you'd never say that. My grandfather...well it's difficult to explain.'

'Are there any other little secrets you've forgotten to tell me?'

'There he is now! Hello, Grandpa!'

Heather made a note to return to this subject.

*

Big Chris and Little Chris had searched high and low for a boat large enough to accommodate the Scholar, Perceval, a boatman, and one of their number. They couldn't find one anywhere. Tony, as the former marine, had been assigned to stalk the three fisherman from a boat hired from the fishing centre. He'd grumbled that the hire boat had a smaller outboard motor than the *Chicka-Dee* and that it wouldn't be able to keep up in the event of a chase.

Perceval had scoffed at the idea and warned, no ordered, Tony to remain at a discreet distance. So, Tony remained about ten fathoms off the port quarter, or something, a little bit behind and to the left.

The Scholar had another successful day. Richard had given up fishing himself. Casting a fly from a boat was a lot more difficult than when standing in a stream, and without a faithful ghillie to tell him what to do Richard was badly out of his depth, so the Irishman fished alone.

Robin Barnes, the local boatman, neither fished nor advised nor contributed in any way. Richard decided to broach the subject of hiring the *Chicka-Dee* but without the services of Barnes himself.

'We'll pay the same. We just need the boat and the tackle. One of our friends wants to come.'

Barnes feigned reluctance, insisted on a sizeable deposit against damage and finally negotiated a large hire charge. The arrangement was made for the following Friday.

The Scholar, with his back to the pair of them, smiled.

*

Big Chris and Little Chris were waiting for them on the jetty. Tony had decided to stay out a little longer. He would justify it as reconnaissance, but really, he just liked being alone on the water. Thinking. Maybe he should buy a little boat. He could take the boys out on it the weekends, well, one weekend in three. The court had been clear about that.

'Any luck?'

'Not too bad. The Scholar here got a couple of nice ones.'

The Scholar didn't react. At least he thought he hadn't, hoped he hadn't. Perceval had his back to him so he wouldn't have seen. The two goons, Chris and Chris, they weren't looking. Nobody saw. If there was anything to see. And he was almost sure that there hadn't been.

*

When he got back to Windmill Cottage, the Scholar went through all his checks again. He was confident that the mobile telephone was still undisturbed in its hiding place in the chimney. He sat on the floor with his back to the door so that he couldn't be surprised. He switched on the phone. Four messages. He read them quickly once and then went back and read them slowly. He read them a third time and then deleted them.

Customs had smashed up a large part of Higgins' operation. Might have been a coincidence, of course, might not. Anyway, it didn't matter. That part of the job was done. He just needed to add a little sugar to the Belfast story, and his mission was almost complete That was just as well because if they knew who he was it was almost time to go.

He assessed his objectives, weighed his options, considered what needed to be done. When he'd thought everything through, when he was sure that he hadn't overlooked anything he drafted a long and detailed text message. He checked it twice, then pressed *send*.

The phone was low on battery now. He hadn't a charger. Too bulky to be hidden in the pub toilet. Too bulky to smuggle back taped to his thigh. It shouldn't matter. If things went according to plan, that would be his last message.

When he'd finished, he replaced the telephone in its hidey hole and covered the false brick with dust, dirt, and cobwebs.

Chapter 24

Frank McBride was rechecking his accounts. And it was making him even grumpier than usual. Frank wasn't a businessman by inclination. He'd never aspired to be one and that the fact that he now had to admit to himself, reluctantly, that he'd become one was due to a fluke of circumstances.

He was only in Rutland because Michelle, his daughter, had moved there with her husband and her children, Maisie and Frankie. And he was only in The Old Volunteer because Michelle's husband had got a transfer to Spain and Frank had found himself homeless. Bernard had bought the pub and installed Frank as manager thus providing him with accommodation.

He could probably have lived with that. But this! This was embarrassing! He was good at it. He was a successful bourgeois. And he hated it.

Frank was Marxist-Leninist. More accurately, he was probably a lapsed Marxist-Leninist in the same way that he was a lapsed Celtic supporter and a lapsed Catholic. He'd actually been born a lapsed Catholic. That was pretty common in his part of Glasgow.

He looked again at the very healthy bottom line and tried to persuade himself that as a paid employee he was still a working man. He was still a member of the proletariat. He certainly wasn't a capitalist. He'd never had any capital for a start. Well, until now.

When Bernard, now he *was* a capitalist, had employed him the old man had insisted to building in a profit sharing/performance bonus scheme into the contract. Frank hadn't expected there to be any profit and so he hadn't objected at the time.

But here it was, in the line below the bottom line, if you know what I mean. In the first six months since reopening The Old Volunteer had made a net profit of nearly sixty thousand pounds. Under Bernard's scheme, Frank checked the figures again. He was due a bonus of £14,617.57.

He was also owed two weeks' holiday.

*

Frank picked up his copy of the *Rutland & Stamford Mercury* and turned for the fourth time to the advertisements on page 47, just before the sports news.

It was absurd. It would be vanity. And there was nothing wrong with his old Ford. In truth, he hardly used it, a few thousand miles a year. He didn't need a new car. And he certainly didn't need that one. He had never needed that one. Nobody had.

But he wanted it. Four years old, reasonable mileage, and he even liked the colour.

When Frank had moved to London in the sixties, all the self-respecting villains had a Jag. They were mostly Mark IIs then, the occasional S Type. It was a gangster's car. Jaguars were a bit edgy, a bit naughty. They were a limousine, of course, used by undertakers and cabinet ministers, but if you wanted to rob a bank or a train, you wanted a Jag for the getaway.

It was different now, of course. Villains drove flashy German cars, Mercs and Beamers, but Frank was old school. He looked again at the price. He could afford it. But could he justify it?

Frank sometimes wondered how people who didn't smoke pipes made important decisions. He reached for his tobacco pouch and took a pinch of McLintock Black Cherry. Today's pipe was a special one, a Meerschaum. He had been running it in for a couple of years now and it was approaching peak performance. The rim had yellowed to a light sepia. The bottom of the bowl was just one millionth of a shade of brilliant white. He struck a match.

Twenty minutes later, Frank had decided that he needed the Jag. It was for an essential work purpose. You might even argue that it ought to be tax deductible, although he doubted that the Inland Revenue would share that view.

*

Frank walked around the car, clockwise, and then anticlockwise. He didn't actually kick the tyres, but that didn't matter. The salesman could tell from twenty yards away that this was going to be the easiest sale of the day. Here was a punter who knew very little about cars but had dreamt of owning a Jag since he was in short trousers. There would be a bit of haggling. Scots accent might let him knock an extra hundred off, important to let the punters feel that they'd got the better of the deal.

The moment that Frank sat behind the wheel he knew that he had to have this car. Six litres. V12. Over three hundred horsepower. Walnut dash. Cream leather and Signal Red metallic. It had a personalised number plate, but he could change that.

He handed over a two grand deposit in cash and arranged to collect the car in a day or two. Then he drove back to Leighton Parva to discuss arrangements for hiring an interim manager to run The Old Volunteer while he was away.

*

It was almost three hundred miles from Leighton Parva, but in the Jag it was a positive pleasure. He only stopped once, to refuel, and buy a mobile telephone. He put it on charge using the Jag's cigarette lighter. By the time he reached Strathaven, it was fully charged.

Frank had never visited the place before. He knew almost nothing about it. It was small. It was just this side of Glasgow. Danny was there.

He knew even less about Strathaven Celtic Football Club. As a young man McBride had stood alongside seventy thousand others and watched Glasgow Celtic win the first of their nine in a row. He moved to London the next year, but he'd been in Lisbon to see them win the European Cup.

Strathaven Celtic would be unlikely to mimic either of these feats. They played in the Lanarkshire Premier League, which is less prestigious than it sounds. The ground itself had one crumbling terrace upon which, in theory, a thousand spectators might gather. They never did. Any crowd in three figures was considered a big night at Strathaven Celtic Park.

It wasn't the click of turnstiles that kept the club in business. It was the pouring of pints. The capacity of the social club was a little less than the terrace, but it was often full. Even on a weekday night, there were at least fifty people in the bar above the changing rooms.

McBride took a stool at the far end of the bar. Both the staff were busy with customers at the other end. He had the opportunity to survey the surroundings properly while he filled his pipe.

It was a long way from The Old Volunteer. If anything, it resembled the Glasgow pub in which Frank had been born and raised. Not so much in terms of decor or the scale but in terms of the atmosphere. Most of the customers were facing a television in the corner. Chelsea was playing Mallorca, and the locals were getting behind the Spanish side in a big way.

Eventually, the young woman who had been serving a group of men at the far end of the bar noticed Frank and walked over. Frank indicated the Guinness pump with the stem of his pipe and the young woman started work. 'One sixty-five'

Substantially cheaper than The Old Volunteer. Frank handed over a Bank of England five-pound note. The young woman eyed it suspiciously and held it up to the light. Who knew what she thought she might learn from this? She then looked Frank up and down, suspicious and unimpressed. Grudgingly, she rang up the sale and gave him his change. She smirked as she put the one-pound notes, carefully chosen to be from three different banks, into his hand. Good luck spending those down in England.

At the same time the other fifty per cent of the bar staff noticed Frank.

Frank knew, knew for a fact, that he was exactly five days younger than himself, but he could easily have passed for ten years older, twenty in bad light. He'd been a big man once, and he was still tall, or would be if you were able to lay him out straight, but in all other respects he seemed to have shrunk. And his skin didn't seem to have kept pace with the downsizing. It was the same colour as the rim of Frank's pipe. He wasn't tanned in an outdoorsy, healthy sort of way. There was nothing healthy about his appearance at all. A life in the tropics can do that to you I suppose.

Frank sipped his pint.

'Francis!'

'Daniel. Or should I call you Father'?'

'Not anymore. Not for a while, actually.'

*

Daniel was Frank's cousin. Auntie Pat's youngest. They'd grown up together, except for those few years when both had been evacuated, Frank to Barra, in the Outer Hebrides, Dan to Drumnadrochit, on the shores of Loch Ness.

At the age of eighteen Frank had been called up for National Service. Daniel was already in the seminary and his service was deferred. By the time he was ordained seven years later his country no longer needed him. Frank was in Customs by then, working at Greenock Docks.

Daniel had joined the Redemptorists, a religious order devoted chiefly to missionary work. Frank saw him occasionally over the years when he was back from Africa or Latin America.

'So, it's true.' The two men were at a table as far as possible from the television. Moira could manage the bar on her own for a while. 'You've been de-frocked.'

'Something like that. I over-emphasised the temporal nature of my pastoral mission.'

'Meaning?'

'They didn't approve of my enthusiasm for liberation theology.'

'I heard that you were leading communist guerrillas into battle in Peru.'

'You mustn't believe all you hear, Francis. I was only giving them last rites and absolution.'

Frank chuckled, 'We're a pair, aren't we?'

'We are that. What brings you here, Frank?'

Frank paused a moment while he re-lit his pipe. 'I want to buy some cigarettes.'

'There's a machine in the corner.'

'About three million a month to begin with, various popular UK brands.'

'You wouldn't be trying to set me up now would you, Frank?'

'I'm retired. I run a pub now. Can't survive on a civil service pension.'

Dan took a packet of Benson & Hedges from his pocket. He took one and pushed the packet across the table.

'Frank, you could never kid me when we were kids and you sure as hell can't kid me now.'

'I'd like to buy from our kind of people.'

'Washed up old commies, you mean?'

'Are there any?'

'I doubt it.'

'Celtic fans then.'

'There might be one or two of those. From over the water. Patriots. Or retired patriots anyway.'

'Sounds ideal.'

'Frank, I'm not going to end up with my kneecaps blown off, am I?'

'I can't rule it out altogether.'

Dan lit the cigarette. He took a second packet from another pocket and pushed it across the table. Frank picked up both packets and examined them, initially individually, and then side by side.

'Very good. Very good. Which one is the snide?'

'The one I'm not smoking. That stuff'll kill you.'

He coughed for emphasis, a long wracking cough that began with a harsh vigour but petered out into a weak apologetic sigh.

'I am sorry, Dan. If I'd known sooner, I'd have come up to see you earlier.'

'You have troubles of your own, Frank. How are Michelle and the kids?'

'I miss them, Dan. I really do. How long do you have?'

'I've seen my last Christmas.'

'Oh, Dan!'

'Never mind that. I think I can put you in touch with some people. What shall I say your name is?'

*

Frank had twenty-four hours to kill in the city of his birth. He returned to his old neighbourhood, but everything had changed. The names of some of the pubs had remained the same but inside, and in some cases outside, everything was different. Hennessy's bar had gone. So had the betting shop on the corner and the barbers where he'd got his first Tony Curtis hairstyle and something for the weekend.

The only thing that seemed to still be there was the pawnshop. It was called something different now, but it was still the same thing. Frank had known it well. Pawn tickets were often accepted at Hennessy's. He'd often seen the same things in the window for a week and then disappear only to be back a week later, sometimes re-hocked by the original owners, sometimes the new ones, or the latest at least.

There had been a trumpet. Frank had coveted it. He'd seen it in the window at least four times, but he could never afford it. Just for old times, he pushed open the door. The bell sounded, the same rusty apologetic tinkle. It couldn't be the same bell. Perhaps it was the atmosphere of penury and desperation that created its own unique acoustics.

There were no trumpets. It was probably just as well. Frank wasn't sure that he could have resisted. It was mostly jewellery. The emphasis was on the lower end of the carat scale. He saw a chunky necklace. It was marked as eighteen carats. There was probably a decimal point missing. He bought it anyway.

Then he headed west. He bought a leather jacket, a nice one, and some silk shirts, black, purple, bottle green. He visited a barber as unlike the one he'd visited as a teenager as it was possible to imagine. The beard was trimmed to little more than a stubble. A young man applied something called wet-look gel and sold him a small jar for an extortionate price.

Finally, at the age of sixty-two he did something unimaginable. Francis Daniel McBride OBE had his ear pierced. Just one.

Frank forced himself to stroll about the city to acclimatise himself to his new look and to shake off the feeling of self-consciousness. He visited three department stores and two toy shops before he found what he wanted. He bought the best and the most expensive child's chemistry set he could find.

*

Perhaps it was the outfit, maybe it was the Jag, it might even have been the gel and the earring. Nearly twenty years after he'd first gone undercover, he was back in the game.

The Watersplash had always been a villains' boozer. Even when Frank had been a kid. It didn't matter how many times it had changed hands or how many interior designers had tried to inflict a new more hospitable, less hostile atmosphere. None of it made any difference.

The current incarnation seemed to think that it was a Manhattan cocktail bar, but oddly one with a whole bank of fruit machines. There were no pool tables or dart boards. Even the most idealistic of The Watersplash's landlords would know better than actually to provide his clientele with weapons.

The two men opposite McBride clearly thought that they'd inherited the mantle of Glasgow underworld hard men. Some people might have been taken in but Frank McBride had seen the real thing. He was faintly amused at their gangster pretensions.

The tall one was wearing mirror sunglasses. What a clown! Notwithstanding a certain amount of neon and whatever the blue one was called the bar was still pretty gloomy. The small one was ostentatiously playing with a flick knife. He'd decided that for the purposes of this meeting he would affect a cigarette in the corner of his mouth. The smoke was drifting up into his face and his left eye was watering. The two of them were more than half blind.

'See you, whit ye need tae understand is ma assosh y ates are verry serious people. Ah'm talking an all tegither daffrant levol o' serious d'ye ken grandda.'

Oh dear! It was going to be like that was it? Frank really didn't have the patience for nonsense conversations with young fools who thought they were Govan's answer to Al Pacino. He dialled up the Glesgae and delivered his little speech in a hoarse whisper so dripping in menace that it was outlawed by several strategic arms treaties.

'Naw! Whit ye need tae ken is that Ah'm nae messin' heah! Ah'm buying top quality geah, and Ah'm paying top dollah. So, Ah dinnae want tae waste ma time wi' the likes ahf ye two wee baw bags. Noo ye gan and call yer mammy or whitver it as ye need tae to dae because I want wan name and wan number. D'ye ken? And if ye call me grandda agin, ye'll be eatin' yer tatties through a straw. So, get tae fuck ya wee gobshite.'

The small one spilled his flick knife onto the floor where it broke in two as if he'd got it in a Christmas cracker. The tall one scuttled off throwing apologies and assurances of deep respect over his shoulder as he went.

Chapter 25

Volunteer Padraig Mac Liam was having a busy week. He'd been ordered to check out of the Harboro Hotel in Melton Mowbray and move to the William Cecil Hotel in Stamford. This was more like it! Five-star stuff! Or four at any rate, leather armchairs, wood panelling, and Stamford was a lovely town. This undercover agent behind enemy lines lifestyle was one he could get used to. He felt like...

And here was the problem. He couldn't feel like James Bond because he was a Brit and therefore the enemy. And he couldn't feel like Michael Collins ghosting around Dublin in 1920 because he was a traitor to the cause. He would have to become his own legend.

His orders were to drive up to Yorkshire and collect a package. Perhaps he would see that woman again, the one with the admirably tight jeans.

Alas, not. He arrived in the car park of the Premier Inn near Pontefract at noon, as instructed. Almost the first thing he saw was the same Vectra he'd seen at Hartshead Moor, and the same man sitting in it.

He was given his instructions and asked to repeat them back…twice. Finally, he was handed a small package.

'This wasn't easy to find. I may not be able to get another one.'

Padraig nodded and weighed the package in his hand. It was lighter than he expected. He returned to his car, placed the package under the passenger seat, and headed south. He had to do a little shopping.

*

The Scholar was now working to a timetable, but he had to be careful. He couldn't afford for Diarmuid Geraghty (a name that would soon be consigned to the dustbin) to do anything that might alert the Brits. Fortunately, the tall Englishman seemed to think that he was his friend. He could use that.

It was working well. He would respond as before to the shorter one, Michael, but become more talkative with Richard. The pair seemed to notice this, without becoming suspicious it seemed, and altered their questioning style accordingly.

If they knew his *nom de guerre*, his professional persona, they would soon know who he was. If not his actual name at least his importance and his history. There was little he could do about that. On one level it didn't really matter. Even if they knew he was still safe while he was talking. They would be content to listen and then confront him when the river of intelligence had run dry.

He had one last thing left to tell them. It was just a question of judging when and how to feed them.

The Scholar spent two days giving them chapter and verse on the dissident republicans of West Belfast. He knew that everything would be checked so, as before, he made sure that it was mostly accurate with a couple of things that were impossible to verify and a couple that were wrong but commonly held misconceptions.

He gave them names, favourite pubs, and meeting places and one or two safe houses, some of which he knew the Brits had already identified. He told them about sources of funding, the identities of cash couriers and the various illegal activities that contributed to everyday expenses. They lapped it up. Especially the tall stupid one.

*

But then, after nearly three weeks, James McKenna aka the Scholar aka Diarmuid Geraghty made a mistake. It wasn't a disaster. It was recoverable. A professional operator always anticipated that something would go wrong, that it would be necessary to have a plan B. It wasn't ideal. It wasn't what he wanted to do. But it was what he had to do.

The problem was that he'd mistimed it. Or rather, he'd failed accurately to estimate how much time it would take to impart his 'Belfast material' and he'd run out of things to say. The truth was that the Scholar was a Derry boy and knew little about Belfast. He'd spent the early part of his IRA career in the city of his birth. He'd spent the last fifteen years or so in a more international role. He had nothing further to say.

He could just make stuff up. He'd been littering the real information with speculation, embellishment, and sheer fiction ever since he'd arrived at Windmill Cottage. But that was the point. The fiction had been seasoning or garnish. The meat had been the real thing, or a version of it. He'd run out of meat.

The Brits knew he was 'the Scholar'. How long they'd known he couldn't tell, possibly since the very start. He'd been trying to think of a slip that he might have made but nothing occurred to him. Perhaps it didn't matter. If they knew he was the Scholar, and if they knew who the Scholar was, and more importantly what he'd done, then this little holiday in Rutland wasn't going to end with handshakes all round and promises to exchange Christmas cards.

While he was talking, he was safe. It was when he ran dry that his problems would begin. And he'd run dry. Well, not quite dry. He had the emergency tank. He had Paschal Carty.

*

The ferry from Stranraer to Larne took a couple of hours and the journey across Northern Ireland took a couple more. Frank skirted South of Derry and crossed the border at Killea. The Good Friday Agreement had changed everything. There was a small sign welcoming him to the Republic of Ireland and nothing more. No border post, no customs, and no soldiers. Half an hour later he was in Letterkenny, the fastest growing city in Europe, according to a sign erected by the council.

He parked the Jaguar outside Dillon's hotel. He was a little early. And the young fool detailed to watch for him was a little late. Frank saw him go in and identified him for what he was immediately. A lifetime conducting covert surveillance doesn't equip you with a great many usable skills, but when you needed them, they were handy to have.

Frank gave him five minutes to get settled. He wanted his actions to be reported. He was going to behave exactly as the man he was going to meet hoped he would. He checked the mirrors. There it was, parked three cars back. Would there be more than one? Possibly, possibly not, it all depended on how far they were going to take him. He'd been told that he would be meeting his contact at Dillon's but come on!

Frank walked into the lobby looking left and right. It would never have done to look like a complete innocent. He saw the young fool sitting at a coffee table in the lobby. He couldn't have been more obvious if he was reading a newspaper with eyeholes cut in it. Frank approached the desk.

'Have you any messages for a Mr Flanagan?'

The young woman was wearing a name badge that read 'Tereza'. There were little flags than indicating that she spoke Czech, German, French, and English. Donegal had changed. She said that she would check and examined a set of pigeonholes where in earlier, less electronic, times there had been a key rack.

She turned in a few seconds, smiling, happy to have been of service, apparently delighted at having to contribute to a stranger's day and facilitating a modicum of satisfaction. Donegal had definitely changed.

'Now,' she said, holding out a white envelope with the word 'FLANAGAN' written in biro. She'd been here long enough to pick up the vernacular.

McBride thanked her and took his envelope to the end of the desk where he opened it. It contained a single piece of paper and a simple message. 'Silver Tassie Hotel, Ramelton Road, 12:30 PM.'

It was now ten past twelve. Frank beckoned over Tereza. She gave him directions and bade him a grand day. He decided he liked the new Donegal.

Frank could have driven slowly to make sure that the following car could keep up but he was a gangster in a V12 Jaguar. That would have been very odd. He passed the golf club and the motorhome showroom doing eighty, but he had to slow down immediately afterwards behind a tractor that in England would be regarded as vintage. Perhaps Donegal hadn't changed all that much. He saw the following car catch-up, saw the look of relief on the faces of the two young men.

The Silver Tassie's bar was almost deserted. Frank selected a tall stool from where he could see most of the bar and most importantly, the door. He ordered a Guinness. A Guinness isn't the beverage to choose in Ireland if you have an urgent thirst. The barman poured about two-thirds and then wandered off. Frank was starting to wonder if he'd been struck down by rapid onset amnesia or perhaps been abducted when he returned and poured the final third.

'Now,' he said.

Frank's fist had barely closed around his pint when he felt a presence beside him.

'Mr Flanagan?'

Frank took a big sip, or a small draught, depending on your view of such things.

'Aye.'

The man looked as if he was about to say something, but the amnesiac/abductee barman had returned. He nodded, and the barman began to pull another pint of Guinness. Frank took advantage of the opportunity to survey his new companion.

He was about the same age as Frank, but the years had been less kind. When you considered what Frank had put his body through in his younger days that was a pretty unflattering thing to say. But Paschal Carty had not had an easy life.

He'd been interned in 1960, one of four hundred rounded up as a consequence of the IRA's border campaign and spent a year in prison. He was interned again ten years later and did another four years in the late seventies. He was no longer in the H blocks for the hunger strikes, but he would have volunteered. In the late eighties, he was sentenced to twelve years and freed as part of the Good Friday settlement.

Even when he was technically at liberty, he was often on the run. He'd had wounds tended by medical students, by vets, and on one occasion by an old woman whose medical prescriptions relied almost entirely on pouring whiskey into open wounds and invoking the aid of the Holy Spirit. He looked rough, but it was a miracle he was alive at all.

The barman had left again or been beamed up by a passing UFO.

'I understand you're a businessman, Mr Flanagan.'

'Aye.'

*

Paschal Carty had reserved a meeting room at the Silver Tassie. That was fair enough. It was his home turf. Frank wondered whether he was going to ask him to strip so he could search for a recording or transmitting device...or a gun. He hoped that he would. The more tests that he would pass, the better.

'What do you want to talk about first? Prices? Payment terms? Delivery arrangements?'

'Product,' said Frank. He put his briefcase on the table.

Paschal nodded at a young man. He'd been the passenger in the car that had nearly failed to follow Frank. He left. Frank produced a set of test tubes from the briefcase, a small plastic petri dish, a set of small filter papers and a scalpel.

'Most people just smoke them.'

'I am not most people, Mr...?'

'Carty.'

'I am not most people. Now I can be flexible about a number of things, but not quality. So let us see if we can find a basis to make further negotiations worthwhile.'

'I don't negotiate, Mr Flanagan.'

Frank was about to reply when the young man returned with a large holdall, the type that football teams use for everybody's kit. In fact, that's what it probably was. There was a small logo, presumably the club's, and a much larger logo for a local animal feed company.

The young man spilled the contents out on the table, a couple of thousand cigarettes in sleeves of two hundred. He smirked at Frank. 'Amn't I clever?' the smirk seemed to say. Well. We'll see.

Frank drew the sleeves towards him and stacked them up into two piles of six. He pulled the first towards him. John Player Specials. He turned the box over in his hands a couple of times and then reached into the inside pocket of his jacket for a pair of spectacles. The young man smirked again but Carty didn't.

Frank examined the box from all angles, then he tore off the cellophane and opened the box. He removed one packet and examined it. After a moment or two, he reached into his briefcase and withdrew a magnifying glass. The packet had an English language health warning on it. Frank didn't trouble himself with that. They were easy to print. Instead, he examined the small print containing the compulsory health information.

The printing was blurred and fuzzy, oh, and there was a spelling error. Frank continued at his slow, methodical pace. The young man was starting to get bored and resentful. Paschal was feeling a blend of irritation, concern and, yes, respect. He was dealing with a pro.

Frank opened the packet and shook all twenty cigarettes onto the table. He withdrew the foil lining and examined it, first through his spectacles, and then with the aid of the magnifying glass. He could feel the atmosphere in the room changing.

Frank had been interviewing people for nearly forty years. He knew how to use silence and the passage of time as a weapon. In Frank's hands it wasn't a sniper's rifle or a stiletto dagger. It was more like a means of suffocation or a way of bringing a heavy weight slowly, inexorably down upon your victim. First there was the alarm, then the fear, then the crushing awfulness of the inevitability, the urge to cry for mercy and the final, total, utter asphyxiation.

Frank selected a cigarette. Taking a scalpel, he slit it open lengthwise. He picked up the filter with a pair of tweezers and examined it.

Using the same tweezers, he stirred the spilled tobacco a little then took a pinch.

He placed the tobacco on the little filter paper, a couple of inches across. Then he reached into his briefcase and withdrew two test tubes. The first contained a blue solution. The second contained a solution that was a sort of rusty orange. Using a pipette he added two drops of the first solution and one of the second to the filter paper. He then stirred the slightly fizzy damp tobacco stew and then brushed the tobacco away.

He held the filter paper up to the light. His face was expressionless. Finally, holding the paper between index finger and thumb he held his cigarette lighter a few inches below the paper, then he held it up to the light.

It was all nonsense of course. None of it meant a thing. The first solution had been copper sulphate from the child's chemistry set. The second solution had been Irn Bru.

Frank took a notepad from his briefcase, helped himself to a Silver Tassie pencil from the jar and made a few notes. Then he drew a second sleeve towards him.

The young man could stand it no longer. 'Are you going to do that with all of them?'

'What's the matter, son? Have you never dealt with a professional before?'

'It's okay, Colm.'

The young man switched to the Irish language, which he spoke poorly, 'He's just an old fraud!'

Paschal's Irish wasn't great either, but he was able to say, 'Just be quiet, Colm.'

'Right, Mr Flanagan, cards on the table, let's talk.'

'Mr Carty, I like your product. It's actually pretty good. The filters in particular, I assume they're genuine?'

Paschal Carty would have liked a drink. But to do that now would be to surrender what remained of the initiative entirely. 'The Lamberts, JPS, Bensons, Silk Cut, and the Embassy. Those are mine. I manufacture them. The Marlboros and the Marlboro Lights, I buy those in.'

'From Spain or Morocco?'

'I buy them in Spain, I don't know their origin.'

Frank pulled a sleeve of Marlboros towards him. 'Carry On.'

Paschal detailed his whole product line. Some he manufactured himself. Some he bought and knew were genuine, albeit they had the health warning in Spanish, others he couldn't vouch for.

All the while Frank was examining and dissecting the Marlboros and dousing them in Irn Bru.

All the while Paschal Carty was mentally calculating the correct price to charge to this Scotsman, and what steps he could take to discover who he was.

After what seemed like an hour but was probably about five minutes, Frank spoke again. 'I'd like to see the factory.'

Colm couldn't contain himself. 'You can't,' he said, before switching back to Irish. 'The Scholar said that nobody was ever to visit the factory.'

Paschal took a moment to remember the right words before replying in Irish, 'Do not tell me what I cannot do. I am the chief here, not the Scholar, and I make those decisions.'

Colm retreated again to the corner, with a petulant look on his face. Frank pretended that he hadn't understood, but the Gaelic Scottish of Barra isn't so different from Irish.

After a few more minutes, they had the basis for a deal.

*

The Vale of Belvoir stretched from Old Dalby in the south-west to Allington in the north-east. It spread over three counties and encompassed about sixty villages almost all of whom had a pub, sometimes more than one. But there was only one place in the vale where you could get a pint at four o'clock on a Wednesday afternoon.

Frank McBride had dispensed with the leather jacket, silk shirts, and the gold chain. It had taken three courses of Head and Shoulders to remove the gel. But the earring was still there, and it was the first thing Monster noticed as he walked into The Wheel Inn. He wisely decided to say nothing. But he couldn't let the Jag go unmentioned.

'Nice car, Frank.'

'I dare say you'll be driving something similar one day.'

Was that a lucky guess? Had Monster let slip at some time in the past that he dreamt of one day driving a Jag? You could never tell with Frank.

In a change from the usual Frank was drinking bitter. That was the problem with visiting Ireland. The Guinness was so much better that you couldn't drink it at home for a couple of weeks afterwards. After the second sip, he had composed himself and got his account straight in his mind.

'Your man is Paschal Carty. He's a real bad bastard from Derry. If you look him up, you'll almost certainly find he's a Fenian, and he's been inside a couple of times. Whether he is still active or not I don't know, but do not underestimate him.

'He stays mostly in Derry, but he has someone running things for him in Spain, someone called the Student, or the Schoolboy. The Irish word is *Scoláire*. He has a factory there too. I told him I wanted to buy at the factory gate and pay factory gate prices. He wasn't willing to do that right away. So, we reached a compromise. Oh, and I'm going to need some money. About twelve grand.'

'For the Jag?'

'No, Christopher. I'm going to buy some fags.'

Chapter 26

Padraig Mac Liam decided that he would do his shopping in Peterborough. He found a shop that specialised in clothing and equipment for people who liked to make their leisure times as unpleasant and uncomfortable as possible. There he bought a woollen hat and a headtorch.

At a second similar shop he bought a mini-Maglite and a Swiss army knife. These were back-ups in case of mishap. He bought a set of screwdrivers and another of hexagonal Allen keys. At a different shop he bought a small set of bolt cutters and a set of spanners with a ratchet. Finally, he bought a dark coloured rucksack.

He returned to the William Cecil just after six, ordered room service, set his alarm for midnight and had a little nap. He would do the job tonight.

*

He'd briefly considered blacking his face with camouflage paint, but wisely decided against it. It would be difficult enough having to explain his presence on the shore of Rutland Water in the middle of the night without looking like a commando.

Padraig's first problem was that the entrance to the fishing centre was blocked to vehicles. It wasn't a locked gate; he could have dealt with that. It was a barrier that rose and fell, like the entrance to a car park, which, he supposed, it sort of was. He couldn't park in the village. It was far too small. The residents would have noticed an unfamiliar car and if he woke anybody, if anybody saw him, well, that wouldn't do.

Instead, he found the entrance to a farm track. It was protected by a rusting gate and secured with a padlock. Padraig treated it as a warm-up. He took a set of lock picks from his pocket, put on the headtorch and set to work. A life spent as a Volunteer hadn't equipped Padraig with many life skills, but he could pick locks. It had been a sort of specialism of his. He was through this one in thirty seconds.

He parked the Mondeo behind the hedge. It was invisible to all but the most inquisitive observers and in any case, he didn't expect it to be there very long. He put the headtorch back in the rucksack, put the rucksack on his back and set off on what he hoped was a diagonal course towards the boat park.

*

What he'd expected to be the easiest part of his task actually proved to be the most troublesome. He couldn't find the bloody boat! There must have been two or three dozen and in size and profile they all looked much the same. He went from boat to boat, tripping over lengths of rope, rigging, and who knew what other nautical bric-a-brac. Each time he flashed on his headtorch. Each time he saw a name at the bow that he didn't recognise.

It was half-past two when he found the *Chicka-Dee*. He paused and listened. Nothing. He put on the headtorch and examined the

THE RUTLAND VOLUNTEER 257

outboard motor at the stern. He would have called it 'the back' or more likely, 'the arse end'. Suzuki, 15 horsepower. These details were irrelevant. He was concerned with the engine cowling and how it was secured.

Aha! He congratulated himself for thinking of the hexagonal Allen keys. The second one he tried fitted. Within five minutes, he'd undone all six bolts and removed the cover. He took out the package he'd been given in Pontefract. It was going to be tight. The gaffer tape was employed again. It just fitted. He replaced two of the six bolts and tested it. Again, tight, but it just worked. But an engine cover missing two-thirds of its bolts would rattle. The gaffer tape again.

And that was when he noticed the set of Allen keys in their own little wallet on the gunwale. He thought for a few moments. He removed the gaffer tape, replaced the four remaining bolts and satisfied himself that the Allen keys were in a sufficiently noticeable position. Ten past three. Time to get out of there.

But first he had to make sure that he'd left nothing behind. There's nothing more demoralising than scrabbling around on the ground in the dark looking for something you're almost sure you haven't dropped. It took fifteen minutes. To the east there was the first signs of the impending dawn. He really had to leave now.

*

He was back at the William Cecil shortly after four. The night porter seemed surprised to see him. What on earth could anybody be doing in Stamford until four in the morning? That had been a mistake. He should have stayed away until the morning shift had come on. He could have pretended he'd just been out for an early stroll. That porter was going to remember him.

But he was tired, exhilarated at having completed another secret mission, but tired. He fell into bed and dreamt of how, one day, he would tell Erin McCrory about this. Perhaps that would be in bed too.

*

The team had had a new car delivered, a Renault Laguna. It was replacing the old Laguna and so Lake decided to give it the same code name; Lisbon. He'd also decided that it would be the car that Monster and he would take to Birmingham.

'So, what exactly is Frank's status?'

'He is a participating informant, and his name is Flanagan.'

'He's behaving a lot like an undercover officer, false name, and everything.'

'Well, he's not. For one thing he's not an officer anymore.'

'They're going to say he's an Agent Provocateur.'

'I know they will, but he's not, I checked with legal.'

'He initiated contact.'

'Yes, but he didn't initiate the crime. They've been smuggling for months. And that factory didn't appear out of thin air overnight. We're covered. Legal said that so long as he didn't provide the opportunity to commit a crime that otherwise wouldn't have been committed, then we are all clear. It's not like leaving a wad of fivers on the pavement. Anyway, there is no such thing as 'agent provocateur' or 'entrapment' under English law. You ought to know that.'

'I do.' Monster grinned. 'I just wanted to see if you did.'

*

Lake had to have the same conversation with Alan Hawkins, the Assistant Chief Investigation Officer. Perhaps he was testing him, too.

'I hope Frank understands that you're in charge and that you're directing things. He doesn't have discretion to make it all up as he goes along.'

'Well, we have explained that to him.'

'That isn't the same thing at all. Anyway, that can't be helped. I hope you realise that we are at the absolute outer limits of my authority and our powers here. Frank has invented the concept of Undercover Retired Officer and you two are going to be quite close to undercover status too. Make sure you know the rules, remember the rules, and don't get carried away.'

It was exactly the speech that Lake would have given if he'd been in Hawkins' shoes, which hopefully he never would be.

'Take me through it again.'

'Frank has ordered twenty master cases, that's twenty times ten thousand fags. It's eleven and a half thousand. Cash on delivery.'

'And where is the delivery?'

'Somewhere near Nottingham. We will be told a few hours in advance. Frank will have the cash. He'll be in his car. Monster and I will be in the video van.

'We'll do the loading. All three of us will have tags in case one of us gets a chance to get near the wagon. There will be a full surveillance team with a technical car nearby. If the lorry leaves empty, we'll let it go. If it still has merchandise on-board, we'll follow it to the next slaughter. We'll retrieve the tag, if we manage to deploy one, at the exit port.'

'Which will be?'

'Don't know.'

'And if everything goes to plan?'

'Then Frank, will be invited to buy at factory gate prices next time. If we're really lucky, at the actual factory gate. Either way, he'll be gathering evidence against Paschal Carty.'

'And we think he's the head man, do we?'

'Seems to be. Frank thinks he's a sort of chairman of the board. The real work and the real direction are done in Spain by someone else.'

'And that is?'

'A mystery, for now. Someone called the Student or the Scholar or something similar.'

*

Bryan hadn't seen the Irishman with those eyes for a few weeks. He was quite pleased. But the Irishman, he'd never learnt his name, had been the only person at the warehouse who spoke proper English. Everything took three times as long with the Spanish. And they would pretend not to understand when it suited them. Still, on balance, it was still better than having those eyes fixed on you. Ander gave him his money and he counted it in front of him. He would never have dared do that with the Irishman.

He was also pleased to learn that he didn't have to drive all the way up through France this time. He was on the Santander to Plymouth ferry. The crossing took nearly twenty-four hours. It was almost a cruise. Maybe he'd meet that driver from Leicester again, what was his name? Alan? Andy?

It would take him all day to reach Santander from Seville. Experience had taught him that the route via Salamanca was best. He'd be in Portsmouth the following afternoon.

Then it was up to Nottingham to drop off and then home for a few days. Easy money, and he wasn't even nervous anymore. He'd made this run a dozen times and never had an issue. Never expected to, frankly.

*

Monster dropped Lake off at the hospital. He was a little early but he'd arranged to meet Bella in the coffee bar, so it didn't matter. It was quite nice to have a few moments to think, actually.

His chief concern was Frank. All informants were bloody nightmares. Participating informants were even worse. They all thought they were James Bond. They would nod at all the right places when you told them what they mustn't do. And then they would go and do it.

And none of them were Frank McBride. The Scotsman had been the first customs officer to go properly undercover. He'd decades of experience. And less than two years ago, he'd been Lake's boss. Could Lake really bring him to heel like a well-trained spaniel. He doubted it.

And if he and Frank disagreed about what should be done? Well, the chances were that Frank would be right and Lake wrong. Except that right or wrong, the responsibility was Lake's. And if it all went wrong...

*

Bella arrived looking beautiful. From certain angles in certain light, you could tell. Of course, the real giveaway was that she glowed with life and hope while simultaneously looking absolutely exhausted.

When they were expecting Caroline, they both agreed that they didn't want to know the sex. Now Lake wasn't so sure. He couldn't have told you why. He would have been equally happy with a boy or girl. But for some reason, this time, he thought that he might like to know. And in an hour, well more like half an hour probably, well...

'They're going to ask us if we want to know the sex, you know?'

'I know.'

'And you don't want to know?'

'No...why? Do you?'

'Maybe, I'm not sure.'

'Well, I don't mind if you know.'

Lake still couldn't decide. During the scan he initially averted his eyes from the monitor but after a while he could resist no longer and took a look. That was no help whatsoever. He'd heard parents taking in hushed tones about how they felt when they saw their unborn child for the first time. He knew that you could tell the sex sometimes.

Absolutely useless! Bella was either going to give birth to the Milky Way or the monitor had become connected to air traffic control on a particularly busy day. He was starting to suspect that it was all cobblers. He couldn't have even guessed how many were in there. He looked away again.

'Well that all seems fine,' said the nurse or radiographer or, well, the scanning lady, while she made notes on a form. 'Now, would you like to know the sex?'

Lake still didn't know the answer to this perfectly reasonable and straightforward question. But Bella did.

'I do but he doesn't.'

The scanning lady gave Lake a look that seemed to indicate she thought a lot less of him.

'That's fine, we're all done here.'

Bella was wiping gel off her belly.

'If you want to pop outside, I'll let Mummy know.'

Now Lake felt terrible. Was he already a bad parent? Scanning Lady seemed to think so. He left the room and ostentatiously stomped down the corridor so that it was obvious that he was well out of earshot.

*

He offered to drive home but Bella told him not to fuss. As they left the car park Lake enjoyed the idea that Bella was going to have to spend the next six months keeping the secret. The slightest slip of the tongue, or a moment spent too long looking at a pink dress or a blue sailor suit in Mothercare and she risked giving the game away.

It would dawn upon Bella soon too. it dawned upon her that she was going to have to guard her pronouns for the next six months. Bella was happily chatting away, making plans for a second nursery, discussing double seat buggies, and whether they needed a bigger car.

'And I suppose we'll have to put his or her name down for a nursery too.'

'I suppose.'

'And we need to have a proper talk about names. Two sets, obviously, boy, and girl.'

Well, this was going to be fun. Bella knew the sex and so she was going to be handicapped in name discussions because she couldn't risk giving the game away by holding her ground for one name and giving in easily for another.

Lake was confident that he would get his way in the end this time. For once he had the advantage. He might not be able to interpret ultrasound images, but he could read upside down. And Bella didn't know that he knew. Patrick Joseph Lake. That had a nice ring to it.

*

They collected Caroline from nursery together. They hadn't told her that she was going to have a baby brother or sister, well, brother, if the scanning lady knew her job. They hadn't told her anything. But she would be asking questions before long. All of which meant that Bella and Joe would have to tell their parents too.

Caroline had wanted orange and pink things for dinner. Bella didn't seem to think this request the least bit unusual. Spaghetti in tomato sauce (orange tomatoes) ham and carrots. She managed to get nearly three-quarters of it in her mouth. Lake volunteered for bathtime duties. He managed to get a piece of carrot in his hair. He couldn't have told you how.

And after all that Bella had managed to make dinner and the pair of them sat down in front of the television. Bella with a pile of year eleven marking, Lake with a head full of things that could go wrong on Operation Bridegroom.

They were watching, well almost watching, a detective drama. It was like all the others. There was a hard-bitten cop. Why are there never any gently bitten cops or delicately nibbled ones? He was known only by his surname. His private life was a mess. He was going through his third divorce. He had a gambling addiction and a little brother who was a petty criminal. Or was he a cocaine addict? Perhaps that was the other one, the one who collected jazz seventy-eights.

Was it necessary to have a chaotic private life and some defining character flaw to be a good detective? Was Lake going to be like that one day? He looked over at Bella, an essay on supply and demand perched on her belly. The flickering lights of the baby monitor over her shoulder.

There were more important things than catching cigarette smugglers. Maybe Monster had the right idea.

Chapter 27

Thursday was Paschal Carty day. The Scholar began with the highlights, an executive summary, you might say. Paschal Carty and the Irish Republican Volunteers were the face, body, and arms of the dissident republican movement in Derry. Particularly the arms. The Scholar could tell from the body language that he had their attention although the two Englishmen both tried to disguise it.

Michael was a bit better at remaining neutral, but Richard couldn't hide his interest. Perhaps it was because his limbs were so long. They sort of exaggerated every movement and every telltale sign. Now that the executive summary had done its job, he began at chapter one. This was his last card. He had to make this story last.

'I assume you've heard of the United Irishmen of 1798...'

*

The Scholar wanted to go fishing again on Friday. Michael didn't think it was a good idea, but Richard somehow managed to imply that by refusing the suggestion he would be conceding that it was Richard who had the rapport and was now the primary interrogator.

He agreed, but made it conditional on winning the pub quiz. He was certain that his grandfather would not permit that to happen a third time despite how motivated the Scholar might be.

He was even more sure when, after the first round, Ron's Team had scored full marks and were in the lead. The topic had been sports and had been arranged (of course it had been arranged, everything was) such that all members contributed. Ron knew a surprising amount about Speedway racing and a less surprising amount about the rules of crown green bowls. Richard was able to contribute some laughably easy answers on the subject of rugby and Heather, who was a keener fan of Manchester United than Michael had appreciated knew which goalkeeper had been killed in the Munich air disaster.

Michael knew what this meant. Their team's lead would be gradually pegged back. They would go into the final round with all to play for, and be pipped at the post. That was exactly the sort of thing that his grandfather would find funny.

But perhaps he was wrong. Full marks on the second round too. A lot of questions about the classical period. Meat and drink to Richard Perceval. Ron's Team's lead actually grew. One or two people knew that Michael was Bernard's grandson. Perhaps he was trying to initiate a riot. It was only at this stage that Michael noticed that Frank McBride wasn't present.

The next round was popular culture. Ron's Team tended to fare poorly on this subject and this week was no exception. Three out of ten but still holding on in joint second place.

Music, five out of ten. Slipped to third.

Science and nature. Heather usually contributed here and she more than played her part. Nine out of ten and they were back in joint first with only the art and literature round to go. This was traditionally the Scholar's specialist subject. Michael and Heather were confident.

Richard, if anything, was overconfident. Ron was his usual impassive self.

Bernard always read the scores before the final round. There were the usual groans from those at the bottom of the list. 'They don't like it Uppingham', 'Shake Rutland Roll' and 'We only came in out of the rain' were all in contention.

A widely respected author of serious literary novels gripped her ballpoint pen a little tighter.

A retired barrister who had defended capital cases at the Old Bailey was sweating slightly.

A head teacher, a retired surgeon, and three Justices of the Peace all shifted restlessly in their chairs.

And at one time or another most of them cast nervous glances at the mysterious Irishman who knew so much about Mark Twain, Marcel Proust, and Anthony Trollope.

But the Scholar! He looked like he was about to experience the most important, the most consequential, the most intense fifteen minutes of his life. His eyes had taken on a new appearance, one that Michael hadn't seen before. He'd seen the watchful (but menacing). He'd seen the thoughtful (but menacing). He'd even seen the triumphant (but menacing). This was something new and entirely different, entirely terrifying. He looked as if he was possessed and not by anything good. Michael wouldn't have been surprised if he started speaking in tongues or if his head caught fire.

And suddenly Michael knew what was going to happen. He gripped Heather's hand under the table like a couple who had reached the top of the roller coaster and now had no choice but to endure the fate that gravity had in store.

By rights, there ought to have been some sort of steward's inquiry. Did The Wombles really count as art and literature? Or Tony Hart? Or

Enid Blyton? Ron's Team scored zero and finished dead last. Michael caught his grandfather's eye. He really hoped that the old man knew what he was doing.

Ron didn't care. Heather was a little relieved, actually. She didn't want the villagers to think that she was benefitting from bias on behalf of Bernard. Richard was in a profound sulk and the Scholar, well, he looked like he'd seen a ghost.

*

Richard escorted the Scholar back to Windmill Cottage, complaining all the way about the hideous low brow injustice of the final round. In particular, the Agatha Christie question had been wrong. By which he meant that points had been awarded for the correct answer according to the television adaptation and not the book.

He was furious and began to wonder whether this was all due to the sinister hand of Michael. He was jealous. That's what it was. He was jealous of the fact that he, Richard, was outperforming him. This was nothing less than sabotage cooked up by Michael Butcher and his grandfather. This would be in the report.

The Scholar was weighing his options. This was a very unwelcome development. But it couldn't be helped. There was no use complaining like Richard. That was what amateurs did. Ranted and raved and looking more and more like Basil Fawlty in one of his more crazed episodes.

He would have to abort. And reschedule. He'd timed all his disclosures for this date. Now he was going to have to pull something else out of the bag to keep the inquisitors satisfied. Fortunately, he'd held something back, just in case.

When he got back to Windmill Cottage, he forced himself to sit on the bed for an hour. People became hasty when things went awry. They always wanted to fix things immediately. Big mistake. Amateur error. Calm was needed here more than ever. He waited another ten minutes for luck, then he checked all his 'tells', listened carefully, and retrieved the phone from its hiding place in the chimney.

The battery was dead. Shit!

*

Bryan knew that as soon as he notified Tony he was at Leicester he would be expected to go to the meeting place directly. So he made sure that he'd had a little rest and something to eat and drink before he made his call.

'You're late!'

'Traffic.' He wasn't going to apologise to that thug.

'You should be here in an hour, got a pen, and paper?'

*

Monster and Lake were checking over Cyclops, the van brought up specially from London. To all appearances it was an ordinary white van like thousands of others seen every day on British roads ferrying plumbers to leaks or brickies to building sites.

If was in any way unusual it was that it was trying not to appear unusual. It bore no markings of any kind, no names of a plumber, joiner, or painter, no telephone number, and no snappy little advertising slogan. People remembered names, they remembered trades, on very, very rare occasions some people remembered advertising strap lines. And so, there were none.

It was a white van. Even if you glanced in through the cab windows it was unremarkable. A couple of empty cigarette packets, a burger wrapper, last week's *Daily Mirror*. And if you opened the back doors. It was just a white van. Unless you looked very, very carefully.

Where the two back doors met, just at the top, in a tiny gap, there was an 8mm lens. In the back of the sun visor on the passenger side there was a 16mm lens. And behind the false bulkhead was the video recording equipment, operated by a set of controls in the glove box.

Monster was checking that everything was working as it should when Lake got the call from Frank.

'Normanton, just north of Bottesford, on the A52 towards Grantham. In about an hour. I'll meet you in the car park of a pub called The Muston Gap, just east of Bottesford.'

Lake glanced at his watch. Then he called Nick Harper.

'Normanton, just north of Bottesford, off the A52.'

'The old airbase?'

'I don't know, maybe. Make sure the team keeps well back.'

*

Frank was waiting for them. The Jag was gleaming and so, strangely, was his hair. Monster regretted that this didn't seem like the occasion to say any of the dozen things that were on the tip of his tongue.

In theory, Lake was in charge. In theory, he was calling the shots. And in theory he should be briefing Frank. But, come on.

'Okay, we'll be going in shortly. Don't try too hard. You are a couple of blokes whose job it is to load and drive a van. Don't try to be gangsters. Don't try to be anything. Say as little as possible. You got the lumps?'

Lake fished three devices from his pockets, each about the size of a cigarette lighter. When Frank had started, well probably some time after Frank had started, tracking devices had been a lot larger and were known as lumps. The technology had moved on but the language hadn't.

'Right, if you get a chance, and only if you get a chance, inside the back bumper. But don't try anything clever. It's not worth it.'

Monster was sufficiently aware of the etiquette to look at Lake.

He nodded and handed one device to Frank and another to Monster.

Frank's phone rang.

*

Frank McBride had never been to RAF Bottesford. But it was still very familiar. There were dozens just like it all over Lincolnshire and the east of England. Frank had spent an unhappy six months at one of them in 1956. Most of the hangars had gone and the control tower was clearly abandoned. If the runways were in anything like the state of the perimeter track it had been a very long time since any plane had landed here.

Bottesford was just like dozens of others, built in a hurry in 1941, intended to last a couple of years and still in limited use decades later. Frank led in the Jag; Monster and Lake following close behind in Cyclops. They were both in the middle of a convoy of six or seven vehicles, mostly Transit vans.

They passed two old buildings that had been abandoned, another in only fractionally better repair that seemed to serve as a lawnmower repair business. Then there was a gap as they swung left past an old dispersal pan. Three more buildings housing small businesses and then a sharp right, almost a hairpin bend, finally a set of gates, opening into a small yard framed by some Nissen huts erected as a temporary measure over fifty years before.

There was no lorry. Monster was wondering how it would negotiate the hairpin bend when it came. Lake was wondering where to position Cyclops to give the cameras the best possible view.

Frank's parking decision was all together more straightforward. He swept in and parked alongside Tony Castle's Jaguar. As a power play it couldn't have been better. To put it in terms that Tony would have understood it was like parking Real Madrid alongside Grimsby Town.

Frank got out of his car. Even the gentle swish, thunk as he closed the door seemed like a statement of superiority. Tony was impressed but determined not to show it. He walked across to Frank using what he thought was his gangster walk.

'Flanagan?'

'Aye.'

'Payment in advance.'

'Where's the wagon?'

*

The other vans had fanned out in what looked like a choreographed fashion. Each had its rear door facing inwards to where the lorry would presumably park. Lake parked Cyclops in the same fashion but made sure that he swept round such that one or other of his cameras could capture the number plates of the other vans.

Drivers and passengers emerged from the various vans. There were nods of acknowledgement but nobody actually struck up a conversation. Lake noticed that everybody was of a type, young men, about the same age as Monster and him and dressed similarly. Tracksuit bottoms were popular. And T-shirts bearing the names and logos of sportswear companies that belied the bodies they concealed.

They were all white. Half of Eamonn Walsh's customers were Asian. That was Leicester, he supposed. That was when Lake recognised Eamonn Walsh, himself. Walsh had been travelling in the passenger seat of a blue Transit. Now Lake thought about it, it seemed like he was actually leading a small convoy of three or four vans The Other Office had told him Walsh had a new supplier. And this was obviously it.

*

They heard the lorry before they saw it. And they saw the cloud of dust before the lorry itself. Bryan pulled in and parked where everybody had expected him. He climbed down from the cab and stretched extravagantly. If he was trying to send some sort of message, he was wasting his time. Tony Castle was already at the back of the trailer.

The doors were opened, and a pallet trolley used to move the first two pallets, oranges, onto the tail lift. The lift was lowered, and the oranges moved to one side. Castle climbed into the trailer. He had a piece of paper in his hand.

Frank remained by his car, but from where he was standing Lake had a good view. He glanced over his shoulder to ensure that he wasn't blocking Cyclops' camera. Those pallets that he could see were wrapped in shrink-wrap. They appeared to be labelled. Castle consulted his list.

'Number one, Gary.'

A pair of men who had come in a white Transit stepped forward. They took one pallet to one side and started to tear at the plastic. A full pallet was fifty master cases, or half a million cigarettes. This one looked less than fully loaded, so 400,000, maybe a few more.

'Number two and three, Steve.'

Two more men stepped forward.

As the two men started to load, Lake noticed that the boxes were labelled as different brands. This operation was slightly more sophisticated than the load delivered to The Walnut Tree. The pallets were prepared for the customers' specifications. It made for swifter unloading at this end and implied that the smugglers had the luxury of time at the other.

'Four, five, six, seven, eight, nine, and ten. Eamonn.'

Eamonn Walsh and his companions stepped forward. Three and a half million fags. Lake was calculating the lost excise duty he was watching just drive away.

Two men in replica football shirts took pallets eleven and twelve.

There was only one pallet left. Frank strolled round to the back of the trailer. He beckoned to Lake and Monster. They walked over in a slight arc to give Cyclops the best possible view.

'That's eleven thousand, five hundred pounds, Mr Flanagan.'

Everyone noticed the 'Mister'.

Frank reached into his pocket and withdrew a doorstep of notes. Monster and Lake lurked nearby in case there might be an opportunity to deploy a tracking device. But the wagon was empty or would be very shortly. It wasn't worth the risk.

They used the tail lift to enter the van. Monster took his time, manoeuvring the pallet trolley into position, giving Lake a few precious seconds to look around. But he saw nothing. The inside of the trailer was pristine. He'd seen dirtier operating theatres.

Other vans were starting to depart. It was less than fifteen minutes since the lorry arrived. Slick. It only took a few minutes to load the twenty master cases that had been Frank's order. They were ready to depart.

'Just a few minutes, Mr Flanagan.'

What was this? This wasn't in the script. Everyone else had loaded up and buzzed off. Frank didn't look concerned, but then he was probably good at that sort of thing. Lake wasn't sure how well he was masking his own growing alarm, so he made sure that he kept his back to Castle.

Monster was a little bolder. He continued to watch Frank and saw the other man hand him a piece of paper. Frank nodded and put it in his pocket.

Lake had been so preoccupied that he failed to notice the lorry driver approaching until he was almost upon him. Unfortunately, he seemed to be the chatty type.

'Haven't seen you lads before.'

'First time,' said Lake. He immediately regretted it. Monster's approach was better.

'What's it to you?'

It wasn't actually delivered with menace, but when you're six foot three and eighteen stone you don't really need to put too much Dirty Harry into it.

The driver decided that he would continue his little amble unpunctuated by a sociable chat with these two young men.

Castle's phone rang. The conversation lasted two seconds. Thirty seconds later it rang again, and a minute after that. He was getting the all-clear from the customers. Lake was impressed. Castle said something to Frank that Lake didn't hear but the message was clear, free to go.

*

'North on the A1. You lead. I've got more mirrors.'

Lake and Monster set off north up a country lane. Monster was driving, Lake doing his best to check the nearside door mirror but all he could see was Frank's scarlet Jaguar. After five minutes they joined the A1 and five minutes after that Frank overtook them indicating left. He turned sharply off the A1. The sign read 'Fen Lane' but it wasn't much more than a track. Lake's phone rang.

'Blue Mondeo, on our tail.'

Lake checked the mirror, there it was.

'First fork or T-junction you go right. He's probably following me but if he goes with you, lose him.'

When van and Jag separated, the Mondeo followed Frank, but not for very long. Volunteer Mac Liam wasn't trained for this and he didn't have a six litre V12 engine. The last he saw of the Jaguar was it travelling south on the A1 at more than a hundred miles an hour.

Chapter 28

Frank, Bernard, and Ron were walking Rocky and Brunhilde along the ridge when Frank's phone rang. Not that phone, the other one. He glanced at the number and decided that it could wait. He didn't need to leave until after lunch and he was determined to enjoy these last few hours.

Bernard had found someone to look after The Old Volunteer for a couple of weeks. They were a retired couple who had run a pub for twenty-five years, Clive, and Angela. Ron or Bernard would look in every day or so to ensure that there were no problems. Ron was looking after Rocky. Everything was settled.

He'd told his friends that he'd been to Scotland to visit family, which was true, if not the whole truth. Now, he said, he was going to Spain to see his daughter, Michelle, her husband, and his grandchildren, Maisie, and Frankie Junior. This was also true. So far as it went. He gave Bernard Michelle's telephone number in Madrid. The old goat would be sure to check, so why not make it easy for him?

When they reached Leighton Parva, he said goodbye to Rocky, fondled his ears, and assured him that he would be back in a few days. It would have been comical if it wasn't so touching.

When Frank was back in his flat above The Old Volunteer, he returned his phone call.

It was on.

*

It was nearly two hundred miles to Portsmouth, but Frank took his time. The next forty-eight hours or so would be the nearest thing he had had to a holiday for two years. He had to fill the Jag with petrol near Luton. The numbers just kept going up.

He arrived at the port in plenty of time and waved a passport at the controls. The immigration officer didn't even glance at it. Within an hour, he had parked on the car deck and was wandering about somewhere in the bowels of the colossal ferry looking for his cabin. When he found it, his first task was to plug his phone in. His second was to find the bar. He wouldn't be in Bilbao for almost thirty-six hours. For the first time in a week, he felt genuinely off duty. He decided that he would leave his 'Frank McBride' phone switched off. From now on, he would only be Daniel Flanagan. He looked at the picture in his cousin's passport. Fortunately, it had been taken a few years ago, before the cancer. The likeness was good enough.

*

Frank stopped at Burgos for lunch. He would be at Michelle's house in the Fuente del Fresno district on the outskirts of Madrid in a few hours, but he wanted to make a small diversion.

The Battle of Brunete, fifteen miles west of Madrid in July 1937, was a serious defeat for the republican forces in the Spanish Civil War. In particular, the XV International Brigade suffered heavy casualties. Among them was the father that Frank McBride had never known.

Brunete is a small town, a big village really. There was no memorial to Frank's father or to his comrades. He didn't know exactly where his father had died. The letter that his mother had carried with her until the day she died didn't provide many details. Shot by a sniper, killed instantly, and that was probably a lie.

Frank walked around for a few minutes. He saw a memorial to his father's enemies, returned to his car, and left.

An hour later he was at Michelle's house. Maisie and Frankie ran out to meet him. They had grown. They were tanned. Frankie was wearing a Spanish football shirt. Maisie was wearing earrings. He was hopelessly, blissfully, totally happy.

'Is that your car, Grandad? It's cool!'

*

The Scholar had been awake half the night trying to think of some way to engineer a fishing trip for the following day, but in the end an opportunity fell into his lap.

Michael's Thursday night report had provoked a reaction back in London and he was awoken at five past six by a text message from Phillipa Templeton, delivered in her usual peremptory tone. He cursed and headed for the shower. He caught the seven twenty and only as the train pulled out of Peterborough did he text Richard with the news.

Richard had had less than his full eight hours too. He'd been writing a report of his own until almost two o'clock in the morning. He wanted to get the tone exactly right. Up until now his reports had focussed on errors and underperformance by Michael. He was happy with his work but if he was to boost his credibility and his reputation as an officer of 'sound' judgement he needed to make a few forecasts. Forecasts that he was confident would prove accurate.

His general theme was that whereas the Irishman, Geraghty, the Scholar, whoever he was, mistrusted Michael but he'd established a rapport with Richard. A rapport based on the mutual respect of two men utterly dedicated to their respective causes, two men of ruthless professionalism, two men whose organisations were lucky to have them. And that's a difficult message to communicate in an understated modest style. It took him several drafts.

The forecast part was easier. If only Michael could be removed from the interrogation team high quality product would be sure to follow. And the evidence of this would be the pure gold he panned from an intimate tête-à-tête with the Irishman as he pitted his wits against the trout of Rutland Water.

But annoyingly, because of that stupid pub quiz he would have to delay that message. There would be no fishing trip, no shared intimacies, no intelligence goldmine. He cursed Noddy, Hercule Poirot, and Great Uncle Bulgaria.

So, when he received the text message from Michael a large sly grin spread across his features. He retrieved his report from his drafts folder, added a couple of sentences and pressed 'send'.

The only flaw in his plan was that Michael had insisted that Tony or one of the Chrises accompany them in the boat. But Michael wasn't here, was he?

*

Tony, it was to have been Tony, wasn't happy at all. He insisted that his orders were that he should be present to keep guard on the Irishman. But the Percevals were not the sort of family to tolerate mutiny from a jumped-up sergeant like Tony. His stubbornness was no match for Richard's breeding. One of his great uncles had had a hundred members of his company killed on the first day of the Somme.

'That is a direct order. And I don't want you splashing about nearby in another boat, either. Remain on the shore. Take some field glasses if you absolutely must but under no circumstances are you to interfere.'

Tony had tried to phone Michael, but his phone was switched off. In the end, he had no alternative but to accede. An order was an order, after all. But he insisted that he got it in writing. Richard signed the piece of paper with a flourish. It felt good. He felt good. Today was going to be his day.

*

Richard and the Scholar collected the rods and tackle and the keys to the *Chicka-Dee* at the shop. More accurately, they collected the keys to the pair of padlocks that secured it to the trailer. Together, they manhandled it to the slipway and launched it. Tony and Big Chris were detailed to return the trailer to the field where all the boats were parked, or moored, or whatever it was when a boat was on a trailer.

The Scholar started the outboard motor and with Richard at the helm they set off into Rutland Water, heading for the spot just north-east of the Hambleton peninsular that had proved so fruitful the previous week.

Richard waited until the Scholar had settled into a rhythm, casting out to the boat's starboard side before engaging him, oh so casually, in conversation. The Irishman was quite forthcoming at first, but as the minutes passed without so much as a bite; he became irritable and less communicative. Richard decided that he would try again once he'd caught a fish or two. He would be in a better mood then.

But half an hour later, the Scholar had caught nothing. Richard saw Tony and Big Chris on the shore. Chris was eating an ice cream. Tony was studying the boat through binoculars. Even at this range, Richard could imagine the scowl.

The Scholar was scowling, too. But he wasn't frustrated with his lack of luck. It wasn't luck. He'd removed the hook from his fly while Richard's attention had been elsewhere.

'Sure, I don't think they're here today. Robin suggested that the other side of the headland might be a good spot when the wind is in the south.'

Richard nodded. He had no idea which way was south. Helpfully, the Scholar pointed to the south-west to indicate what he hoped was a more favourable fishing ground. Richard turned and tried to start the outboard motor, but it failed to respond to his enthusiastic but inexpert yanking.

'There's knack to it. Let me try.'

Richard was reluctant to surrender, but he also didn't want to humiliate himself further. He and the Scholar swapped places. The Irishman got the motor running at the third attempt. He didn't want to embarrass the man. And so, with the Scholar now at the helm the *Chicka-Dee* headed off south-west until after ten minutes he announced that they'd almost reached the spot that he wanted to try.

Richard didn't notice that the headland was now between the *Chicka-Dee* and Tony and Chris on the shore. Neither did he notice that there wasn't another boat within a thousand yards. That was when the engine cut out.

The Scholar tried twice to start it again without success.

'I think there's probably a bit of weed in the carburettor. Robin warned us about this.'

Richard didn't remember. But in truth, he'd paid very little attention to the angling chat between the Scholar and the *Chicka-Dee*'s owner.

'I'll have it fixed in a second.' The Scholar had already loosened a couple of bolts. 'Ah, yes, a bit of weed. That's all.'

The Scholar turned back to face him. His eyes, usually so empty and dead were now alive with excitement. No, not excitement. His eyes were alive with joy. In his hand was a Beretta 418 automatic pistol. Small, easy to conceal, and in this case, fully loaded.

The first bullet entered through Richard's open mouth. The second went directly between his eyes. The third was probably unnecessary, but the Scholar delivered it anyway, point blank, right temple. He manhandled the body over the side, started the engine, and headed for the sailing club on the far shore.

*

Tony and Chris looked at each other. Sound travelled over water, but it distorted it, too. And neither was used to the report of a small calibre gun like the Beretta. But they didn't hesitate. They were running for the car even before the flock of startled gulls had ceased ascending.

The Scholar opened the throttle up. He'd rehearsed these moments in his mind. Four minutes to reach the shore. He saw Mac Liam cut the engine and leapt over the prow as it slid up the beach, making a noise like tearing calico mixed with a poorly serviced lawn mower. The two raced across the lawn in front of the clubhouse to the car park. The Mondeo was parked facing the exit. It was away and gone two minutes before Tony and Big Chris arrived.

*

Diarmuid Geraghty was gone forever. Within two hours, Anthony Corscadden was checking at Stansted airport for a flight to Rome. An hour after that, he was in the air.

Rome has two airports. The Ryanair from Stansted carrying Corscadden landed at Ciampino. The Turkish Airlines to Istanbul left from Fiumicino. It was carrying the same passenger, but this time his name was Timothy Madden.

Michael had been in Phillipa's office when the news came through. Richard Perceval was dead. The Scholar had fled. And to make things worse the team in Northern Ireland couldn't find Paschal Carty.

Phillipa received the information with pursed lips. She looked as though she'd just received some mildly frustrating news. As if a train was cancelled or her favourite shade of lipstick had been discontinued. She pulled a sheet of paper towards her and started making a list. After she'd added two items, she looked up at Michael with an expression that clearly said something on the spectrum between, 'Why are you still here?' and 'Get out of my sight.'

The Scholar had been on the run for twenty minutes. It was probably too late to catch him. The all-ports bulletins that are so popular in films and television shows aren't actually that effective. But it had to be tried But realistically? Ordinary looking man, average height, age approximately forty, could be travelling under literally any name in the world and might be headed anywhere. It would need a miracle.

The details were still unclear, but this had been a well-planned and well-executed escape. He would be sure to have a false identity. It would probably be a passport, an Irish one in all probability. It was likely that he would want to leave the country. Spain was a likely destination, but he was unlikely to travel there directly.

Her list focussed instead on containing the situation in Rutland and in particular on the press. A team was despatched to Windmill Cottage to go over the place with a fine-tooth comb. Chris, Tony, and Chris were summoned back to London. They would be debriefed and then suspended for the duration of an internal inquiry after which, who knew?

Michael was sent to a room in the basement where he was asked questions for six hours by a man he'd never seen before, and never wished to see again. At the end of this he was asked to hand over his identity card, building pass, and mobile telephone. At ten o'clock he found himself standing on the pavement in Vauxhall wondering what he was going to do with his life. How easy would it be to find a job with a two-year gap on his CV where the words, 'failed spook' ought to be?

He caught the night bus home and spent three hours staring at his bedroom ceiling. It didn't help.

*

In the morning, he headed for Rutland. Maybe he should tell his grandfather everything. It was likely he knew most of it already. It was possible that he knew more than Michael. The old man had eyes and ears everywhere. Margaret for a start and who knew who else?

But what could the old man really advise? Michael had been de-briefed. He was to all intents and purposes suspended, although the word had never been mentioned. His ability to influence events was now zero. He would either be found to be at fault, or he wouldn't. Or somebody would have to be blamed and he fitted the bill. Richard Perceval was probably a fallen hero now, he thought bitterly.

And could he expect sympathy and understanding from Grandpa? Almost certainly not. Anyway, that wasn't why he was heading for Rutland. He wanted to see somebody who knew nothing of his professional life. He wanted to see someone who wouldn't ask any questions but would stroll with him hand in hand through the fields discussing the merits and de-merits of different breeds of dogs. Yes, their relationship had reached that stage.

Michael hadn't really had a relationship before. He'd had girlfriends. He'd thought at the time that those episodes were relationships. But they'd all been short-lived. And they'd all ended the same way, with the woman sadly listing his inadequacies, character flaws and failings, and Michael generally agreeing that her points were perfectly valid and fair.

This was different. At least he didn't have to lie to Heather about his job anymore.

'I'm unemployed. I had a job. I made the most catastrophic of all imaginable cock-ups. And now I'm unemployed.'

But perhaps he wouldn't tell her that today.

Chapter 29

When Paschal Carty was a small boy, he'd seen an RAF Catalina crash into Lough Foyle. It had presumably been out over the Atlantic looking for U-boats. He never found out what had gone wrong. Perhaps it had simply run out of fuel. But he never forgot the sound it made. Or the sight of it cartwheeling across the surface of the water, parts large and small breaking off and performing their own terpsichorean accompaniment.

His friends had all agreed. They were never going to get into one of those things. For the first thirty years of his life, he didn't even have the option. Holidays had been a week in a boarding house at Bundoran, the seaside town across the border in Donegal. It was always on the week in July when the Orangemen and the Apprentice Boys were marching about Derry.

He hadn't had much opportunity in the second half of his life, either. He'd spent nearly half of that in prison. And he didn't so much have holidays more, periods in hiding in various safe houses. All of which meant that in the spring of 1999, in his sixty-third year, he was boarding a plane for only the third time.

He'd made a couple of trips to Turkey nearly twenty years ago and he had hated flying then. He wasn't looking forward to it now, either. Even his enemies, and he had plenty of those, would concede that Paschal Carty wasn't a cowardly man. He'd assembled primitive and unstable bombs, taken part in fire fights and endured interrogations at the hands of the police and military. But he was frightened now, as he boarded the Ryanair from Dublin to Seville.

And it must have showed because the flight staff were so attentive, so sympathetic, and so reassuring. Part of him was grateful, but most of him resented it bitterly. He wanted to stand up and shout, 'I am Commandant Paschal Carty, Commander-in-Chief of the Irish Republican Volunteers and I am afraid of no man.'

But he didn't.

Dublin airport had been unfamiliar and bewildering enough, but Seville was worse. Everybody seemed to know where they were going. And they were all in a hurry, or purposefully striding to some very important and familiar destination. Paschal couldn't even find the baggage carousel.

This wasn't his world, not his generation. The Scholar would have navigated his way through this as smoothly and serenely as the little yachts on Lough Foyle. Thank God there was nobody here to witness his discomfiture and...his weakness. And nobody ever would. He found his luggage, found customs, and emerged into the arrivals hall determined to look like what he was, a powerful man in complete control.

Ander was waiting for him. A small man holding a large sign upon which was written 'PAT'. Paschal strode over. The two shook hands and Ander took Paschal's luggage. This was more like it. He led him outside to where a Mercedes was parked illegally. The driver leapt out hurriedly and opened the rear door, 'Commandante,' he murmured as Paschal got in.

Ander had entered the back seat from the other side.

'We will take you first to your hotel, Commandant Carty.'

Definitely more like it.

*

He approved of the hotel too, The Colon, in the heart of the old city. A reservation had been made for him under his own name. He hadn't bothered to get a false passport. Ander promised to return the following morning at nine.

He spent the early evening wandering about the old city slightly perplexed that none of the restaurants seemed to open until nine. In the end he was forced into the last resort of the Irishman abroad, the Irish bar.

It was on the Calle Adriano and Paschal hated it before he'd even crossed the threshold. It was even worse inside. There was a bicycle bolted to the wall the Christ's sake! He handed over a great many pesetas, he had no idea how much that was in real money for a pint of Guinness. It was surprisingly good but it didn't alter his mood. His life had been spent fighting for Ireland, and who cared? What had it all been for? A Disneyfied boozer with bodhran's scattered about between tin plate advertisements for Barry's Tea and Tyrconnell Whiskey?

When he'd finished it was near enough nine o'clock and he went in search of a restaurant where the menu had pictures of the fare on offer. He could at least point in any language.

*

The following day was better. Ander picked him up in the Mercedes. There was no sign of the other man. Paschal had never caught his name. They crossed the Guadalquivir River and headed north. After about an hour Ander turned off to the right towards the foothills of the Sierra Morena. The villages became fewer and further between and then so did the individual buildings. A good place to bury a body. But not today, it was too warm.

Finally, they turned off through a pair of rusting steel gates and up a track that tested the Mercedes' suspension. Then Paschal saw it. There was a sign. If Paschal had been able to read Spanish, or if it wasn't rusted and faded, he would have known that he was approaching what had once been the Almaraz brothers' steel wire company, specialists in coat hangers, and shopping baskets. Except they were all plastic now and the brothers had fallen out when times got tough. They'd been relieved to sell the place to the Irishman with the dead eyes.

Ander pulled to a halt in a cloud of dust. It was eleven o'clock.

*

Before the tour and inspection Ander insisted that it was time for coffee. 'We can use the chief's room,' he said.

Presumably this meant the Scholar's office. Paschal wasn't crazy about him being referred to as 'the chief'. He liked it even less when he saw the office.

The room was substantially larger than the house in Creggan where Paschal had grown up. At one end was a conference table in rich, dark mahogany that could have seated twelve. At the other end was a desk, also in mahogany, that looked like it might have previously belonged to a Rockefeller. In front of this desk were a pair of chairs and a coffee table. Ander gestured towards these but Paschal instead went and sat behind the desk. The chair was just like the one JFK had used in the White House. Paschal had seen pictures. A small kernel of resentment started to grow. Was this where the movement's money, his money, had been spent?

Ander went to the door and shouted something incomprehensible. It didn't even sound like Spanish. He returned to the chairs in front of the desk.

'Welcome to the Almaraz brothers' factory,' he beamed.

'Who are the Almaraz brothers?'

'That doesn't matter. They are gone. But the chief thought it was better to buy the whole business just to get the site. The company is owned by another company in the Isle of Men.'

'Isle of Man.'

'Are you sure?'

Paschal Carty was beginning to dislike this man. Just then the coffee arrived. Paschal looked suspiciously at the very small cups. He watched as Ander added three spoonfuls of sugar and did the same himself. Actually, that was quite good.

*

When they'd finished Ander took him on a tour of the factory, starting with the delivery bays.

'Here is delivered the papers and the filters. Next door we receive the cardboard for the boxes, the cellophane, the ink etcetera. Finally, over here is delivered the tobacco.'

'Virginia or Turkish?' Paschal felt that he ought to demonstrate some knowledge of the tobacco industry.

Ander shrugged. 'Tobacco, just tobacco. We do not sort it or grade it. Everything is the same, Marlboro Light, JPS full strength, all the same. Nobody complains. We get it from Morocco.'

The Spaniard, although he wouldn't have called himself that, led Paschal through the doors into the factory itself. There was a steady drone and hum of machines working. Despite the large fans in the ceiling the heat was stifling. Paschal felt himself starting to sweat, but nobody else seemed to mind or notice.

'These machines we bought from a factory near Pamplona. They cut the tobacco. Here we add the ammonia, the sugar, the levulinic acid.'

'Why?'

'Is make better. Standard ingredients, smoother, taste better.'

'Do you, we, have different recipes for different brands?'

Anders just laughed.

'When the tobacco is treated, we load into this machine. It rolls the cigarettes.'

He reached into the machine and pulled out a paper. He showed it to Paschal.

'Today we are making Silk Cut, see?'

Paschal could see that something was written on the paper, but without his reading glasses...

Anders continued leading him past a machine the size of a caravan. A man in overalls, a cigarette stuck to his bottom lip, was fussing at a control panel. A conveyor belt ran to another slightly smaller machine.

'Here we add the filters. Very good filters, we buy them from the same company that produces for the real manufacturers. They think we export them to China.'

Paschal nodded; it seemed like the thing to do. They were deep within the factory now and the noise made it difficult to follow what Ander was saying. Behind the second machine was a hopper that funnelled the cigarettes into another conveyor. But instead of following the route of the cigarettes Anders led him across to another part of the factory.

'This is the print room. We print the papers, the cartons, everything. The chief bought these machines in China, brand new, very reliable.'

'Are the cigarette machines not reliable?'

Ander shrugged. 'They are old. We have to maintain them very carefully. They need to be stripped and cleaned every week.'

'What's our output?'

'Normal day...five million cigarettes, if we don't have to change brands too often.'

'I thought you said it was all the same tobacco.'

'It is, but we change the papers, the cartons, takes maybe half an hour. Normal day we make two million one brand in the morning, three million another brand in the afternoon. We could make more, maybe ten million in a day but...the machines, they are old...and we can only make as many cigarettes as we have filters, cartons, cellophane.'

'So, twenty-five million cigarettes a week?'

'Approximately.' Ander shrugged again.

Paschal did the arithmetic in his head. He was impressed.

*

When they returned to the office Paschal said that he wanted to review the accounts. Ander said that he would arrange for them to be brought in but suggested that first they have lunch.

The Mercedes swept out past the old, rusted gates, and turned right, not in the direction from which they'd come. Paschal thought that this was just as well as he hadn't seen anything that resembled a restaurant or even a café in that direction. He was just starting to prepare himself for another long journey through the dusty foothills when they reached El Pedroso, a smallish village that Ander described as a city.

They pulled up outside what Paschal would have called a café, but which described itself as a restaurant. Specifically Ignacio's Restaurant. There were a few plastic tables and chairs on a shaded terrace, but

Paschal was relieved when Ander led him into a dark and cool interior filled with heavy wooden furniture.

Through a pair of swing doors at the back emerged a middle-aged man wearing a vest that exposed his hairy shoulders and wiping his hands on an apron that looked as if it had been used to clean a tractor.

He was obviously the proprietor, possibly Ignacio, although the sign above the door was so old that Ignacio might have been his grandfather. He greeted Ander as if he were a long-lost son. A big hug, and then a slightly smaller one for Paschal who still felt as though he was being crushed by a bear. The man called into the kitchen. The waiting staff had to be hugged and then a woman less than half Ignacio's size was introduced. She was about a hundred years old. Perhaps she was the wife of the original Ignacio, or maybe life was just very hard in the Sierra Morena.

Paschal and Ander were shown to a table and the menus theatrically swept away. Paschal didn't understand a word, but the general message conveyed through extravagant gestures and beaming smiles was that the usual bill of fare wasn't suitable for such an important guest and that Mama herself would prepare something special.

The something special seemed to be mostly pork, served with potatoes fried in olive oil, a green vegetable that Paschal didn't recognise and black pudding, although the Spanish called it Morsey-something. This was all washed down with the coldest beer that he'd ever known. Paschal was starting to understand why the Spanish had invented the Siesta. He was full, content, and very slightly drunk.

*

On the journey back to the factory Ander filled him in on a few more operational details. The factory functioned from Monday to Friday and Saturday mornings were spent cleaning, servicing, and maintaining the machinery. Three men were employed in the print shop and three on the factory floor. Ander served as supervisor and the office staff consisted only of his wife, Bixenta.

In addition to all these was Mikel, the driver who collected the previous day's product each morning and took it to a small warehouse in El Garrobo, on the road back to Seville. Supplies, tobacco, paper, cardboard, etc. were also delivered to the warehouse and taken to the factory by Mikel.

Apart from these nine people and 'the chief', whose real name Ander didn't appear to know, nobody ever visited the factory.

Paschal was very aware that he'd invited the man he knew as Daniel Flanagan to inspect the place in a few days' time. Maybe he could blindfold him for the journey.

Chapter 30

Sunday morning, Ron, with Rocky, had called on Bernard for their usual morning walk, when Clive, the relief manager of The Old Volunteer hurried over the road. He wanted to clean the beer pipes but couldn't find the key for the cupboard containing the fluid. Did Bernard perhaps know where it might be found?

Bernard shook his head. But Ron had an idea.

'Frank cleans the pipes on a Sunday afternoon. Key might be in his Sunday jacket.'

Frank worked every hour that The Old Volunteer was open and more besides, but Sunday evenings were his time. He sat at the bar, always on the same stool, and he wore a Donegal Tweed jacket, a sort of a visible indicator that he was off duty.

Bernard conceded that it was worth a try. He allowed himself to be led back to the pub while Ron played with Rocky and Brunhilde. Sure enough, in Frank's wardrobe was the tweed jacket. He would hardly need that in Spain in spring. Frank reached into the right-hand pocket. He pulled out a packet of cigarettes, Benson & Hedges. The packet was open, and one was missing. Very odd. Bernard had never known Frank smoke anything other than his pipe, or pipes, because he had a collection.

In the left-hand pocket, he found a set of keys. Not for the first time Ron had proved to have a sharper mind than most gave him credit for. While he might have left school at fourteen, he regularly set crosswords for *The Times*. Bernard would occasionally tease him by calling him ''Rutland's leading cruciverbalist'.

Clive tried one in a cupboard door and smiled his thanks. Bernard returned to Ron, Rocky, and Brunhilde and set off down the Oakham Road to the stile.

But his mind couldn't let go of the packet of cigarettes. It was odd. And the bright red Jaguar was odd. And Frank had bought a leather jacket. A few days ago, when they'd been walking Bernard had thought that perhaps Frank had had the lobe of his left ear pierced. There was no earring of course, just the hint of a hole. But his eyes were those of a man who was almost eighty. He'd dismissed it at the time. But not now. It all indicated one thing. The silly old fool (Frank was seventeen years younger than Bernard) was going undercover again. He resolved to address this when he returned home.

Bernard and Ron's usual walk was just under three miles. They'd been able to do it in just under an hour. Ron almost certainly still could but Bernard was slowing down. He was also pretty tired by the time he got home to find a white BMW parked in his drive.

*

Michael had told Heather as much of the truth as he dared. He was off work for the foreseeable and planned to spend some time in Leighton Parva, either staying with his grandfather at The Old Vicarage or...

Heather didn't allow him to finish the sentence. She took him by the hand and led him upstairs to show him the half of the wardrobe she'd allocated and the drawer she'd cleared out for his benefit. Well, eventually she showed him.

She'd shooed him out of the house at lunchtime. She was going to cook a proper Sunday lunch and that couldn't be achieved with him in attendance. Heather wasn't a great cook, and this would be the first time she attempted anything really tricky, like roast parsnips. It would be messy. It would be loud and there was a good chance that there would be a lot of bad language.

Michael decided that he ought to pop in to see his grandfather. He was slightly surprised to see the BMW and more surprised when he learnt to whom it belonged.

'Hello, Mikey. You know Margaret, of course.'

'Hello, Michael, I've just been telling your grandfather about Friday. Oh, don't look so glum. I'm sure it will be all right. Death, taxes, and being badly let down by a Perceval. The only certainties in life. They'll have to go through the motions but really you needn't worry. A nice paid holiday for a couple of weeks.'

Michael was sure that she meant well. And there was a very good chance that she was right. None of it was his fault. He'd insisted on one of the guards being in the boat. Tony would confirm his account, he was sure. But if they were looking for a scapegoat, he knew that he fitted the bill.

'What was it all about Mikey? Dissident republicans, was it? Fighting like cats in a sack? Disclosing the locations of each other's arms dumps?'

'Nothing so exciting. Cigarette smuggling mostly.'

'Really? So that's what they're up to these days.'

And then the subject moved on. Michael learnt a tiny bit more about his grandfather's history and a little about Margaret's too. She'd been in Berlin, 'working in the office' she'd said, which she almost certainly wasn't. Or perhaps she was, and she'd a husband 'in the field'.

But Bernard's mind was elsewhere. His friend was going undercover to infiltrate a gang of Irish terrorists, the most dangerous of whom was now at large and knew that Frank wasn't whoever it was he was claiming to be. He needed to be warned.

He excused himself and went to his study. He called Frank's mobile, but it was switched off. So, he called the number he had for Frank's daughter, Michelle. She told him that she'd just missed him. Frank had told her that he had some business in Seville and that he would be back in a few days. Bernard tried the mobile again, same result.

Michael remembered something that he hadn't had time to do in London.

'Did you meet Ron?'

'Oh yes,' said Margaret. 'Nice to be able to put a face to the name.'

Michael's face must have looked puzzled.

'It's in your file.'

'What? Why?'

'You really don't know?'

At that moment Bernard returned to the drawing room.

'Grandpa, who exactly is Ron?'

The old man paused. For a second Michael thought that he might be genuinely lost for words. He appeared to be holding a difficult internal debate with himself and it didn't look like fun. An onlooker might have thought that he was wrestling with a particularly acute episode of indigestion. Perhaps that's what he always looked like when, shorn of other options he'd been forced to tell the truth.

'Ron...Ron is the loyalist, truest friend for whom you could ever wish. And the bravest man that you will ever meet.'

'The bravest?'

'Yes. You should be very proud of him. He is your great uncle. My brother. Half-brother.'

*

When he returned to Primrose Cottage, Heather was just emerging from the kitchen. She seemed pleased with herself. Presumably she hadn't noticed that she had a piece of parsnip in her hair.

'You're just in time.'

Michael tenderly removed the parsnip. Well, he did his best. Cary Grant would have struggled to remove a root vegetable from a girl's hair and carry it off with panache. He waved a bottle of claret his grandfather had given him.

'It's an eighty-two.'

'Is that good?'

'I think so. I was clearly expected to look impressed.'

'And did you?'

'Not in time, I fear. But I managed grateful pretty well.'

'Yes, well, you're good at grateful, aren't you?'

*

Heather was proud of her first attempt at a Sunday roast. It was true that some of the vegetables were a little underdone, and some a little overdone. But Michael said that the range of textures of the vegetables added interest to the dish.

And the beef, or most of it was perfect. And almost anybody could mistake tartare sauce for horseradish. The labels on those jars were far too small. And Bernard's wine was very nice. Michael looked across the tiny dining table in the tiny dining room at Heather. The operation had been a disaster. His career was probably in ruins, despite what

Margaret had said. But perhaps that didn't matter. Perhaps he could stay in Rutland, stay with Heather, find a job doing...well there must be something he could do.

He was just about to ask Heather whether she'd recommend a career in teaching when he heard the front door bell. Heather frowned, rose, and walked past him to the hall. She returned seconds later, whispering.

'There's a little old lady at the door. She says she needs to speak to you urgently.'

It was Michael's turn to frown. He rose, wiped his lips on one of Heather's grandmother's napkins and went to see.

It was Margaret. Of course, it was Margaret.

'Oh Michael, I'm so sorry to disturb, but I had to tell you. I very much fear that your grandfather is going to do something terribly, terribly foolish.'

'And you want me to speak to him? I very much doubt he'll listen to me.'

'No, dear. He's already gone.'

*

Hans-Hubert Kalbach, known for years as Berti the Limp, had had an interesting life. He had been born in Berlin in 1956, a year after his father had returned from the labour camp in Siberia, and two years before he died, weakened, and diminished by the ten years he had spent there.

Berti hadn't been much of a student. All the teachers agreed that he was an intelligent boy, but he never exhibited any desire to conform or play by the rules. But he came of age when the German economic miracle was at its zenith. There was work for everybody, even Berti. He got a job for the city council, working on the bins.

A workplace injury and a strong trade union together ensured that he had a job for life. He didn't have to work too hard. He had plenty of time to explore other sources of income.

And that had been all he was thinking of when he'd been approached by the Englishman. He later learnt that he was a colonel in British Military Intelligence but at the time he was just a man offering a few Deutschmarks for easy work. Berti became one of Bernard Taylor's couriers. Later he was used for other little tasks, not too difficult, not too legal, but well paid.

When the wall came down Berti had enough contacts to exploit the situation. Berti always knew someone who could perform a task, obtain an item, do a favour...for a price. Some people would have called him a fixer. Some people would have called him a petty crook. Bernard called him an invaluable contact.

Berti became rich, but he was shrewd enough never to advertise his wealth. He lived in a modest apartment, drove a battered Opel. His only extravagance was a trip to a clinic in Switzerland. Berti the Limp hadn't limped since 1994.

He'd sort of assumed that this would be his life. Until he met Valeria. She'd been in Berlin celebrating her divorce, if *celebrating* was the right word. They kept in touch even after she returned home. She came to see him a couple of times. He went to see her a couple of times. The third time he stayed.

They were married now, and had twin sons, Alvaro and Mateo, as well as Valeria's daughter, Daniela. Valeria had a successful jewellery design business. Berti had regular work as an agent, finding holiday homes in Andalucía for wealthy Germans. They had a nice apartment in a fashionable neighbourhood of Seville. For the first time in his life Berti was properly respectable...almost.

Because Berti couldn't help himself. He liked the low life, sleazy bars, questionable acquaintances, dodgy deals. Two evenings a week he permitted himself a little time in Seville's equivalent of his natural demi-monde. He still knew people; he could still do favours.

He'd been surprised when he received the phone call from Bernard and even more surprised when he learnt that his old paymaster was in the Alfalfa bar in the Calle Aguilas.

*

The Englishman looked old. He wasn't dressed appropriately for the Andalucian spring and was sweating lightly. He'd once been the most formidable, the most powerful, and the most ruthless man Berti had known. Now he felt slightly sorry for the old man, sipping a glass of Cruzcampo beer and studying a dish of olives with an expression of mistrust.

'Brigadier.'

'Hello, Berti.'

'Is this a social call?'

'No.'

'Then I will need a beer also.'

They waited until a pretty young girl wearing an apron and very little else placed two beers on their table. Berti raised his glass and fixed his eyes on Bernard's. The eyes were tired.

'To business!'

Each took a sip.

'Berti, I'm looking for an illegal cigarette factory. It's probably run or at least managed by an Irishman, maybe more than one.'

'Brigadier, this is not your usual line of work.' He was too diplomatic to say that at his age he shouldn't have any line of work.

'And when you find it, I'm going to need a gun, two would be better.'

'Bernard!' He was Bernard, now. 'Bernard, this is not Berlin. This is not my city. In Wedding or in Kreuzberg I could put one in your hand in an hour. Here? Here I am a respectable citizen. I am in the holiday home business.'

'And ammunition, naturally.' Bernard had never been good at accepting 'No' for an answer.

'Large calibre, not a pop gun. It's not just for show.'

Berti shrugged, 'I'll ask around.'

'I'll be here. Every day between six and six thirty.'

'Very well. Bernard, I do not wish to be indelicate...'

'A million pesetas. Half now.'

An envelope changed hands under the table.

'I will do my best.'

*

Berti already knew about the cigarette factory but had elected not to tell Bernard. Partly because to reveal information as easily obtainable is to devalue it, and partly because he still had enough residual fondness for the old Englishman to want to talk him out of whatever foolishness he was determined to undertake.

Seville didn't have a large Basque community, but Berti knew where to find them in a little bar just off the Calle Iguazu near the Real Betis stadium in the south of the city. He was well known there. The barman was a friend. He would pop in later, after he'd gone to see the armourer.

*

The following day Bernard was back in the Bar Alfalfa, dressed a little more appropriately this time. He'd almost given up. It was actually just after half-past six when Berti arrived. He had a small shoulder bag and from the way he carried it, its contents were heavy.

'Let's take a walk.'

The men walked in silence for ten minutes down the Calle San Jose until they reached the beautiful public park, Los Jardines de Murillo. It was still warm and so they selected a bench in the shade of some trees.

'I have found your cigarette factory. It is in the hills outside the city. Very remote.'

'Thank you, Berti.'

'But I do not think it is run by the Irish. It is run by a bunch of Basques. Serious people.'

'ETA?'

'Could be, who knows? But either way, they're very dangerous people, Bernard. And you're not as young as you once were.'

'How do I find this factory?'

'It is called Almaraz Brothers and on the road between Castilblanco and El Pedroso. But Bernard, it is isolated. You cannot approach it unseen. And these are dangerous men.'

'Thank you, Berti. The other thing, have you something for me in that bag?'

'Bernard, please don't.'

Bernard reached into his pocket and withdrew an envelope. He put it on the bench between them. Berti shook his head. Bernard said nothing. After a minute, Berti picked up the envelope and walked away. The shoulder bag he left behind.

Chapter 31

The Scholar had expected things to move slowly in Istanbul and he had been correct. Friend had to be introduced to friend. Countless cups of dark, sweet, gritty coffee had to be consumed. Assurances of imminent meetings had to be acknowledged and appreciation expressed even when he knew that those assurances were worthless.

He knew that he was being watched. That was good. It was a test he could easily pass. He had plenty of time on his hands. He saw the Hagia Sofia. He haggled over the price of carpets in the grand bazaar. He visited the Blue Mosque, fair enough, that was spectacular. Eventually he got what he had made the trip for, an appointment to meet the man known as 'Demir'.

The Scholar felt like he was in an *Indiana Jones* movie. The noise, the smell, the smoke. This was supposed to be in the European half of the city. It didn't feel very European to him. There were people everywhere. Everybody either seemed to be in a hurry or completely immobile. How many of them were Demir's men? He suspected that if he made too sudden a move, he would probably find out.

Ayaz led the Scholar to a café just off Taksim Square and promised that Demir would be with them at one o'clock. That hour passed, and the next. It was a quarter past two when Ayaz rose from his seat.

'Mr Demir will see you now.'

He made the tiniest indication with his eyes. His head didn't move at all.

A man at the next table, an unremarkable man, probably in his late fifties, the Scholar didn't notice him sit down. He wasn't the noticeable type. Perhaps he had been there when he arrived. He rose now and took the seat vacated by Ayaz, who strode off into the crowd and disappeared in seconds.

'I am Demir. And you are the Irishman who wishes to meet me.'

'Yes, I have a message for you. From an old friend of yours.'

The following morning, the Scholar took the flight to Madrid. By lunchtime, he was three-quarters of the way to Seville. He decided to press on and eat later.

*

Frank met Paschal Carty in the lobby of the Colon Hotel. Paschal had the feeling that the Scotsman he knew as Daniel Flanagan had got the better of him in Donegal and so he took the opportunity to score a point by emphasising his opulent lodgings. Ander was outside in the Mercedes. That helped too. Paschal and Frank sat in the back. When they reached the outskirts of the city, Paschal offered him a sleeping mask bearing the logo of Gulf Air.

'You understand, security.'

Frank put it on, settled back, and relaxed.

They reached the factory just before eleven. Frank removed the sleeping mask and wiped his forehead with his handkerchief. It was a warm day. There were half a dozen cars parked outside the factory, parked in the shade, which made it easier to read their number plates. Ander led them inside. They took the stairs up the 'the chief's office'. 'The staff only work a few hours on Saturday. Most of them will be going home soon. We can take a look around the facilities then. In the meantime, can I offer you some refreshment, Mr Flanagan?'

Paschal took a seat behind the large desk, 'Now, what would you like to know?'

'Let's start with prices.'

'Let's start with quantities.'

Frank took his pipe from his pocket. He slowly filled it. 'Have you a match?'

Paschal hadn't but Ander, who was doing his best to remain inconspicuous at the far end of the room hurried over with a book of matches. Frank thanked him, lit his pipe, and put the book of matches in his pocket. Bar Ignacio, El Pedroso.

'I'm happy with the samples I've seen so far. I'd like to take a few from here as well. If those are also satisfactory then I would want five thousand master cases a month. To be collected here, in Spain. I'll arrange transportation, distribution, and sale. And I'll sell where I choose. None of your other customers' markets are off limit to me. Now. Price?'

Paschal was doing the sums. Fifty million cigarettes a month.

'Perhaps we could take the tour now and find you a few samples.'

Ander gave Frank almost the same tour that he'd given Paschal a couple of days earlier but didn't share quite as many details. Frank asked a few technical questions. He inspected the printing machines, the cigarette papers, nodded approvingly at the filters. He picked up some raw tobacco, rubbed it between his fingers and appeared satisfied. He was in danger of overdoing it. He insisted on taking half a dozen packets of cigarettes from among the stock waiting for collection. He said that he would test them later.

Paschal had remained in the office, sitting behind the big desk, feeling very pleased with himself. He assumed the same proud proprietorial air that grandparents do when small children achieve small triumphs or when a racehorse of which he owned a tiny share romped home in a Wednesday afternoon novice hurdle at Uttoxeter.

Flanagan was a serious man. This was a big customer. A professional who knew his business. A man who wanted fifty million cigarettes a month. And who had found him? Not ' he chief', not any of those low-lifes from England, not the Basques. He had. Commandant Paschal Carty, Commander-in-Chief of the Irish Republican Volunteers. Who was 'the chief' now?

Frank was happy, too. He had all the information he needed. If he'd been forced to, the number plates, and the book of matches, would have led him to the factory, but he didn't need either. There had been a sticker on one of the emergency exits. Frank didn't read Spanish, but it looked like some sort of certification from an official safety inspection. That didn't matter. It had the name and the address of Almaraz Brothers. He now knew the location of the factory.

His mission had been completed. Frank knew everything he needed to know. One phone call to outline what he'd learnt and then he could go back to Madrid, see Michelle, see his grandchildren.

And that's what would have happened. If he'd left an hour earlier.

*

Bernard had driven past the factory. He'd seen and counted the cars outside. He found a little spot a mile or two down the road where he could see them leave. One by one he counted them as they drove past. It must be half day on Saturday.

Then he saw the Scholar in his hire car.

'That's not good,' he muttered, half to himself.

*

The Scholar had taken the stairs directly to his office. There was a little gantry outside, a relic of the days when one or more Almaraz brother liked to survey his kingdom and make sure that his staff weren't slacking on the job.

On the factory floor below he heard Ander, speaking in English, which was unusual. Then he heard the reply, a Scottish accent. Then he saw him. He stepped back before the Scotsman could see him and pushed open the door to his office.

His uncle was sitting behind the desk. He didn't like that for a start. And he was looking smug. He didn't like that either.

'Who's that downstairs?'

'Hello, Jimmy. Nice to see you. No, don't thank me. Springing you from the clutches of the British security services, no big deal.'

If anything, he was even smugger.

'Who. Is. That. Downstairs?'

'Oh him, that's our newest and our best customer.'

'Who is he?'

'Name of Flanagan. Glasgow originally but based in England now.'

'Are you sure?'

'I've seen his passport, Jimmy.'

'I've had a dozen passports. That means nothing.'

'Listen, Jimmy. He's a serious player. He wants to buy five thousand master cases a month.'

'How many has he bought so far?'

'We're at an early stage. He's serious, Jimmy. He tested the fags with chemicals and everything.'

'So, you brought him here?'

'He was blindfolded, Jimmy. Try to remember who you're talking to. I'm your commanding officer. And I've been on active service since before you were born.'

The Scholar turned away, he walked to the far end of the room, leant on the windowsill, and stared out at the mountains. He managed his breathing, but his knuckles were white.

'Who introduced him?'

'Some friends in Glasgow.'

'That man's name is not Flanagan. His name is McBride. He's a publican in England, in the little village where I was held. And he knows my face. What the hell is he doing here? No. Don't answer that. Let's find out.'

The Scholar walked the length of the room, past the desk, and crouched on the floor where there was a little safe. He spun the dial, entered the combination, and opened the door. Paschal had turned to see what he was doing.

'Jimmy, don't be hasty. Fifty million cigarettes a month. Think what we could do with that money.'

The Scholar cocked the gun. His eyes were like a pair of coals in the face of a psychopathic snowman. He opened the door of the office taking care to remain out of sight of the factory floor and shouted something in Spanish.

*

When Paschal and the Scholar reached the loading bay Frank was already sitting on a plastic chair, the type you see outside every second bar and café in southern Spain. It doubtless bore the logo of a brewery or a soft drink manufacturer. He was facing out the open side of the loading bay. The mountains stretched out before him. A buzzard circled overhead, lazily gliding on the thermals. The sun was low in the sky, away to his right. Ander was a little to the side. Frank could almost ignore the revolver. Almost.

The Scholar nodded and Ander moved behind Frank. He felt his hands being tied. Not rope, something else, electric cable possibly. Frank alone wondered why there was a second chair. Ander knew. The Scholar knew. Paschal didn't seem to have noticed.

'And now you, Uncle Paschal.'

'What?'

'Sit down. Put your arms behind your back.'

'You can't be serious.'

'Or I'll shoot you where you stand.'

'James! Jimmy! Don't be crazy!' Paschal spread his arms wide, the universal gesture of conciliation, or an appeal to reason. He took a step forward.

The scholar levelled the pistol. At this range he could not miss. But that was not the issue. It was a matter of whether he would, not whether he could. Paschal looked into the eyes. And he knew. He sat down and placed his hands behind his back. Ander stepped behind him. It was electrical cable.

Paschal decided to try again, 'Jimmy!'

'I know, Paschal. I know everything.'

In the eighties he'd been selected for the Nutting Squad, punishment beatings for those who didn't pay protection, executions for informants, kneecapping for drug pushers. All on the orders of Paschal. Or Mr Easter as the heroin suppliers of Istanbul knew him. The man who controlled the Derry heroin trade. The man responsible for the death of Joseph. The Scholar's baby brother.

The Scholar nodded at Ander and walked away. By the time he had reached the door Paschal Carty was dead.

*

Bernard heard the gunshot, saw the birds take flight. He was almost eighty. He'd been a widower for almost two years. Why not here? Why not now? He had been a soldier for most of his life, time to be one again.

*

Ander turned his attention to Frank.

This is the part in the movie where the villain treats everyone to a monologue, going over the key plot parts for the audience, tying up loose ends, that sort of thing. Ander didn't do that. He wasn't a movie villain. He was the real thing. He just pulled up a chair and sat in front of his prisoner. Frank could almost see the thought process. He'd been made a witness to a murder. He had to die. He would know this. Therefore, any attempt at interrogation was futile. But the Basque was in no mood to talk anyway.

'*Any second now*,' thought Frank, Ander would conclude that the smart thing to do was to shoot him and disappear. Any second now. Now.

Ander stood. He swept away the plastic chair. He stood back, levelled the gun.

His finger tightened on the trigger. Frank closed his eyes. He heard the gunshot. This one sounded different. But he could still hear it echoing. Was he dead? Was this what it felt like? He heard a second shot. So, he wasn't dead. Why not? He opened his eyes.

Ander's expression hadn't changed. There was no shock, no alarm in his eyes, not even a puzzled expression. He looked like he always looked except for two entry wounds in his forehead, like a pai of crimson carnations blooming on a time lapse camera. His gun arm was at his side. He made no effort to raise it. A third shot. This time he fell. The gun clattered on the floor.

Frank heard footsteps behind him, felt hands working on the knots behind his back. He twisted to learn the identity of his rescuer.

'You!'

'Arr!'

And in the background, they heard the sound of the Scholar's car driving away.

Chapter 32

Lake had assumed that with Frank undercover, despite it being outside of the technical definition he couldn't help thinking of it in these terms, there would be no activity. Frank had to be safely out of harm's way before Customs started arresting people and seizing cargos.

He was therefore surprised when he got the call from the Other Office.

Lake had spread an Ordnance Survey map over his desk. Monster and he were examining it together. Tony Castle would be receiving another consignment of cigarettes the following day. This time they knew the location of the slaughter.

'Assuming it's the same wagon, it's due into Portsmouth at ten in the morning. That's three and a half hours, minimum.'

'He might have another drop off to make first.'

'It's possible. Also, he may have to have a break. But what counts is that he can't be here before one thirty. Two or three is more likely.'

'Agreed. And based on last time we're looking at, what? A dozen arrests?'

'Which means we need twice that many troops. I don't want anything like a fair fight. Not after what happened to Steve.'

'So, we aim for twenty-five officers?'

'Yes, and a couple of Old Bill too.'

'Where are we going to put a dozen prisoners?'

'Yeah, well, we'll need to speak to them about that too.'

Lake had never thought of it in those terms. So far as he was concerned, he was a temporary Senior Investigation Officer, with the emphasis on temporary. But so far as Lincolnshire police was concerned, he was a Detective Superintendent, which technically, legally, he had to concede he was.

And in the police, if a superintendent wants back-up, well, that's what he gets.

*

Kesteven Rugby Club was busy on Sunday mornings, when there would be a couple of hundred children learning the rudiments of the game and a similar number of parents sheltering in the clubhouse clutching polystyrene cups of coffee and bacon rolls. The large car park would be full, the single gate unlocked for the occasion.

It was fairly busy on Saturdays when the adult teams played and on one or two evenings a week when they trained. But on a Tuesday afternoon there was nobody there at all. If you could manage to by-pass a rather flimsy padlock you had access to a huge area in a remote location. The road was little used. The nearest building was more than half a mile away.

Bryan Sharpe's lorry arrived at ten to three. There were half a dozen Transit vans in the car park already. Tony Castle was leaning against his Jaguar, smoking, and chatting idly to Eamonn Walsh.

*

And ten minutes later, just as the first van was loaded and ready to leave a little procession swept into the car park. As well as the customs cars, there was a police car, a minibus full of coppers itching for a punch-up and even a dog van in case somebody decided to make a run for it across the first team pitch. Most of the twelve men present stood, rooted to the spot, too surprised to move. Even Tony Castle, who claimed to have taken on the Ajax Ultras singlehandedly in 1980 didn't fancy the odds.

Only one man wanted to provide the police with a little sport. Bryan Sharpe had leapt back into his cab and was trying to hide in the sleeping compartment. The police sent a German Shepherd named Dylan in after him and he came out squealing and citing the European Convention on Human Rights.

Twelve in custody, six and a half million cigarettes seized and Lake had made a mental note that German Shepherds would never appear on his list of potential family pets.

*

The following morning the Other Office notified Lake that there would be no further intelligence forthcoming on Operation Bridegroom and the active investigation side of the case should be considered closed.

'But everybody's very pleased with the work you've done.'

'Are you ever going to tell us why we did it?'

'Nope.'

'Would it be anything to do with inter-agency cooperation by any chance?'

'You've done well, Joe. Don't blot your copybook by asking stupid questions.'

'And Frank?'

'Frank's fine. Don't ask him any stupid questions either.'

Epilogue

Michael had been summoned to Phillipa's office. He assumed that he was going to be fired unless she intended to strangle him with her bare hands. That was definitely a possibility. He went over the past couple of weeks in his mind. It wasn't a pretty story, corpses littered over two countries.

He might just about be forgiven for his grandfather. I mean, everyone knew he was completely uncontrollable. He wasn't sure what he was going to offer as an excuse for Ron though. The truth wouldn't sound good. 'Oh, we took the seventy-five-year-old along because we thought he'd be the best shot.'

Well, he was.

Phillipa didn't look pleased. That told him nothing. She never looked pleased. She invited him to sit. There was properly a trapdoor under the chair, a chute leading to a shark tank, or a bath of acid or something.

'Well, Michael. You've had a busy couple of weeks.'

She raised her left hand. Oh no, she wasn't going to do that thing where she counted disasters on her fingers was she?

'Richard Perceval, slain in the line of duty, shots fired in Rutland. In Rutland. Have you any idea what it's like to impose a D notice in a place where dark work at the flower arranging is considered front page news?'

Bit harsh, he thought, but she was doing that thing with the fingers.

'A dangerous terrorist escaped from our custody despite two intelligence officers and three armed guards.' The second finger.

Now that was very harsh. Michael had actually been sitting in Phillipa's office when the Scholar had escaped.

'Ander Ugarte, ETA terrorist, wanted in Spain, and France, also dead courtesy of the captain of your pub quiz team.'

Now she was just being unfair for the sake of it. Third finger, though.

'The leader of the Irish Republican Volunteers, dead.' Fourth finger.

Now that definitely wasn't fair. Ander Ugarte had shot Carty.

She'd reached the thumb. Perhaps she was going to stop now.

'And the Scholar, the most dangerous man in Ireland, possibly in Europe, having spent a couple of weeks drinking the taxpayers' coffee is now, who knows where.'

Michael was wondering whether she was going to start on the other hand.

'Can you even begin to imagine the diplomatic mess? The Spanish want to know if it was our agents. What am I supposed to tell them? 'Oh yes, we're using geriatric hit men now.' You are a very lucky boy, Michael.'

Michael thought perhaps he'd missed some critical detail. He wasn't quite ready for this gear change.

'Yes, very lucky. You see small cock-ups, even medium size disasters require me to go crawling to the chief, the chief to go on bended knee to the minister and there has to be a sacrificial lamb or two at your level. But this isn't a small cock up, is it? It's a colossal catastro-fuck, isn't it?'

Michael thought that was probably fair.

'Which means that we have to take another approach entirely.'

'We do?'

'Yes, Michael, when we have a disaster on this scale our only option is to declare it a triumph, emphasise its secrecy, and give medals to everybody concerned. The greater the fault, the bigger the gong. Why do you think so many retired service personnel are knights?'

Michael was having a little trouble following.

'Now, your grandfather is already a knight. Frank McBride won't accept one. And frankly I don't know how we'd justify knighting Ron Godsmark, a retired painter and decorator. We thought about an MBE for services to cruciverbalism, but he won't have it. Anyway, what are you supposed to give a man who has already won a Victoria Cross? So, that just leaves you.'

Ron had a VC? Ron! Michael was confused, were they going to knight him?

'Don't be stupid, Michael.'

She was reading his mind now; this wasn't good at all.

'Naturally you're going to have to be promoted. Close your mouth, Michael. The security detail backed you up and that fool Perceval wrote a memo declaring how clever he was and how he was going to break all the rules because he got along so well with the Scholar. So, you're off the hook.

'The promotion comes with a salary increase. You should be able to buy quite a nice little flat in town without having to sell Primrose

Cottage. You and your young lady will have somewhere to visit at weekends. I said, close your mouth, Michael.'

A NOTE FROM THE AUTHOR

Thank you so much for reading The Rutland Volunteer. I do hope that you enjoyed it. If you did, please leave a review as it will help to bring Frank and his adventures to a wider audience.

Cigarette smuggling had begun again in earnest after the creation of the European Single Market in 1993 and by the end of the century it was taking place on a grand scale. Some of the more enterprising gangs actually established their own factories and manufactured counterfeit versions of popular brands.

The ratification of The Good Friday Agreement led to the creation of a number of republican splinter groups, but the Irish Republican Volunteers is entirely my own invention. Other groups did dabble in cigarette smuggling.

Smuggling is also the subject of the fourth book in the series. Frank and Bernard will return in The Rutland Legacy.

The world of Frank, Bernard and Leighton Parva would not exist without the inspiration of many of my former colleagues and would never have been brought to the page without the support and encouragement of my friends and family.

In particular, I would like to thank Eddie, Ace, Chris, Tony, Nick, Tobin, Bonnie, Fiona, Sue, Ewa, Mac, Joe, Beth, Charles, Deirdre, Teresa and Liam, The Disaster Triplets and above all Fina.

Join my mailing list

Mailing list subscribers get free books, a bi-monthly newsletter and The opportunity to enter quizzes and competitions.

They will always be the first to learn of Michael's writing plans, new books and projects.

Sign up at https://www.michaeldaneauthor.com/

MORE FROM MICHAEL DANE

The Rutland Legacy

A gang of disaffected young men from Dresden stumble across a hoard of gold.

A new celebrity resident arrives in Frank McBride's world.

A neo-Nazi network of lawyers and assassins enters the story.

And unexplained journeys are being made by an aircraft designed for secrecy and stealth from a tiny airfield in Rutland.

Frank McBride sees it all unfold but he has a separate mission of his own,

Printed in Great Britain
by Amazon